Torso

Denise Danks is a journalist and screenwriter. She is the author of the Georgina Powers series of computer crime novels, the latest of which, *Phreak*, is available as an Orion paperback. *Torso* is her sixth novel. She is married with two children and lives in London.

By the same author

THE PIZZA HOUSE CRASH
BETTER OFF DEAD
FRAME GRABBER
WINK A HOPEFUL EYE
PHREAK

Torso

Denise Danks

VICTOR GOLLANCZ

LONDON

First published in Great Britain in 1999 by Victor Gollancz
An imprint of Orion Books Ltd,
Orion House, 5 Upper St Martin's Lane,
London WC2H 9EA

A CIP catalogue record for this book
is available from the British Library.

Typeset by SetSystems Ltd, Saffron Walden, Essex

Printed and bound in Great Britain by
Clays Ltd, St Ives plc

For Glimmer and Yankee Leader,

to whom I told this story on one crazy trip
to San Francisco

Chapter One

Stella. Stella. Stella. Steven says her name in his head. A hiss and then a flick from the top to the bottom of his mouth with the tip of his tongue. Stella, la, la. Hair, skin, breast, belly and thigh, his sweet cat of a wife. She is soaking up the late afternoon sunshine and the attention of three serenading guitarists. Her face is impassive as she looks towards the sea, but from time to time she looks directly at him and he can see himself reflected in her sunglasses. His face is a blank page. His eyes are mirrors in which she can see herself.

The straps of her sundress have slipped off her shoulders and her skin is as smooth as butterscotch. His mouth is closed and he doesn't make a sound as he vibrates his tongue against the back of his teeth. She is tapping her feet as she threads her fingers through her thick black hair. She's a little drunk, but so is he. He goes over it in his head and thinks he can find a beginning, but the beginning is too far back and all he can hear is the music. She sang to him like a siren and now they make love, all the time. He wakes her up because he cannot sleep with longing for her. Sometimes, he tells her, he can almost see themselves making love. He thinks it must be one of those out-of-body experiences, but Stella says it's just a biological trick wired into human nerve endings so that people won't panic when they're close to death.

The light is bright and the music grows louder and more meaningless. He decides it's time to go, and peels off a couple of thousand pesetas from the thick wad of money he has in his pocket. The guitarists stop and proffer wide, well-rehearsed, well-meaning smiles, but because it's more money than they expect, they start up again, their harmonized voices soaring and trembling against the clatter and strum of their instruments. He waves them away and they leave, ambling through the empty cafeteria, their smiles fixed and persistent, their fingers playing softly over the strings.

He leans forward towards her and draws his fingers against her skin.

'Come on, baby, let's go.'

'Oh,' she says, whining like a child.

'Come on. I'm tired of the sun.'

She drops her head back, exposing her throat, and he lifts his hand to where the pulse trembles slightly against her skin.

'You've been watching me,' she says.

'What else is there to look at?'

'The sea. The birds. The little boats. The end of the summer season.'

'I'm not a tourist.'

'You've been watching me, haven't you, and now you want to go somewhere.'

She sighs and stretches up before pushing her sunglasses on top of her head.

'I'm hungry,' she says.

'For what?'

'For what. For food,' she answers, and settles back again to face the sun. Her eyebrows are black feathers. Her mouth rests slightly open so he can see her tongue inside, wet as a little pink fish. Stella, la, la.

She starts to speak.

'I was thinking of someone,' she says. 'What with the heat and everything. Someone from a long time ago. This guy. He was much, much older than me.'

'How much?'

'Ten years.'

'You were?'

'Fifteen, maybe sixteen.'

'What about him?'

'He sent me photographs of himself. You know, Polaroids.'

'How nice. Do you still have them?'

'They were three photographs of his cock. One from the front, one turned slightly and one from the side. He'd put oil on it so it shone.'

Steven takes out some papers and a tin of Golden Virginia and begins to hand-roll himself a cigarette.

'Why'd he do that?' he says.

'Because he missed me.'

'I meant the oil. Why'd he do that with the oil?'

'To make it look nice, of course.'

'Nice?'

'Bigger, bigger,' she says and laughs.

Steven lights the cigarette and picks strands of loose tobacco from his lips.

'And did it?' he enquires.

'It looked as shiny as a fried sausage. Absolutely edible. A perfect work of art. He had no head either,' she says, and as an afterthought, 'In the photographs.'

'What'd he do? Get a kid to hold the camera?'

She pulls the shades back down on to her face and sits up.

'You're too disgusting, Steven.'

He laughs this time, and feels the sun burn his hands. He can hear her foot still tapping against the metal table and a slight breeze blowing through the striped canopy above their heads.

'I'm hungry,' she says, but he says, 'Let's do the business first,' without knowing that his sweet life is about to turn to vinegar.

As he pays the bill, she moves out of his field of vision. It might have been the breeze, the final fading of summer, or the alcohol in his blood, but he feels the warmth leave his body. He buttons up his jacket against the sudden chill and follows her, out of the sun and into the shadows of a narrow street, where he loses sight of her again, just for a moment. He feels himself rise up and hover about above the town like a bird caught in an updraught. Down the street a little, outside a small, old building, his hawk eyes focus suddenly on a crumbling male torso balanced on a plinth that is scabbed with rusty moss. He feels his chest tighten and his breathing quicken as he scans the stump of the pitted neck, the butchered arms, the disintegrating line of the thoracic cavity and her black hair pressing against the thick, fore-shortened thighs as she hides from him, shaking with excitement at her little game of hide-and-seek. Stella. Stella. How wonderful you are.

Chapter Two

He lay next to her on the bed, listening to the hiss of garden sprinklers. The blinds were drawn and the morning light was bleeding into the room around the edges of the window. She was staring at the ceiling, not bothering to say that it didn't matter that she hadn't come, or worrying that he hadn't come.

The digital radio cut straight to a cautionary traffic report. The El Toro Y, which is such a fearsome intersection of freeways that commuters have undergone counselling in order to cope with it, was causing difficulties for morning traffic converging from the 405 and the 5 south to San Diego and north to Los Angeles. There would be at least a dozen nervous breakdowns that day, but the traffic would not affect her. Her work was a five-minute drive towards the ocean, and his latest job interview was at the offices of a plastic surgeon, thirty minutes along the coast road.

The bed dipped and he turned to watch her walk naked across the bedroom towards the bathroom. But for a collection of communication devices: the clock radio, a television, a VCR, a telephone, a fax, a computer with modem, and, of course, each other, they lived alone. He heard the shower start and when he heard it stop, Steven Gates threw back the sheet that covered his own naked body and got up to follow his wife into the bathroom.

'I'm having bad dreams,' he said.

She didn't look up.

'At night, or just any time?'

'Any time.'

'What about?'

He didn't answer, and she continued rubbing at her skin with the towel. She glanced at him, and at his lean, scarred body and his sick-looking face.

'What do you expect?' she said.

He leaned against the door frame, taking the weight of his body on one extended arm and watching her dry herself, until she held a towel up to her body and frowned.

'Don't look at me,' she said, and pushed the door shut so that he had to step back quickly to avoid getting caught. He gazed at the shell-coloured paintwork, feeling her silent presence on the other side of the door.

'I'm going for a swim,' he said, but she didn't reply.

She listened without moving until he had gone, and then retched unproductively into the sink. When the nausea had subsided, she ran the cold tap and splashed her face a few times before checking her reflection in the mirror.

'Baby grow,' she thought, 'baby grow. Grow. Grow.' She smoothed her left hand over her firm right breast. Another ten years, Stella, she told herself, another ten, and then you'll have to spend some money.

Steven watched her legs. She was walking down from the house and around the edge of the pool, calling his name. He pretended he couldn't hear. The morning sun warmed his shoulders and each time he raised his head, he could see her legs rising up into the body of her smart, red suit. As the cloth moved rhythmically over the nylon sheaths of her stockings, he became keenly aware of the radio sound of her voice, the tungsten glare of the sun on the pool and the cool, streaming touch of water. The sunlight hit his eyes and he was blinded, sensitive only to the call of her voice and the colour of blood. The experience was quite magical, he thought, and despite her irritation, he was going to make it last at least a couple more lengths.

'Do you need me to drive you?' he said, finally dragging himself up on to the side of the pool. She had lit a cigarette, and with her dark hair and black eyebrows, she looked more than a little Italian.

'No, I don't. You've got an appointment, with George.'

'I haven't forgotten.'

It occurred to him that he knew exactly where his wife's groin was under the suit, and exactly what colour her pubic hair was and how it was waxed into a thin tuft like a well-fed caterpillar. She had one leg turned out, and she was gripping her arm tight against her chest as it supported the elbow of the other.

'It's a job, something you can do,' she said.

'Oh, splendid.'

She sighed and drew on the cigarette. He noticed that her lipstick had left a moist stain on the filter tip.

'You can wear the new clothes you bought,' she said.

Steven reached back for his towel and rubbed at the back of his neck and under his arms.

'The new clothes *you* bought.'

'Oh, for God's sake, Steven.'

'For God's sake what? Jesus, what is it? It's not a job at the bank, is it? It's not even a job at McDonald's.'

She flung her cigarette into the flat water and began to walk away. He stared at the crimson imprint of her mouth and the trail of black ash it left floating on the surface. He watched the extinguished cigarette dance on the ripples like a little boat, listening all the while to her gold heels clacking on the tiles until they stopped and she called back to him.

'I just want you to make an impression,' she said.

He didn't turn his head and he didn't answer. He waited. The sound of her heels started and then stopped again, and then her voice, more gentle, more reasonable, called his name. He looked up.

'Don't forget to floss, will you? They hate our teeth,' she said.

The property had survived the fire that had swept through the canyon a year ago. Steven and Stella were among the lucky few. A neighbour had had the good sense to plant sturdy, indigenous vegetation that had protected both their homes from the worst of the blaze. Down the road, the charred trunks of cypresses and palm trees stood like wires around the blasted basins of the swimming pools that were all that was left of villas worth half a million dollars and more. Chimneys stood alone, bricked and fireproof, but no walls remained, and the markings of floors spread out like the chalk outlines of Saturday-night homicides. Steven said it reminded him of Pompeii, only without the heavy casualties. He was right. On the boardwalk and in the pavement cafés, people spoke of collateral damage and the one man who had died trying to save a pet. Stella would listen in silence, and imagined she could still smell burning.

Through the numerous miniature rainbows spread by the water sprinklers on their lawn, green shoots pushed through the blackened aloe. A hammer slammed into a foundation far away, and trucks rumbled in and out of the valley. A year on, the rebuilding had begun and a candlelit evening of remembrance had already been held by the traumatized residents of the town. As the procession had passed by, Steven had whispered mischievously in Stella's ear, 'Mind that flame.'

She had not laughed.

Across the deep canyon, the sand-coloured hills lay as low and indifferent as lions resting after a morning kill. He glanced at them from time to time as he stood naked in the kitchen diner, placing slices of sourdough in the toaster and waiting for the kettle to boil. He liked to eat toast with English marmalade. Stella had made a pot of coffee but he liked to drink tea, even though the slightly saline water wasn't right for it. These were old and comforting rituals in this strange, bright land. The radio was tuned to one of the non-stop West Coast music and chatter stations. It barely registered, like the background hum of constant traffic on the intersecting freeways, but it was part of the ritual even though it wasn't BBC Radio 4, which managed to draw its listeners' attention with moments of silence. That morning, however, one particular news item engaged Steven enough to make him stop what he was doing. It concerned a house painter and former Orange County resident, John J. Famalaro, who had been arrested in the state of Arizona.

He had stashed a woman's body in a freezer that he kept in a rental truck parked in his driveway, and, it transpired, had transported the corpse around the area for three years. While she lay like a side of beef in the truck outside his home, he had passed the time inside the house, watching videotapes of TV missing persons. A woman who had employed him to decorate her house on the actual day of the murder related her experience in a voice that was both appalled and excited by her chance encounter with the indifferent killer. He *had* been distracted that day, she remembered, all too clearly now, and she pointed to the proof. Look, the paint, she jabbered, just three years on, look, see, it was peeling. Worse, she had recommended him to her friends. The reporter conspired with her to recreate the full horror of the woman's brush with death, and with the perfectly understandable social embarrassment at having endorsed a workman who was not only dangerous but also distracted.

A self-congratulatory advertisement for a major car rental firm followed, with enough air time to pay for the news of Famalaro and a fresh revelation that the term *OJ* had replaced *Whoomp – there it is* as the most popular saying on the street. To OJ, to beat up, as in a domestic dispute. To Shapiro, to convince somebody. To Famalaro, thought Steven, to forget to undercoat.

He heard her footsteps coming back.

'The car keys aren't there,' she said.

Steven continued to spread butter on a second piece of toast. The butter was never quite right, either.

'They're complaining about the paint job,' he remarked as she pulled open the kitchen drawers and cupboard doors, slamming them shut.

'What?'

'Famalaro. The killer. He painted houses. Not artistically, you understand, decoratively.'

'I sit in my car and I know I have them there. Today, they're not there.'

'You always leave them in the ignition. It's a bad idea. I've told you.'

'What are you saying? Someone took them? Why take the keys? Why not the car?'

Steven shrugged and continued eating. Stella looked at him.

'I'm being followed. I know it.'

'How so?'

'I can feel it,' she said.

'Famalaro's in Arizona. He won't be back until next week, care of the Orange County authorities, so it's definitely not him.'

'Ha bloody ha.'

'Be proud, my darling. The big stars are falling over themselves to get a stalker. This year's must-have accessory is a fucked-up little friend drooling about the place.'

'Where's my spare?'

'It's like getting an Oscar, good as. I could open a *chichi* store on Melrose so people who didn't have a real one could buy tell-tale stalker accessories, like trainer markings for the flower beds. I wouldn't need a job then.'

'Where's my spare?'

'Where indeed? Where indeed, Stella? I, for one, would like to get to know him better.'

She stopped searching for a moment. Steven had her attention.

'Are you going to introduce me? Do I have to do it myself?' he said.

'I haven't the faintest idea what you're talking about.'

'We're a pair, Stella. Siamese twins. Joined at the heart. Remember?'

She looked inside a Native American Hopi-style jug. The keys were in there.

'Remember,' he called after her as she hurried out to the car. He listened for the ignition and the sound of the engine moving off down the hill. He listened to the sound fade, and thought of Famalaro and the overwhelming feeling of relief he must have experienced by finally disposing of his conscience and meeting his deepest needs. Stella drove away in a temper, punching the short-code number of her lover into her mobile telephone.

Inside a darkened room, the reels of a German tape recorder began to spin. The walls were covered with black and white photographs. These were no studio portraits, with an unconnected smile and a hand resting on a tilted cheek, as eyes focused at some point behind the photographer's right ear. Each one of these was a long-lens, grainy snap of the subject, unaware: shopping, driving, at the beach, at the gallery, in restaurants and coffee shops, loosening the heel around her shoe, scratching her arm, lighting a cigarette, making love – and not always to the same man.

One photograph lay on the desk. It was of Stella and the man with whom she now spoke as she drove too fast down the steep and winding road towards the sparkling ocean. He wore his hair long, and her fingers were caught in it as she kissed his mouth in a moment of tender sexual contact that had been stilled by the expansion and contraction of a mechanical iris. On the desk, beside the photograph, lay a razor blade and a roll of yellow tape.

'Michael? It's me. Michael. He knows,' she said.

'Oh man.'

'He has someone on the case. I know it. Someone's watching me all the time.'

'Tell him. Tell him about us and leave him. I want you with me.'

'I can't.'

'I want you with me, Stella. I want you with me. Stella, do it.'

She tried to concentrate on the sharp descents of the road ahead.

'You'll have to cut me another key for the studio.'

'It was on there?'

'Yes, it was on there.'

'Tell him. Why can't you tell him?'

'I don't know. I just can't; don't ask.'

The reels of tape spun round and round as Steven dressed for his interview. He stopped for a moment by the large bedroom window to watch the morning sun dance on the blue water of the swimming pool. There was quite a breeze, and the ripples moved like fish breaking the surface. Steven gazed at the restless water until it grew still and frozen, like a thought caught in a loop of memory. His body tensed as the feeling of déjà vu crept along his nerve endings. In the time-slip of his mind, he imagined he saw a figure sitting by the marble edge of the pool: a dark man in a light suit who was drinking black coffee from a small white cup.

'It's simple, my friend,' the man said. 'We take the boat and we pick up the delivery. We come back and you go home with even more money. What is your problem with this? It's a great deal.'

Steven took off his sunglasses. He was not afraid to look this man in the eye. On the contrary, he wanted the man to look into his.

'My job description is the problem,' he replied, 'and it goes like this. Deliver the boat. Check. Get paid. Check. Get on the plane. Check. You see, Duran, all I have left to do is get on the plane.'

Stella was leaning on the wall of the terrace, admiring the view of the valley from the white villa. She liked the way the underside of the deep green leaves of the olive trees looked like silver when the wind blew.

'You talked to Charlie?' Duran enquired.

'I talked to him.'

Duran glanced across the pool at Stella. Her sundress was lifting in the breeze. She hooked one ankle over the other, and her leather sandal flapped against the sole of her foot. He opened a flat pack of untipped cigarettes and lit one. He had a gold lighter.

'You have to show me how to use this boat with its computer. I have no brain for these complicated pieces of modern equipment. You show me how it works, for free, you know, all part of the service.'

'No, not for free, all part of the sale.'

Duran laughed and pointed his finger at Steven.

'Charlie's sale. Nothing to do with you. Give me the product demonstration I want, and you, you personally get an extra five thousand. You can bring your girl.'

'My wife.'

Duran glanced at her.

'You can bring your beautiful wife.'

Steven leaned back a little in the chair and then forward again. He rested his elbows on his knees and watched the dead berries float on the water like black beetles in the orange reflections of the dying day. He spat a stray tobacco leaf on to his fingertips.

'I'll take ten,' he said. 'It's worth ten.'

Duran laughed.

'Come on. Get real, man.'

'Ten. That's it. Or my beautiful wife and I take the plane.'

Chapter Three

As he sat opposite Dr George Peyronie, Steven wondered if
the overweight plastic surgeon felt as uncomfortable in his
new clothes as he did in his. There was a small bronze of a
truncated male nude on a glass shelf behind him, and a
painting of a headless female form on the wall. Stella would
have supplied both, Steven was sure of that, because Dr
Peyronie didn't look like the kind of man who would go out
looking for this stuff. He knew shit about it, any of it: office
decor, interior design, art for offices. He could afford to pay
other people to know, like he paid someone to choose the
suit he was wearing according to whether his Color Me
Beautiful palette corresponded to Winter, Spring, Summer
or Fall, or his aura, or whatever damned thing it had to
coordinate with this year. Steven bet himself that the only
thing the doctor had gone out and bought, personally,
through individual choice, was the Rolex on his wrist.

'Steve, what can I tell you about this business?' he said,
shutting off his computer and shuffling his papers into a neat
stack. 'You see these love handles here?'

He grabbed at the flesh under his shirt.

'Lipo.'

He hefted a tubby leg up on to the desk.

'Calf implants.'

'They look very natural,' Steven conceded.

The man tweaked irritably at the cloth of his trousers.

'These are mine. I'm making a goddamned point, for Chrissakes. I'm saying it's what I *do* nowadays. It ain't just the ladies. Men. Men come to me all the time. It's good business, Steve. No, excuse me, it's *unbelievably* good business. Human bodies, my God, how many? And how many rich ones? And not one perfect. Hey.'

He took his leg off the desk and clasped his chubby fingers across his chest.

'You know what the big thing is now? Dicks. Dicks, Steve, R Us. Believe it. You ever thought about that?'

'Circumcision?'

The doctor seemed more surprised by the statement than the misunderstanding.

'You still got a foreskin?' he said.

'Haven't you?'

'No way, man. A foreskin is goddamned un-American.'

'I hope I'm not breaking the law.'

'It ain't the law.'

'Astonishing.'

The doctor paused. He knew exactly what the man was getting at with his sarcastic tone. He even agreed to a certain extent, but he nevertheless felt a surge of irrational patriotism, an inbuilt desire to defend his country's judicial honour.

'Guess that's why we Yanks are a good lay, Steve.'

Steven sat impassively and seemingly uncomprehending. George felt the need to explain. He jerked one hand back and forth.

'You get desensitized. Less likely to unload early?'

'Oh. I didn't realize,' Steven assured him.

'Come on. How do you restrain yourselves, you British?'

'We don't. We're very sensitive, very selfish bastards. Us British.'

Dr Peyronie relaxed back in his chair.

'I was talking about penile implants, Steve.'

Steven feigned a little interest.

'Is that the new thing?'

'It's the new thing but it ain't new. They've been doing it for centuries in India. They start on the boys when they're small. Slice the skin of the penis and insert a pebble, then another, then another, one at a time. The skin heals over.'

Steven asked if he could smoke and the doctor said no. There were regulations. Steven had to hold his hands together and twiddle his thumbs while his companion continued with his explanation of the ancient practice of genital mutilation. Steven considered it just another misunderstanding in the endless search for eroticism, and found his attention drifting towards the headless woman in the painting.

'Size counts,' the doctor explained. 'Don't fool yourself, Steve, size definitely counts. I know all about the coefficient of expansion, but the overall starting point of your schlong, that counts. And those people have always known that. You've seen their books, you've seen their temple drawings. They *know*.'

The painting was a superior watercolour. The overall effect was of an anatomical sketch, yet it was a mystery as to what exactly the viewer was looking at. From where Steven was sitting, it was as if the woman was pleasuring herself, glimpsed through a crack in a door. The painting was entitled *Siesta*.

'Those pebbles are extra. They massage from the inside and they hit the spot. The fucking Holy Grail. Can you imagine how they negotiate for those dowries over there? Say, here's my son for your daughter and the ten goats, but listen up: he's a five-pebble man and she's going to be happy for the rest of her life, so what do you say to throwing in the field by the well?'

Steven was staring at the woman, the curve of her hip and the slight swell of a breast under her lifted arm. The doctor tapped at the skin under his own eyes.

'I had the fat removed here. I was looking a little tired. See?'

Steven looked at him.

'I think that's my wife,' he said, nodding at the picture.

The doctor stared at the painting and back at Steven.

'No kidding? That's Stella?'

'I think so.'

'Gee, I'm sorry.'

'What for?'

The doctor felt forced to look away, up at the painting again, because Steven was looking at him now and not at the nude. The man was goddamned disconcerting.

I hear you're good with boats, Steve,' he said, composing himself at last.

'I've had some experience, yes.'

The doctor squinted his little blue eyes at the man sitting opposite, and began to wonder what it was with these lowlife Brits that they made you feel inferior even though you were worth a zillion times more than them.

'Or you wouldn't be here, right?' he offered.

'It's not that I don't enjoy your company, George. I can call you George, can't I?'

'Sure,' the doctor replied with a weak smile.

It was a forty-foot sea cruiser with an awning at the back. Steven considered the console with its excessive clutter of electronics and then looked out across the busy bay. The morning breeze had eased and a haze of brown smog had settled over the water and smudged the horizon into the urine-coloured sky. Somewhere, at the back of his head maybe, he could hear a droning like that of a boat engine, and Duran's astonished voice emerged from his memory.

'Three photographs of his dick? Are you serious? What kind of guy thinks of that? You ever do that for her, Steve?'

Duran took the fishing knife and started to hack at bread

and cheese. When he'd finished dividing it up, he poured some more brandy into their glasses. The two men were pleased with each other, with the way the night had gone, but Stella was sulking. She hadn't wanted to come in the first place, and their shared success was not hers. She drank with them but without joining in with the celebration. She had heard Duran's question and she was waiting to hear Steven's answer.

'Why should I?' he said. 'If she wants a look, I've got it right here.'

Duran thought that was pretty funny, but Stella pulled a face. She walked over to one of the bunk beds in the cabin and slumped down on it. He nodded over at her and lowered his voice as he sat down close to Steven.

'It doesn't bother you? Her other guy?'

'Guys. Other guys. No, it doesn't bother me.'

Duran tore at the bread.

'No? You never think about her with them?'

'I didn't say that.'

'Friend, it would drive me crazy. She's a beautiful woman. Men come on to her all the time, yes? Look at her, like an animal, a cat. You could lick her fur. You understand me? You're a lucky man.'

Both the men looked over at her. Her arms were stretched above her head and her dress had edged up to show the triangle of her cotton underpants, like a little blue-white sail in the moonlight. The boat was on autopilot, and the bales of cannabis were roped and on board. Steven struggled to keep his eyes open and his head from tipping backwards. He turned his face to the sky and saw two stars falling out of the black-and-diamond night. As the boat headed north-wards around the coast and beat against the slight swell, the urge to close his eyes became irresistible. Duran lit a cigarette and took another drink. He kept his eyes open.

*

'What do you think?' George said, coming up the steps into the cockpit and looking out across the marina like an admiral over his fleet. 'I take the fishing stuff out, but fuck the fish, Steve, you know what I mean? It don't bother me. So long as the ladies are happy, there's booze and it's hot, I'm happy. You worked these before, Steve?'

'Sure have.'

'Great. I don't want to bother with nothing. This is my pussy boat. That's it. They love it. They take their tops down, they point their perfect tits at the sun and we all have a ball, I tell ya. But, hey, you sail the boat, my friend, so you only get to watch.'

The good doctor laughed but Steven did not. He didn't even look as if he was paying attention, and George began to wonder whether the favour he was doing Stella was turning out to be more trouble than it was worth.

'He's not been well. He needs a break, George,' she had pleaded, and, with what was on offer, who could refuse? He wondered if Steven knew.

'You can set the rods, you know, keep busy,' he said, and Steven turned his eyes towards him.

'Sure,' he said, and walked out of the cockpit and down the steps on to the lower deck. He looked into the darkness of the cabin. The boat was almost identical. He stepped back, almost colliding with the doctor.

'You OK?' George said.

Steven nodded and moved past him away from the cabin.

'I'm fine. Nice boat.'

George rested his hand on Steven's arm and lowered his voice to a more intimate level.

'Stella tells me you served time.'

Steven sucked at his bottom lip.

'In some foreign slammer, a bad business with some blow. I'm not worried about that, Steve, you understand?' George continued.

'Thank you,' Steven replied, taking out some papers to roll a cigarette. He was grateful for the breeze out on deck.

'This isn't just a favour to her, I really want you to know that. I need someone good for this boat.'

'I can handle this boat all right.'

George stood by him, leaning his hands on the rail.

'How was it, Steve?'

Steven wet the cigarette paper lightly with his tongue.

'I don't understand,' he said.

'You know, over there. Inside.'

'George, may I call you George?'

'Sure, call me George, Steve. I said you could call me George, didn't I?'

Steven struck a match in cupped hands and drew on the flame. He inhaled deeply and blew the smoke into the pale sky.

'George,' he said, 'my hosts were the product of a culture that gave us the Inquisition, Franco and Julio Iglesias. How do you think it was?'

The good doctor shook his head.

'Man, they spoiled you, huh?'

Steven smiled and said, 'They sure did.'

Chapter Four

She slipped from her position on top of him to lie underneath, and he began pushing so hard that her head slid away from the comfort of the mattress and dangled off the edge of the bed. The harsh sun cut into the room from a crack in the curtains and shone directly into her eyes. She closed them tightly and turned her face into the shadow of his body. Michael took this as a signal, and pumped his pelvis with increasing vigour until he could hold on to his ecstatic rise no longer. He collapsed on to her with a bellow that sounded like a suffering animal.

Her eyes had opened while his eyes had closed. His body was wet with sweat, her skin was dry, but she wasn't offended or frustrated as he shuddered against her barely exercised body. On the contrary, she felt reassured by her power. She had also felt a slight thrill that perhaps someone was in the wardrobe, or standing behind the drawn curtains. It had perplexed her too, because she hadn't planned it.

She waited for what she considered a decent interval to allow for emotional descent before tapping Michael's shoulder. He moved off her and she rolled over and sat up. Taking the sheet with her, she walked to the window and pulled the drapes back swiftly and suddenly. No one was there, and no one was down on the fire escape either.

Michael lay back on the bed and watched her.

'Maybe if you could relax,' he said.

'I do.'

'It's me, then.'

Stella sighed and turned to gaze across the large airy studio that was divided into open-plan living and working quarters. The wardrobe doors were ajar.

'Stella,' Michael insisted.

'It's not you.'

'What then?'

'I just don't, Michael. I don't do that.'

'It makes me feel like a dog.'

'Why?'

'I get satisfaction. You get none. It's one-sided if I can't make you come. I need to make you come. That's what would really do it for me.'

'Why a dog?'

He knew she wouldn't let it go. Instead of talking about her and him – *About us, I'm talking about us!* Michael thought – she'd want to know what he meant, exactly. She was so damned literal. He sighed and stared up at the distant smoothness of the high ceiling.

'Why a dog?' she insisted.

'Fuck the dog,' he said.

'You don't have a dog.'

Michael groaned. Stella gave a little laugh and then got serious so as not to irritate him any more. Her timing was good.

'I get satisfaction in my own way,' she said.

Michael pushed himself up on his elbows to face her.

'I'm in love with you. I make love to you while I have sex, Stella. What do you do?'

'I do love you.'

'What do you *do*?'

'I satisfy you.'

'I want to satisfy *you*.'

'You do.'

'Don't patronize me.'

Stella scooped up the sheet as if it was a ballgown and dumped it on the bed. She walked over to the table and collected her watch and clipped on her earrings, before bending down to gather up her scattered underwear. He watched with rising anxiety as she dressed.

'Tell me what to do,' he pleaded.

'You can't do anything,' she replied, and leaned over his naked body. He could smell her perfume and the heat of his own body on her. She hadn't showered. She never showered after. She went home to her husband with his smell on her. She kissed him on the lips and straightened up.

'It's me,' she said. 'Just forget it. I have to go now.'

Michael stood up and grasped her.

'My skirt,' she protested.

'Tell me, am I a dog? Am I? Am I just an animal to you?'

She pushed him away and brushed herself down. The colour red would show everything.

'Of course not. It's something I don't do, Michael. Not any more,' she said.

'What? Like drink? Like smoke? With me?'

He was running his fingers through his hair as if he could pull a solution to his frustration from inside his brain.

'With him? Did you just give it up, or something? What about him? Is it something you don't do with him?'

Stella slicked on her lipstick.

'You really don't want to know what I do with him,' she said. He appeared doubly pathetic to her, with his arms flailing, completely naked in body and emotions. He watched her snap her handbag shut.

'I do. I'm sick with it. I want to know what you do with him. Tell me.'

'Michael, don't,' she said with a little more sympathy, but she might as well have speared him with a hatpin.

'Get out. Go on. Leave me alone,' he said, but she was

already walking towards the door. He should have let her go but he couldn't. He ran after her and caught hold of her, pulling her to him. She didn't resist. She put her arms around the man and comforted him instead, like a mother would a child.

'Baby. Baby. Sweet baby,' she said, her eyes glancing at the wardrobe.

Stella had felt someone watching them while she had lunch with Michael Revere, and in the studio while they were making love. She had looked around more often than usual as they had driven to the restaurant, thinking that she might catch a glimpse of whoever it was she felt had been following her for the past week or so. The person who had, maybe, taken the keys from her car.

'Get someone on to it, whether he has his own PI watching you or not. Get your own man,' Michael had said.

'Or woman,' she had replied.

'Whatever, get the best.'

'I'll get the worst. I want him to be noticed.'

Michael sighed.

'OK. I'll shut my mouth for a while, what do you say? I wouldn't want you to contradict my suggestion for a place to eat. Slow down. Jesus.'

She had gunned the car through the lights and was looking in the rear-view mirror. Steven had been standing by the traffic lights and he was running after them.

'Steven. It was Steven. He saw us.'

'Now what?'

'Let me think.'

'Be my guest. All I can think about is what he's thinking.'

The video camera was connected to the computer, and the screen reran three-quarters of an hour of afternoon sex between Michael and Stella. In the background, an audio-tape played a telephone conversation.

'How'd it go?'

It was Stella's voice.

'Great,' Steven replied. '*Dr Peyronie wants me to take him around the bay while he does this year's models.*'

'*It's something, Steven.*'

There was a long pause, a hiss on the tape. Steven spoke first.

'*Guess what?*' he said.

'*What?*'

'*You'll die when you hear this.*'

'*Come on,*' she said, plainly irritated.

'*George says I can watch the action. Maybe do some fishing.*'

'*I hate you.*'

'*Come on, where's your sense of humour?*'

'*I hate you.*'

Steven began to sing a low, bluesy tune.

'*Woman shut your mouth, don't advertise your man. That's how it goes, doesn't it?*' he said. '*Do you sing the blues, ba . . . by? Advertise your man? Those things I do so well.*'

'*I could murder you.*'

'*Do me a favour.*'

The tape was stopped and fast-forwarded to another conversation.

'*I hate him. He hurts me,*' Stella said.

'*Don't get so upset,*' Michael replied.

'*I can feel him slicing at my life. He's taking it away piece by piece.*'

'*Your life is your own. Your sweet, sweet life is your own.*'

'*Is it?*'

'*You can exist without him, believe me.*'

'*Can he exist?*'

Her voice sounded uncertain, and then she seemed to gather herself.

'No, *he doesn't exist. He's a ghost. He's less than that. He's a trace of a ghost,*' she said.

Her voice became bitter and dry, and with little more than a whisper to herself, she added, '*Of an old, old painful love.*'

Michael waited this time.

'*What about me?*' he said. '*Do I exist? Now. In you. Do I? Do you love me? Do I exist?*'

'*Yes, Michael,*' she said, '*you exist.*'

A finger caught the tape and dragged it across the recording head. The manipulation distorted the recording, and a deep and monstrous voice growled until the tape accelerated into normal speed and Stella's voice flew up like a melodic butterfly.

'*Yes, you exist, Michael. You exist.*'

The tape was edged back and forth until the exact moment of transfer from Michael to Stella. A yellow mark divided the lovers and a razor sliced them apart. The small piece bearing Michael's voice was carefully marked M, detached and discarded. It fell to the floor on to a pile of many more small pieces of tape, each also marked M.

Another section of tape eased back and forth over the tape head. Another man's voice growled, '*Do I exist?*'

'*Do I exist?*'

'*Do I exist?*'

'*Do I exist?*'

It was marked and cut, and in between, where Michael's voice had been, a section of fresh tape replaced it. The distorted voice repeated Michael's question.

'*Do I exist?*'

The tape picked up speed, and Stella's clear and natural voice answered.

'*You exist. You exist.*'

The tape spun on untrammelled until Steven's voice said, '*You sing the blues, ba . . . by?*' and Stella replied, '*I could murder you.*'

The tape was pulled back and forth.

'*You sing the blues, ba . . . by?*'

'*I could murder you.*'

'*You sing the blues, ba . . . by?*'

'*I could murder you.*'

'*I could murder you.*'

'*I could murder you.*'

Another yellow line marked the spot and another razor cut split the tape.

Steven swam naked in the pool and waited for his wife's return. He could hear Stella's laughter in his head. She had been giggling as they had got out of the cab. He could remember the way she looked, giddy with mischief, sweetness in his sight. He felt a sudden ache in his chest as if the life in him was being squeezed from his heart.

'*Or my beautiful wife and I take the plane. I don't fucking believe you, Steven.*'

'*God, he fancied you. I swear he paid an extra five just to have you come along.*'

'*You're not going to do it, are you?*'

'*For ten grand? I very much think so.*'

'*Come on, we're not criminals. Steven?*'

'*We deliver stolen boats. I guess that makes us chartered accountants.*'

'*We don't steal them, we're not criminals. Did you really speak to Charlie?*'

'*Nope.*'

'*Let's take the plane, please, Steven.*'

'*What would you buy with ten grand, Stella?*'

'*We're not criminals, Steven, not really. Please, let's take the plane.*'

He dived to the bottom of the pool and looked up through the blue water. A shark circled overhead. Its white belly was wide and smooth and its inwardly pointing teeth glistened in its primitive cartilaginous maw. There was meat in its mouth, and, as it swung its head from side to side, the fish appeared to be half man, half beast. The blood spread on the water like the colour of his wife's suit. He broke the surface in a panic, and Stella was standing there in her swimming costume with her back to the sun.

'I saw you,' he said, breathing heavily and wiping his face.

She folded her arms.

'Where?'

'You ran a red light.'

'What were you doing there?'

'I'd been to the police station.'

'Oh, Steven.'

'About *your* little problem, not mine.'

Stella held out a bottle of suntan lotion and Steven hauled himself out of the water and carefully dried his hands.

She lay on the lounger while he massaged her skin. He couldn't help but view her in parts: here leg, there thigh, here tricep, there bicep, here pelvis, there pubis. The slick shine of sunscreen brought out texture and shape like a light varnish on a fine piece of furniture. His hands folded around and under the musculature as he silently kneaded and smoothed her flesh. It was an erotic contemplation he had always enjoyed. He used to have the same blissful pleasure when he had been allowed to soap and wash her in the bath. All that had stopped years ago. She knew how to punish him.

'Why are you letting me do this?' he asked.

'Because I know you want to.'

'What is it *you* want?'

She sighed.

'At this moment, protection from the sun. Easy, not so rough.'

His loving hands moved over her body.

'I think you want protection for him. You don't want me coming between you and him.'

'Get on with it, Steven.'

He pressed his fingers into her back and watched the dimples form.

'You have to be familiar with the contours. You have to *know*. Does he really *know*?'

Stella didn't answer. The massage was quite pleasant, but she knew the timing had to be perfect, otherwise he'd think there was real forgiveness in her act of permission.

'If you neglect a patch, the tiniest area,' he said, 'you spoil the overall effect, the homogeneity of colour and texture. Worse, you expose a point of entry and something can get in. If that happens, you expose the skin to damage. The skin, this skin, is a very, very delicate organ.'

Stella lay with her eyes closed but was no longer relaxed. She had felt a slight tension in his fingertips.

'I could ask him myself. I could explain things to him. I could tell him all about it.'

'Don't threaten me with that,' she said, sitting up. She took the oil from him, spilled some into her hands and rubbed it haphazardly into her shins. He slipped his sunglasses over his eyes.

'You need me to watch. You said so,' he said.

She rubbed in more oil and smoothed it down over her feet.

'You won't let me, and you fake it with him. You need me to watch.'

'I don't fake it. Not with him. What do you know? You get everything second-hand. You get what I choose to give you. What do you know?'

'Don't make me laugh,' he said, anger creeping into his voice. 'I kept my mouth shut. I did hard time. I did six fucking years and you flew home.'

Stella covered her belly protectively with one hand and pointed at the pool with the other. The sun still danced brightly on the water.

'Isn't this gratitude?'

He stared at the pool and tried not to look at her. The water moved in front of his eyes, his head ached and a pain gripped his chest once again.

'I'm hooked, Stella. I'm spinning through deep water and it's getting so I can't get back . . .'

'Oh, shut up, Steven.'

'Our life was so sweet. You want me to tell him how sweet? That Mister fucking Dream House on the Prairie dog? You want me to tell him? You need me to watch.'

Stella stood up and her shadow fell over him.

'You got tired of the sun, remember?' she said. 'You got what you wanted and now you're getting what you deserve.'

She took two quick steps and dived into the pool, kicking strongly underwater so she wouldn't have to hear him calling her, shouting at her. She didn't expect him to come after her like he did, his hand catching her leg.

They tumbled violently round and round each other like fighting fish. He was too strong for her. She fought but she was losing. Water began to enter her mouth and nose and she began to choke and panic. It was all over. *It was all over.* Her mind was in turmoil. This wasn't the plan. She couldn't lose, not this time. She felt his arm hook around her neck and her frantic hands scratched at his skin. The realization that this might be a final defeat flooded over her, until the hatred and bitterness within swelled like putrid yeast and gave her the strength of rage.

Their struggling bodies broke the surface of the water together and she felt her feet touch the bottom. It was a chance, and she steadied herself to take it but he had already released her. They stood gasping in the shallows, the water around them tormented with whirlpools and waves. She didn't speak, and he said nothing as she waded away from him in long strides towards the steps and ran up to the house. He waited in the fading sunshine and heard the door slam and the car's engine start before walking to the house with some urgency. His body was still damp under the towelling robe as he replayed a short stream of video images. A couple made love in jerky motion. He liked to direct the action. If he so desired, he could make them stammer in coitus or hurry them along. He jabbed at buttons with his fingers and thumb.

The reels of a tape recorder spun around.

Stella's voice, breathless, frantic and angry, spoke, almost drowned by the sound of a speeding car.

'*He tried to kill me. He hurts me. He hurts me, all the time. I want to kill him. I want him dead. I want him dead.*'

'*Leave, Stella. Please leave him,*' Michael replied.

'*I can't.*'

'*Tell me.*'

'*I can't.*'

'*Why?*'

There was a pause.

'*You love me, don't you?*' Stella said.

'*I love you, you know that. I love you.*'

'*Kill him for me.*'

All was still and silent in the room, apart from the sound of an internal fan cooling the computer system, the tape hissing over the heads and the deep, regular breathing of someone listening.

'*That's crazy talk. Cool it,*' Michael said at last.

Stella gasped and panted.

'*I can't breathe,*' she said.

'*I'll come and get you.*'

'*No.*'

'*I'll come and get you, Stella. Stella?*'

The line disconnected but the tape spun on.

32

Chapter Five

Detective Lee Johnson had leaned against a grey filing cabinet and gone through the motions of listening. Johnson was about forty, forty-two, black, neat, trim. He worked out. He liked to look good and smell good, but, all the same, he couldn't bat away the recurring feeling he kept getting nowadays of being all toned up with nowhere to go. The Brit was a little younger, fit enough, Johnson noted, but there was a sickness in his movements, and for what he was here about today, his eyes were too dull and indifferent.

'The keys the first time she mention it? She didn't say what else got her thinking?'

'No. If anything did, she didn't tell me. She might tell you, though.'

'You two not getting along, Mr Gates?'

'She's sleeping with someone else.'

Johnson rubbed his lips. He'd give the poor guy five minutes and tell him the force didn't handle this stuff. Steven spoiled the policeman's timetable when he started to roll a ciagarette.

'I don't mind all that much, providing she saves a piece for me,' he had said, and Johnson took a better look at him.

'She thinks I have a private detective on the case, but I haven't. I don't need one,' Steven had continued.

'How do you know your wife is having an affair, Mr Gates?'

Steven tried to light his ultra-thin roll-up a few times but it wouldn't take.

'I've been feeling a bit . . . left out,' he said. He gazed directly at the detective and picked tobacco from his tongue. 'You know how it is.'

The way he said it had bothered Johnson, for he did, indeed, know how it was. It had been three years since Ella and he had split. He moved away from the filing cabinet and sat opposite the man. He straightened his cuffs and ran a finger around his stiff collar. He was going to take some notes.

'What does your wife do, Mr Gates?'

'She deals in art and fucks the artists when she can. They aren't as faggoty as you think.'

'You think it's one of them?'

'One lovelorn, paint-bespattered prick following her around? Yes, it's possible. She is quite lovely.'

'What do you do, Mr Gates?'

The two men gazed at each other.

'I worry about her,' Steven said at last.

'For a living.'

'I . . .' Steven cast about for the right word. 'I sail, that's right. I'm a jolly sailor.'

Johnson clicked his pen.

'OK, since you're clearly very concerned about your wife, Mr Gates, we'll get on with it. Let's have some details.'

'How's Famalaro?'

The detective looked up.

'Sir?'

'The painter and decorator.'

'What about him, sir?'

'Safely under lock and key, is he?'

'The details, sir, if you don't mind.'

*

Now, as he stood in the man's lounge watching the man's wife, Lee Johnson understood a little of Steven Gates's concerns.

She moved about the room wearing a swimming costume and a thin robe. It was, Johnson conceded, warm for the time of year, but even so, up here in the hills it was cool enough to dress up a little. He wasn't complaining, exactly. Mrs Gates, dressed, would be easy on the eye; almost undressed, she made you want to look and get caught looking.

'Nice house,' he said.

She didn't bother to thank him for the compliment, nor did she bother to agree. She looked through a handful of papers that she held in her hand as if she was giving him a chance to think of something smarter to say.

'The fire didn't get to you?'

'Not to the house, no.'

Johnson felt duly admonished.

'You know a lot of people, Mrs Gates?' he said.

'Art is a networking business, detective,' she said.

'Art *dealing* is a networking business.'

She stopped flicking through the paperwork and looked up at him.

'You make it sound like a crime.'

'It's the job. Makes people feel guilty when we say "good day". I was expressing an opinion.'

'Oh, were you? In that case, let me ask you, what is the point of being an artist and never selling your work?'

'Fact you sit and doodle in your room all day and no one knows about it, doesn't mean you're not an artist.'

Stella didn't reply. She reached out her hand and touched the sculpture that stood on a plinth in the living room. She cupped what appeared to be the testicles of the abstract three-dimensional study before drawing her fingers over it and moving away. The seemingly involuntary action had made the little hairs that curled at the back of Johnson's head prickle up.

'All art requires an audience. It's a form of expression, of communication, detective,' she said, and then, a little irritated, she added: 'This is a waste of time. I really *do* think my husband has hired a private detective to follow me. There is no stalker,' she said.

'Maybe so. But why would a private detective take your car keys?'

She had no answer to that, and Johnson continued.

'I've had a look around. You could tighten up the security around the back here. No one's been in the house, right?'

'I don't think so.'

'You didn't have the house keys with the car keys?'

'No.'

'Anyone else's?'

Stella put her hands inside her robe and rested them on her hips so Johnson got a better look at her black swimsuit. She wasn't that tall but she had great legs, and, he thought, there was some meat on her. He hated it if there was a triangle of space between a woman's thighs and her crotch. She didn't have that, and her breasts didn't need much help from the cups of the costume, either. His eyes flicked once, down and up, until she caught his gaze and held it. A raised eyebrow brought him to his senses.

'Your husband thinks you're having an affair,' he said.

'I am,' she replied, and walked out of the room and down towards the pool.

He stood on the terrace and watched her dive into the water and disappear. She swam the length of the pool underwater and appeared a few seconds later at the far end. As she stood, her hair fell straight down her back and shone like black satin in the sunlight which shimmered on the rivulets that ran down her skin.

Johnson slipped on his shades and walked down the steps to the side of the pool towards her.

'Your husband says you have a lot of affairs, Mrs Gates,' he said as he stood at the edge of the pool and looked across at her.

'The water's beautifully warm, detective.'

'Is that true, Mrs Gates?'

'He'd like to think that,' she said, leaning her back against the side and moving her hand back and forth through the water. She turned her head towards the sun and closed her eyes. She looked like a poster girl, only her head hadn't been directed to inch this way or another, her arm hadn't been moved just enough to accentuate her breast, her lips weren't made up, her hair wasn't gelled, her nipples weren't iced and nothing was faked. The woman was a natural, and a pro.

'I wouldn't like to think that,' he said.

She kept her face towards the sun.

'You wouldn't like to think about me with other men, detective?'

'I wouldn't want to think of my wife with other men.'

She cupped her hands and splashed her face before immersing herself and flicking her feet so that she propelled herself backwards and away from him. He walked along the side to keep up with her.

'Happily married?' she said.

'I'm divorced.'

She smiled for the first time, and turned over on to her stomach to breast-stroke towards him. She put her hands on the side, splashing two or three drops of water on his highly polished shoes as she crossed her arms and grinned up at him like a kid.

'And do you still think about her with other men?' she said.

She had a wide mouth and her teeth were slightly uneven. That small imperfection shocked him. He'd seen forty-year-old women wearing orthodontic braces. He'd seen seventeen-year-olds with breast implants. The only help this woman looked as if she had was a shaved armpit, and when he thought about that smooth crevice, he thought about his tongue licking it and his teeth biting her flesh. He wondered how old Stella Gates was, and as he looked down at her, she held out her hand for him to haul her up out of the water. The cold wet touch of it disguised the warm sweat on his palm.

She sauntered over to the lounger and picked up her towel, drying herself quickly before passing it to him for his hands. As she slipped on her robe and tied the belt tight, she said, 'The truth is, he'd prefer to think of me with lots of men.'

He followed her back into the house.

'I don't get it,' he said.

'Lots of men is OK, detective. Just the one creates a rival. Just the one is dangerous and threatening in a way that many are not.'

Johnson understood the point only too well. He had, after all, something in common with the curious man who had sat in his office the other day, and it gave him no satisfaction to admit it. She offered him a beer, which he refused.

'Coffee then?' she said, and he watched dumbly as she made it, feeling self-conscious as his fingers touched hers when he grasped the cup. She smoked a cigarette and stared out of the window. She didn't look so much like a movie queen now without the sun on her body. She looked tired and touchable.

'Do you have children, detective?' she said at last, without looking at him.

'I do.'

'Do they look like you?'

'Every one but the last.'

He heard her breath catch as she inhaled. She held her

arms around herself as if she was suddenly feeling the cold. Her lips were a little blue.

'Say your husband had hired a PI. Why should he come to us with this story about someone following you around?' Johnson asked.

She dragged the smoke into her mouth again over her slightly crooked teeth and continued to stare out of the window.

'Good question, detective. Good question, but it doesn't make me feel any better.'

As he left the house he knew exactly what Ruth was going to think.

Detective Ruth Dandy was twenty-seven, white and freckled as a new-laid egg, and was as good a cop as he was, probably better.

'You're kind of quiet, sir,' she said when he got back.

Johnson said nothing. He sat at his desk and thought about Stella Gates's teeth, her lips, her skin and her husband.

'This the Gates thing? Come on, make my day complete: does *she* think it's Famalaro too?'

Johnson leaned his elbows on the desk and peaked his hands in front of his face.

'Sir?'

'I don't think *he* thinks it's Famalaro. It's called irony. The Brits go on about it all the time. They say we don't appreciate it.'

'That's because it sounds like plain old sarcasm to us.'

'She thinks her husband has a PI on her tail.'

'So why'd he come to us?'

'Exactly.'

Johnson sat at his desk in silence as Dandy typed up a report. After a quarter of an hour, she stopped and looked across at him.

39

'What she like?'

Johnson didn't reply.

'Line forms to the right, huh?' she remarked, and got on with her work.

Chapter Six

The art gallery by the beach glowed and bubbled against the apricot glow of the dying sun like a little glass of champagne clasped in a soft hand. A minimum purchase from the collection on display would set a prospective buyer back ten thousand dollars, but most of the pieces were tagged for a whole lot more. The more they cost, the more people liked them. It was good business, and Stella had 'personalized' the service the gallery offered. It was perfect for anyone with the wherewithal, but without the will to submit themselves to the uncertainty of relying on their own taste. Stella 'assessed' her clients. She would then buy the right products for them according to a number of criteria, not the least of which was how much their contemporaries might be willing to pay. She'd been promoting Michael Revere for at least a year. She posed for him, she slept with him, and this evening she was showing him off.

It wasn't a hard sell, given the quality of the work and Michael's Native American good looks. The silver about his neck exuded just the right amount of ethnic danger to make him a collectable with the property developers and plastic surgeons in Newport Beach, the richest area of the richest county in the richest state in the richest country in the world. The fact that he was an Italian American from New York was neither here nor there. He had impressed in any case by reason of being 'a close friend' of Robert De Niro, whom he referred to as 'Bobby'. That and the fact that he'd been a junkie but was now clean added to his creative persona, and gave him an engaging aura of controlled instability.

Stella was working the room. She made her English accent more pronounced because she knew how much people liked it. There was no detectable regional dialect or urban idiosyncrasy in her voice. Instead, it spoke of an aristocratic gentility and sophistication that was as pleasing to the ear as the blue and white of Wedgwood was to the eye, and just as misleading a representative of that distant, yet seemingly familiar, nationality.

'This is *beautiful*,' the woman said, reaching out to touch a collection of entwined limbs of stone entitled *Dismemberment*. The piece was placed before a painting which it echoed. Under normal circumstances, Stella would have been striving for maximum eye contact as her client spoke. She was, however, distracted by the sight of Steven making his way through the crowd towards Michael.

'I have to be able to understand. I have to have something to work on, something that relates to me as a person first. Don't get me wrong, I like it to push the envelope a little, but sheep's entrails in glass, this installation stuff, well, I just don't know. This is about sex, right?'

' . . . About the power of love, yes,' Stella replied. She could see her husband and her lover apparently conversing. She focused on them, but could not tell if the even banter was going to spark into something more violent. She didn't want a scene. On the other hand, if it happened she could certainly capitalize on it. She wasn't sure what kind of damage limitation she could exert over the stock, however, and she wondered if an early intervention might just provoke a situation which would be, on balance, best avoided. She didn't like not knowing what Steven was telling Michael. She felt a rising anxiety, as if someone was reaching out their fingers to pull at a loose but vital thread from her clothing. She started forward just as Steven shook Michael's hand and moved away through the exhibits of stone and metal and glass. Stella glanced back at the woman.

'I'm sorry, you'll have to excuse me,' she said, and the woman nodded reassuringly and watched her go, her eyes tracking her to see what, exactly, was making Stella push anxiously through the crowd.

'Are they still an item?' the woman said, leaning towards her husband, who was intently observing a complex piece entitled *Conjugation*.

By the time Stella had woven her way across the room, her husband had gone and Michael was in conversation with someone else, who was telling him, from what Stella overheard, about an actress who had been chosen for an Altman movie because she had *real* breasts. As soon as the man saw Stella, he smiled.

'Lovely as ever, Stella.'

'Ossie.'

She smiled and air-kissed him gently on either side of his face.

'Michael?' she said, still smiling, her hand slipping across Michael's back. He shook his companion's hand.

'Catch you later,' he said, and they edged slowly through the pressing crowd towards a quieter spot.

'Take it easy,' he said.

'What did he say? Shit, I need a cigarette.'

'Take it easy. He was cool.'

'Cool? He was cool? How about you?'

'It was OK, Stella. He introduced himself.'

'He tried to kill me today, to drown me, don't you understand? He's unstable.'

'Let's go outside.'

'What did he say?'

'Not now. C'mon Stella, look around. Not now.'

She gave him a look that was a cocktail measuring one

part hostility with three parts anxiety. The former was enough to unseat his confidence.

'Stella?'

'Later,' she said, and walked away from him. Michael thrust his hands disconsolately into the pockets of his linen suit, and stared at her back disappearing into the throng of art lovers that gazed at his depictions of her body and soul in more than one medium and dimension. It was a good hour before she spoke to him again.

The night breeze tugged at her clothes and whisked the noxious trail of her lit cigarette into nothing. She was wearing his jacket over her shoulders as they stood outside the gallery after everyone had left.

'What did he say?' she demanded.

For Michael, the anticipation of this showdown had quite taken the sheen off his evening. He would have liked to go back to the studio and smoke a joint or two, to try to find his bliss with her. Instead, they were snarling at each other in the street. She was making him feel that he'd done or said the wrong thing. He could tell her that her husband was crazy but she didn't want to hear that. The devil, as they say, was in the detail.

'What did he say, Michael?' she replied.

'He said . . . I didn't understand what he said. He's crazy.'

'What did he say?'

'He tapped me on the shoulder with the catalogue and said, goddamn, I think this was it, "You are Colly Cibber, and I claim the *Daily Messenger* prize".'

Stella stared at him and then began to laugh.

'At first, I thought he said you are Kato Kaelin. Kato Kaelin? Oh, *right*,' Michael muttered.

'He's got a bloody sense of humour, I'll give him that,' Stella replied.

'Kato?'

'My husband. My husband has a sense of humour.'

Michael was getting angry. It was evident that he knew more about O. J. Simpson's house guest than the novels of Graham Greene. He knew exactly who Kato Kaelin was. Everyone knew.

'I don't get it. Who the fuck is Colly Cibber?'

'He's a character in a work of fiction. Rather like Kato, I suppose. What else did he say?'

'He introduced himself.'

'Right.'

'Small talk. He said he'd heard a lot about me. He was polite, and I got the message.'

'What message?'

'That he knows about us.'

'We know that, Michael.'

'He was cool. I stayed cool. It's OK. Man talk. I wanted to break his neck all the same.'

'Then why didn't you? Why don't you? Break his neck.'

Michael sighed.

'He was OK, Stella. He told me to look out for you. He said you were being followed and he'd been to the cops about it. He cares about you. Isn't that kind of touching?'

Stella crossed the road without him. She walked quickly up the hill towards the underground parking lot. Michael stood and watched her go, with the increasing frustration finally putting paid to the good mood brought on by the success of the show. He still couldn't work out what he'd done wrong. There hadn't been a scene, the crazy bastard had been wild-eyed but civilized. You had to hand it to these Brits, he had thought. They knew how to be goddamned civilized. He could understand why Stella might be angry, but why at him? He didn't understand either of them. Was she really afraid? Had the guy OJed her so bad? She had to leave him. He had to make sure of that, now especially. Everything was different now, and he had to protect her.

The traffic was heavy with cars looking for spots outside

the restaurants and by the time he, and the thickset man with the camera who had been watching them, made it across the road to follow her, she was out of sight.

Steven stood outside the empty gallery and watched them disappear. When they had gone, he turned to look at the fragments of bodies that were balanced on the spotlit plinths inside. One kept his attention longer than any of the peep shows to which he treated himself from time to time. It seemed pointless going to those places any more. He'd put the coin in the slot and the girl or woman would stand up and writhe about for a few minutes, until the flap dropped and he had to pay for another look at her exposed body, her flesh, her breasts, her perspiring buttocks and barely veiled pudenda. It was a pointless pursuit of pleasure, because invariably his head began to ache with boredom and he would start to fantasize that the female inside the cubicle was Stella, and if he chose the option of a male occupant too, he could almost come with their help and a little imagination. But he could do that anywhere. He could do that at home.

He stared at the torso behind the thick glass. It was lit so that gentle shadows were formed by its delicate contours. The piece comprised a section of the trunk, an amputated arm and severed leg, and all manner of trivia was attached to it so that the effect was of something found in the crevice of a rock by the seashore; of an organism that had refused to rot but had, instead, become at one with an alien and deadly environment. His face reflected in the glass was tense with unbearable remembrance, and his eyes searched for some relief in the dismembered parts of his wife that were set about the gallery, pressed against the anonymous remnants of strangers. *Michael Revere: An Installation of Memories*, the showcards said.

Steven's gaze finally settled on a luminous painting of a curved pitcher of flesh that held within it, like a goldfish in a bowl, a small, complete child, uncurled, its limbs and arms spread as if it had dived willingly into the warm pool in which it found itself. The child's eyes were open and they stared wetly at him. He seemed to recognize the eyes, even the face. He cocked his head this way and that and his heart beat faster and faster until a headlight caught in the glass. He turned away from the painting of the child, wiping his lips like a man gasping for a drink, and hurried away from the gallery.

He drove his Ford Blazer home through the dark canyon and up the steep hill towards the sky and its indifferent stars that glimmered with the hard light of winter. He could hear sea birds calling as he sat in the off-road vehicle and clutched at the steering wheel.

Michael finally caught up with Stella in the parking lot. She was stooping to open the car door, and as he bent to kiss her neck, there was a whirring and a continuous clicking followed by an explosion of light.

Stella spun around and pushed Michael out of the way before lunging at the shadow behind the flash.

'Hey! Hey lady, take it easy. Hey lady,' the stranger pleaded.

'Not now, my God. Not now.'

'Hey, quit that. Hey. I'm only doing my job, for Chrissakes.'

Michael watched Stella pull the film from the camera and then looked over at the dishevelled fat man in his late forties, who was wearing a brand-new raincoat and who continued to make entreaties for the return of his property.

'Who are you, pal?' Michael said, making a grab at the man's lapels.

'Leave the coat. Leave it, OK? Don't put your hands on me.'

'I asked you who are you?'

'Leave him, Michael.'

He ignored her.

'Who the fuck *are* you?'

'Ray Deedes. Private investigator.'

'Who hired you?'

The man kept his mouth shut even as he choked in Michael's grip.

'You asshole,' Michael said as he released him and glanced at Stella and then back at the detective.

'Oh, man,' he said as he took Stella's arm and guided her into the car.

'Hey! Hey! Wait a minute. What about my camera? That cost money!' Deedes called after them, but his words were lost in a squeal of tyres on concrete.

'Jesus, Stella. Him?' Michael muttered, looking at the receding bulk of the man in the rear-view mirror.

Two hours later, Steven felt his wife slip into their bed.

'Does he love my beautiful wife?' he enquired.

Chapter Seven

Stella was sick for the second time the next morning before she told Steven she was pregnant. It was as if a bolt had dropped into place in a steel wall in his head and locked him in for ever.

He had tried to make love to her, but it was the same old thing. She'd stare up at something behind his shoulder while he pumped away at her, getting lonelier and lonelier until it was a relief to roll off her. She had got up to go to the bathroom almost immediately and he had heard her vomit. He knew that he had known all along, but just hearing her tell him, hearing her say the words made it real knowledge. The morning sickness should have confirmed it for him but it didn't, because he knew how he revolted her. He expected the *thought* of him revolted her enough to make her heave into a basin in the bathroom behind the closed door. He knew that.

Sometimes, though, in her eyes he'd see a look that he remembered. A hesitant look, something like love, that would appear and then disappear like a wild thing in an ancient wood. He would try to remember what he might have been doing or saying at the time that look appeared so that he could get it back, but he never could get it back. The fabulous beast never took the bait or came to his call. It only came unbidden by him and undesired by her, and nowadays she was too strong for it.

He lay on the bed and watched her dress, and he could see the Michael-baby, like the child in the painting, complete and uncurled, its limbs and arms spread as if it was skydiving into the world. A couple of months at most, he thought. No. It probably looked like a primordial fish, too primitive for a casual observer to guess at its future. The relentlessly multi-plying ball of cells would have reached that milestone of mammalian evolutionary history that was marked by the simple vertebrate. So complex, yet deemed so simple that it didn't count. It didn't. She could kill it now if she wanted, rid herself of it, flush it away. He never thought for a moment, though, that it could be half him, and he couldn't bear anything that was just half her. He watched her cover her body and felt his personality fading away to nothing. Two hours later, when she had long gone, he rang Michael Revere and asked the artist to kill him.

'Say something,' an unnerved Michael said to Stella over lunch. She shrugged her shoulders and sipped at the soup.

'I'm starving,' she said.

Michael leaned back hard against the cane chair and almost knocked the laptop off the table behind him. He apologized to the startled writer. The pavement café was packed as usual. The storm in the night had blown away and left a clear, warm day in its wake. Stella caught the eye of the young waiter with the ponytail and ordered more rye bread.

'I suppose I'll have to stop smoking,' she said.

'The guy needs serious therapy. He's losing it.'

'No. He's always had a pretty good feel for what I want. Whether he ever does it or not is another matter.'

'I can't believe you said that.'

Stella stopped eating and dragged her cigarette pack towards her and thought better of it. The tables of the restaurant were too close together anyway, and it would cause unpleasantness.

'He tried to kill me. That's a hell of a lot worse than me just *wanting* him dead.'

Michael didn't answer, but he was beginning to wonder if Stella might not be exaggerating about the other day. It had been going so well. He had had the best professional year of his life since Stella had picked him up, modelled for him, guided and then promoted him. She had very definite ideas about what she called the 'psychology of art', and he was a good enough technician to put her ideas into practice. *The psychology of art. An installation of memories.* It sounded good in the brochures too. *Michael Revere: An Installation of Memories.* He had no real idea if they were his memories or not. She had convinced him that the visions she had were part of a shared memory and that was why people would come. She was right. And now she was pregnant.

It wasn't what he had planned, nor, in truth, what he had wanted, not yet. She said it was his, but doubt gnawed inside him. Worse than that was that the relationship had moved on to another stage before it had completed the first. From now on, she would be focusing on her baby and not on him, and he hadn't made her answer to him, explain herself. He was still full of passion. He ached when she was not there. Michael thought about her body. It had never been entirely his, and now it never would be.

'Did you hear what I said?'

'Why don't you leave?'

'Leave my house?'

'Yeah. Leave your house, and Steven.'

She turned her face towards the pale winter sun and sat back from the table.

'What would be the point?'

'I beg your pardon?'

Stella dropped her sunglasses down on to her nose and glanced at him. He was angry.

'Michael, if someone's following me then they are following me. I move to your place, they follow me there.'

She shoved the glasses back up her face and returned to her sunbathing. Michael tapped his fingers on the glass of the table. The smell of *caffè latte* and vegetarian lasagne was in the air.

'OK. I understand that, but your husband's crazy. You tell me he tried to kill you. He calls me and asks me to kill *him*, for Chrissakes.'

'So did I. I asked you to kill him. Does that make me crazy?'

'You weren't serious.'

Stella didn't reply.

'Aw, come on, Stella.'

'You don't believe me, do you?'

'I . . .'

'He did try to kill me. He tried to drown me.'

Michael looked across the table at her. She'd switched the focus and he'd missed the beat. She leaned down and grabbed her straw hat from the top of her leather bag. Stella never wore a baseball cap, and timed her exposure to the sun carefully. Despite her Mediterranean complexion, she avoided the deep tan she could easily get and which was so common hereabouts. She would shudder at the sight of the volleyball players down at the beach. She despised their leathery hides, their straw-coloured hair and 'ripped' torsos the colour of tea, the men and the women.

'They lie about on the sand and sweat, or play ball and sweat, all day,' she had insisted. 'It's all physicality. They have no range.'

'It's foreplay,' Michael had said. 'Display, courtship, you know, different folks.'

'They're so bland.'

'Not to each other.'

Stella had fallen silent, and then after a while she had stroked his chest thoughtfully and ventured, 'We only like our own kind, is that it?'

He looked down at her upturned face and should have said yes, but he knew that he was not her kind and no matter how much he wanted her, she was a familiar stranger. She was not his kind, and the more time he spent with her, the more perplexed he became as to what, exactly, *was* his kind. In fact, he was beginning to doubt himself. Who was Michael Revere? All he knew was that if she wasn't around, he wasn't much.

'I'm going back to the studio,' he said.

'I have an appointment,' she said, and got up from the table. He stood up and helped pull out her chair, and, as she kissed him, her tongue flicked into his mouth.

'Come to me after work,' he whispered.

'I can't do that tonight,' she replied, and he watched her leave, his hands stuffed disconsolately into the pockets of his baggy chinos and his hair blowing randomly in the breeze.

Ray Deedes shuffled through the photographs he had taken and took a sip of beer. He could see the boat from where he sat. He knew that it belonged to Dr George Peyronie, a plastic surgeon, twice divorced with no kids and a medical reputation that belied the fact that he liked his entertainment unsophisticated. The guy might look like a jerk but he had plenty of satisfied clients, no outstanding lawsuits against him and pocketfuls of dough. Deedes had a file on him anyhow, just in case.

Steven had seen Deedes arrive on the quayside and take a seat at the café. He'd recognized the fat man straight away, even though the detective wasn't wearing his raincoat. He'd seem him many times before. He'd seen him outside the gallery waiting for Stella with his camera. The man had always appeared so incompetent that Steven assumed he must have another source of income.

Steven bent his head as he entered the cabin and opened his tin of rolling tobacco. He sat inside and smoked until he heard his name.

'Steven Gates? Mr Gates? Sir?' Deedes called out from the quayside.

Steven picked some tobacco from his tongue and stepped outside. The man that stood below was sweating profusely and waving a brown envelope.

'It's Deedes, Mr Gates. Ray Deedes.'

Steven stepped back into the cabin.

'I got information, Mr Gates. You might be interested. Mr Gates? Can I come aboard, sir?'

Steven reappeared, pulled the tip from his cigarette and tucked it behind his ear.

'The owner wouldn't like it.'

'George Peyronie? Dr George Peyronie?'

'That's right.'

'I know George.'

'He still wouldn't like it,' Steven said and disappeared once more into the cabin. Deedes called out to him.

'It's about your wife. Mr Gates?'

Steven stepped out on deck and Deedes waved the brown envelope.

'State your business, Mister Deedes.'

'I have information for you.'

'I don't think so.'

Steven turned away and Deedes decided to hurry it up.

'She's seeing someone else. Your wife, sir. I have more pictures,' he said.

Steven turned back and leaned on the rail. He stared down at Deedes and spoke simply to him.

'I know. She knows I know. He knows I know. She knows I know he knows. Now fuck off.'

Deedes waved the envelope again. He was acting up as best he could.

'I have photographs. You get my drift, Mr Gates? I have photographs. You like photographs, don't you, Mr Gates?'

Despite a sharp tingling of anticipation, Steven sighed and affected a reluctant amble down the gangway. He took the envelope from Deedes, who used the opportunity to light himself a cigarette. Steven inspected each photograph carefully. They were all of Stella with Michael Revere. The two of them going into Revere's apartment; the two of them up at the house; walking in the street; a few wild shots outside the gallery; a few mouth-to-mouth kisses.

'You're going to have to do a lot better than this to make a living out of me, Mister Deedes,' he said, and dropped the photographs into the sea. They both watched as the entwined lovers floated for a few minutes and began to sink.

'I got others, sir, and tapes,' said Deedes, handing Steven his card.

'What sort of tapes? Video?'

This was more interesting, something he could watch.

'Audio.'

'I'll think about it,' Steven replied.

The detective paused for a moment and waited for a last-minute change of heart that didn't come. As he turned and walked away, Steven tucked the card into his back pocket and watched the ungainly man. When he had disappeared from view, Steven turned quickly and gazed anxiously into the water. He searched for the discarded photographs but they had gone. He heard her voice instead, intruding into his present like a comet returning from the past.

'Or my beautiful wife and I take the plane. I don't fucking believe you, Steven,' she said.

The cab pulled away and they were in the alleyway. Stella giggled as he pulled her close to him. He smelled the fragrance of jasmine and cigarette smoke in her hair.

'He fancied you. I swear he paid an extra five grand just so you would come along,' he said, and kissed her neck. She had pushed him away.

'You're not going to do it, are you, Steven?'

He stuck his hands in his pockets.

'Steven? Are you?'

'Who me? For ten grand? What do you think?' he said.

'We're not criminals. Steven, come on.'

'We deliver stolen boats, Stella. What does that mean? That we're chartered accountants?'

'We don't steal them. We're not really criminals. Did you really speak to Charlie?'

'Nope.'

She kissed him then, and Steven could taste that kiss on his tongue and in his throat. He could smell the sea, he could smell her, her skin, her hair . . .

'Let's take the plane,' she had whispered, and he asked her what she'd buy for ten grand but she wouldn't answer.

'I'd take you down to Morocco,' he whispered back into her ear. 'I'd buy you a boy, like the boy from the old town. How'd you like that, my beautiful, beautiful wife?'

Stella wriggled away and lifted her skirt for him there in the street.

'What would you do with the nine thousand, nine hundred and fifty you'd have left, husband mine? What would you do with that?'

'I'd get a film crew,' he said, and they had laughed. She came towards him and dug her fingers down behind the belt of his jeans, dragging him to her.

Steven's hand went to his belt, but her hand was no longer there. He stared down at the mud-coloured sea, took the roll-up from behind his ear and put it between his dry lips.

Stella drove her sports car into the carport and switched off the engine. The air was cooler because of the breeze blowing in off the ocean. It was about ten o'clock. The gallery shut at nine, and she had tidied up and left almost immediately for home. The show had gone well and the orders were coming in. It had been a busy day. She leaned back a little in the seat and gazed at her own dark reflection in the windscreen. She'd found a good technician in Michael, someone not entirely bereft of creativity and who could be guided. That was important, especially now, with the way she was and the way she felt. She stared into the blackness until she was overwhelmed with a tiredness that made her feel almost sedated. She could have slept there and then in the chilly cocoon of the car, but she shook her head, gathered up her handbag and folder of work and opened the door. The keys were still in the ignition, and Stella watched them swing in the lock for a couple of seconds and then opened the door again. She didn't want to look as if she was asking for it. She had them in her hand and was locking the car when she heard the sound of a loose stone against metal. She stopped and listened again.

The wind was blowing through the blackened palm trees. It was a soft, papery sound that creaked and sighed like a sailing ship, quite different to the bell-ring she'd heard. She locked the door and edged out of the port, keeping her eyes focused on the far shadows beyond the snout of the moonlit car. She heard footsteps behind her.

'You OK?' Steven said, knowing better than to touch her. She'd jumped away from him and was breathing deeply to regain her composure.

'I heard someone,' she gasped.

'Sure it wasn't me? I came out when I heard your car.'

'Did you? Maybe I'm just spooked.'

'Stay here,' he said and walked towards the carport and into the darkness.

She waited for a good while. The wind had picked up and clouds were racing past the wintry moon. She wanted to get into the warm, but she was doing what she was told for a change.

'Steven?' she called into the carport, but there was no answer. 'Steven?'

She was about to run to the front door when he returned from around the back of the house. She remembered the door to the house at the rear of the carport, and realized he must have used that. She felt a fool.

'Go inside,' he said.

'Anything?'

'Nothing, but I'm sure if it was old Mr Deedes he'd have fallen in the pool by now.'

'You sick bastard,' she said, and walked past him into the house.

At about that time, Ray Deedes had been sitting in his office, smoking a cigarette and listening to Stella's voice playing out of a tape recorder.

'He tried to kill me. He hurts me all the time. I want him dead.'

'Leave Stella, now.'

'I can't.'

'Tell me.'

'I can't.'

'You kill him, for me.'

Deedes stuck out a nicotine-stained finger and pressed rewind.

'You kill him, for me.'

The gumshoe sucked thoughtfully on his cigarette and flipped the tape out of the machine. He leaned back and took another and pressed it into the machine. Jerry Lee Lewis sang out, *'Chantilly lace . . .'* and Deedes tapped his fingers on the desk.

Chapter Eight

When Stella parked her car at the meter near the fifties-style jukebox-and-chrome-fitted cantina, she saw Ray Deedes waiting for her. She passed him on the steps that led up to the gallery but he followed her like a fly after a horse's tail, right through the room and into the back office.

'I've come for my money,' he said.

She asked him to excuse her and indicated that he should wait outside the office. She walked back through the gallery towards the large glass door, locked it, slid the *Back in Ten Minutes* sign into its holder and returned to the office.

'I will pay you, Mr Deedes,' she said, flicking on the security camera console. 'Send me the bill, and whatever I owe you for the camera. I'll let you out in just a moment.'

Deedes made no move to leave.

'He wasn't interested in the photographs.'

Stella ignored him.

'I've got a proposition for you,' he said.

'I don't want to hear it.'

'Let's talk over a couple of margaritas.'

'I don't drink.'

'You look like you might.'

She folded her arms against her chest. The fat man had a genial, lopsided grin on his face and a businesslike look in his eyes.

'I got some tapes, Mrs Gates. You might like to hear them. What do you say?' he said, and pulled a miniature tape recorder from his pocket, placing it on her desk.

He gestured to her white leather office chair. She sat down and listened to the transcribed outpourings between her and Michael Revere as they were played back to her.

'I was upset,' Stella said, when the tape stopped.

'Sure you were.'

Deedes sat on the edge of the desk, his bulk closer to her than she might have liked. There was an organic smell to him, reminiscent of the backyard of a greengrocer's shop, and as he leaned towards her, Stella found the faint odour of rotting vegetables both repulsive and inexplicably nostalgic. She remembered the smell of an overweight body like his in a windowless room like this that smelled of earth and potatoes. She had retreated into a corner then, but twenty-five years makes a great deal of difference. She didn't need to push or plead or struggle any more. It had never worked then, the pleading or the struggling. Better to do what you were asked and learn to put on a show. Better not to tell. What they wanted, they got, until Stella found a way to use what she had learned to hook hearts and reel men in like fish. Reel them in like she had Steven, who had once stood apart from all the rest, and which made everything he had done since so much worse.

The look in her eyes was enough. Deedes eased himself off the desk and stood in front of it. Stella stood up and handed him back the tape recorder.

'I'm not paying you anything for the tape, or the original. My husband and I had had a fight. People say that sort of thing all the time. If you think I'm paying for this, you're pathetic,' she said, trying to contain the rising nausea that threatened to overwhelm her.

'I know that, Mrs Gates, I ain't stupid.'

Stella got up from her chair and opened the door of the

office. There was a water cooler by the door and she took a plastic cup and filled it. Deedes stood by the door.

'What do you want then?' she asked.

'I want to know if it's true.'

Stella filled the cup again. The water was icy enough to make her head ache.

'And if it is?'

'I want to know what it's worth to you, to get what you want.'

Stella smiled.

'Are you offering to kill my husband, Mr Deedes?'

'For a fair price.'

'And what is that fair price nowadays?'

Deedes bit his bottom lip and showed his yellow teeth.

'Ten grand.'

She placed her hand on her stomach as if the baby had kicked.

'I hear that's about what it's worth,' she said.

'You do? Well then, have we got a deal?'

Stella walked away from him and stood thoughtfully by the writhing mass of limbs that she had suggested to Michael should be entitled *Dismemberment*. She stared down at it and then at her unwelcome companion.

'Have you ever killed anyone before, Mr Deedes?'

'I was in 'Nam.'

'In stores?'

'We got a deal, Mrs Gates?'

'No,' she said, walking briskly to the door and flipping out the ten minutes sign. She turned the keys, flicked back the bolts and showed the fat man the exit.

'I'll give you three minutes to get out of here before I call the police.'

Deedes laughed and shook his head.

'But we did business together, Mrs Gates. They're gonna love all the weird shit I got to tell.'

*

She sat alone in the gallery, talking on the telephone and toying with a paperknife. When the exhibition was dismantled most of Michael's work would be shipped out. The painting of the child was not for sale. Michael wanted to keep it.

He was missing her, he said. He was worried. He didn't want her to be alone.

'I have to be with Steven tonight.'

'Oh, you have to? You think he can look after you after what he asked me to do? He's crazy.'

'He's my husband. I have to be with him tonight.'

'What about me? It's different now.'

'Don't be so sensitive. I'll call you,' she said and put the phone down hastily before he could say, 'Love you.'

By three o'clock in the afternoon she felt hungry again, even though she had eaten more at midday than usual. She closed the gallery and drove up the hill to the white restaurant that overlooked the ocean, where she and Michael sometimes went to eat fried oysters and drink tequila in glasses rimmed with salt and lime. The sun was shining and the sea rippled in the light breeze. She could easily have walked. It would have taken twenty minutes, but people didn't do that, not even in Laguna, so she drove and spent twenty minutes in traffic instead.

She ate her sandwich outside, and watched a wedding take place in a white gazebo shaped like a dovecote that was situated close to the cliff's edge, among some ornamental gardens. The wedding was almost formal by Californian standards, with the men wearing lounge suits and the women ornate cocktail dresses trimmed with cockerel feathers and studded with faux crystals and sequins. As the guests crowded around the plump bride and groom, who were both dressed in white satin, the priest raised his hand solemnly to deliver a Native American blessing with as much *gravitas* as if he were reciting from a commercial greetings card. As the couple embraced, a small man in a white suit played a keyboard and sang, 'I Swear', in perfect harmony with a tall, beautiful girl who strummed a guitar.

Stella watched the guests group for photos and noticed one woman in particular. She stood apart and was struggling to open a packet of cigarettes. When she had succeeded, she searched around desperately for a light, until a tall man, who was smoking a substantial cigar, leaned over and helped her out with a flame.

In the background, a Latino artist was hanging a few animal face masks painted on palm fronds in and around a hedge. When he had finished setting them here and there, he produced a short screech on his trumpet. The wedding guests ambled past him and Stella into the restaurant, the musicians hurrying by with their kit to set up inside. The Latino, Stella noticed, had a puckish look about him, and, when he wasn't playing the trumpet or dabbing bold colours on to the large leaves, he scanned a tattered copy of *National Geographic* magazine. He had already painted a lion and an elephant based on photographs that he had found within, and the two beasts stared out through the clipped-leaf canopy of the neatly trimmed hedge. He had also painted a variety of tribal masks, more African than South American in influence, and, as a sop to Hallowe'en, three ghastly witches, which he had leaned against the hedge too.

There were still quite a few ageing tourists about, enjoying the late season, and the general opinion from those who passed by was that the lion was the best. Certainly, the woman in the black dress, who had accepted a light from the man with the cigar, liked that beast the most.

'How much for the lion?' she enquired, letting the last of the guests overtake her.

'Sixty.'

'The elephant?'

'Forty.'

'How much for the two?'

'One hundred.'

The woman considered his precise mathematics.

'I'll give you eighty.'

'One hundred,' replied the Latino before puckering his lips for another toot on his trumpet.

'Oh, Miles,' he sighed, 'Miles baby, I need to practise.'

'Come on. The lion for fifty. I really like the lion.'

The Latino stopped playing.

'I can't. It's a unique work of art.'

Stella paid her bill and walked over to the railings a little way from the action.

'Everyone likes the lion,' she said to the woman, and the Latino glanced across at her.

The woman in the black dress screwed the remains of her cigarette under her heel.

'I'll go in and ask my husband,' she said.

Stella pointed to a small but highly coloured tribal-type mask tucked into the lower part of the hedge.

'How much is that one?'

The Latino was beginning another work of art and was skimming through his magazine for more inspiration.

'Forty.'

'It's nice,' Stella remarked.

The woman in black returned with her husband, a pugnacious type with a short hairstyle. He stared at the finished fronds in the hedge.

'How much for the lion?'

'Sixty.'

'The elephant?'

'Forty.'

'The two?'

'One hundred.'

'I'll give you eighty for the two.'

'A hundred.'

The husband caught sight of the three lurid witches, luminescent in orange and black.

'How much for the Hallowe'en masks?'

'Seventy-five.'

The man turned to his wife.

'Three for seventy-five, see? We could have them on the porch to scare the kids.'

'I'd really like the lion, honey.'

'Offer him fifty,' he said, and went back inside where the wedding troubadours had begun to sing a popular song about love and the building of bridges. Another aged tourist passed by and remarked to *her* husband how much *she* liked the lion.

'You want it, honey?' her husband said, and his wife smiled and shook her head while the woman in black waited anxiously by the railings. She lit another cigarette and tapped her foot. A tall man smoking a large celebratory cigar stepped outside. He put his arm around her.

'You're missing the party.'

'I want the lion, and the elephant, Charlie. A hundred dollars.'

Charlie blew smoke around her and assessed the beasts in the hedgerow. He made an accurate, if heartless, assessment of what he saw.

'The two ain't worth fifty together, seventy max. Look, honey. I know a bit about art. My sister is an artist. Does stuff you might not want to put on your walls, but it's definitely art. Hey, fella, you going to let me squeeze you on this one?'

The Latino had begun on another frond. The big guy made his offer and was firmly refused.

'No deal,' the Latino said.

'You got to do a deal, man. This is America.'

The Latino was unmoved. Stella lit a cigarette herself and offered one to him, which he refused. The sun was beginning to set and it was getting colder.

'I'll have the funny little mask over there,' she said, counting forty dollars out of her purse. The lion stared out from the leaves and the fading sun made a tiger of his mane. The Latino felt the need to explain.

'People have to pay for art. It's unique. They won't get another.'

'You'll paint another,' she said.

'It will never be exactly the same. The animal comes out of the leaf and the leaf becomes the animal. Today is not a hungry day for me, so they can pay the price.'

He gave an eccentric toot on his trumpet. 'Miles. Oh Miles,' he sighed, 'that was *bad*.'

Stella looked down at the curve of her belly. He was right. It is never the same. The animal comes out of the leaf and it is never the same. She felt comforted and protective. This time she wanted to see its face. This time it wouldn't be him.

'I'll pay the hundred dollars for you, honey,' Charlie said to the woman in black, but looking over at Stella.

'I'll pay for you,' he said, flicking open his leather wallet, and the woman moved closer to him as if to breathe in its smell.

Stella drove back to the gallery with the hideous mask she had bought on the seat beside her. She worked for a couple of hours on the books and inventories for the show, and before she set the alarms and left, she slipped the paperknife absent-mindedly into her handbag.

The black detective had asked her if she carried a gun and when she had said no, he then asked why didn't she think about it?

'I'd miss.'

'Not from close range.'

66

'I'd wound him and he, or she, would have a chance to kill me, and anyway, it's just not the done thing.'

He had laughed at that, and mimicked her accent.

'Not the done thing? What does *that* mean?'

It means that carrying a gun is vulgar.'

'It could keep you alive, ma'am, how vulgar is that?'

She had raised her hand to touch her breast, and rested the other on the curve of her belly. 'I feel very safe here, in this country. I don't need a gun,' she said before he could catch his breath.

'Thirty shootings in LA on a Saturday night,' he said. 'You just got to be in the wrong place . . .'

'But I would have to be very unfortunate to be shot, detective, now wouldn't I?'

Johnson began to shake his head but she had continued.

'It would either have to be someone I knew, a domestic situation. That's typical, isn't it? Or it would have to be a random act. People have made themselves so secure you have to go looking for danger. The freeways and money create the geography here. There are no public spaces, apart from the beach and the campuses, nor public transport that is happily used by everyone and not just the Latinos and the poor white trash. You never have to meet anyone who is not like you, unless you employ them, of course.'

That's when Steven Gates had walked in, seemingly out of nowhere, and said, 'Like a painter and decorator, for example', and Johnson had stood in the room feeling like a man caught in a game for two players, the rules of which were eluding him.

Chapter Nine

She pulled into the carport, killed the lights and remembered to take the keys from the ignition. There was music playing loudly inside the house. She could hear the melody and *fol derol derol* voice of a fey English pop star who was singing that he'd been to hell and high tide above the aggressive beat. It brought back memories.

Steven was sprawled on the couch in the lounge. He appeared to have drunk a bottle and a half of wine and consumed a joint, while three-quarters of another lay extinguished in an ashtray. The case of a porn video lay open on the floor and the TV screen was filled with static. Stella slid the palm-frond mask over her face and leaned over him. The guitars jangled and the Englishman sang about all men's secrets, idle hands and the work that the devil found for them to do, and she sang along.

Steven did not stir. She lifted the mask up slightly so she could see his face a little better. She preferred to watch him while he was asleep and unable to monitor each tiny response in her. Even though, because of the deep lines that were permanently etched above his nose and ran in grooves down to his mouth, even in sleep he never looked at rest or at peace. And why should he be at peace? she asked herself, as she took the paperknife out of her handbag. He seemed quite unconscious as she leaned over, his breathing even and extended, but as her hair fell forward, his hand reached up to touch it. The gesture surprised her. He didn't open his eyes, but his tender movement had produced a sudden painful yearning inside her. She had to control a seductive urge to kiss him.

She rested the knife and the handbag on the table before pushing the mask off her face and on to the top of her head. She took the joint from the ashtray and picked up a heavy gilt table lighter. It was Steven's, a cheap souvenir rather out of place among the tasteful objects that she had bought to furnish the room. She read the engraving on the side which said 'Granada', and weighed it in her hand before flicking the lever down to strike the flame. Like the song, the trashy object sparked a memory that leaped back a decade.

The first toke burned the inhibitions from her senses, and she smiled as she sashayed across the room to stop the music. The sound disappeared, but as she loosened her blouse and turned to Steven sleeping on the couch, the words and music seemed to play on inside her head.

There was a moon. She could see it submerged in the pool like sunken treasure, and, up in the sky, all the stars were arranged like little messages from the past. She stood by the French windows and inhaled more marijuana. Steven rolled his the old-fashioned British way, with five cigarette papers stuck together, a sprinkling of tobacco and a cardboard roach, instead of the local method which eliminated the tobacco and comprised a miniature roll-up of pure grass that Stella found impossible to handle. When they were more serious about drugs, they had never bothered with paper at all. Steven used to burn pellets of treacly hash on the end of a cigarette, or pressed between two hot knives so that they could suck the smoke together. They always made love afterwards in what seemed like an intimate sea of sensation. Her fingers tingled as she recalled her memories, and her eyes picked out the moonbeams spilling in through the glass. The blade caught the light as she pulled the palm frond over her face and leaped across the wooden floor, her breasts shaking in her black brassiere, her swaying arms stretched out. She danced until the song in her head finished and she stood before him, slightly out of breath, her heart beating fast and her arms lowered. It was usually impossible to step into a room while he was asleep and not wake him, yet he lay still: the drug that could reveal all manner of sensations to a wakeful eye, in sleep had dulled his five senses and his sixth. He was unresponsive to her, vulnerable. She pulled the mask from her face and placed it on the table before picking up the knife.

'Oh, well,' she sighed, tucking it into her belt. 'Can't wake the dead.'

She retrieved the mobile phone from her handbag and went outside, down to the pool where she lay on a lounger and finished the joint.

As she stared up at the bright, sad sky, she thought about the woman in black and the man who had paid a hundred dollars for her heart's desire. What would she be doing with him now for just one hundred dollars? And what had her husband lost by driving such a hard bargain? The woman would learn from that humiliation; she had to, Stella thought. She had to learn what it meant to be beholden, to be without merit or power other than in her sex. She had to taste the bitter juice of that knowledge. At a white wedding, the woman in black learned that she had sold herself at her own, and everything since had been trafficking. The woman had to learn to stop preying on herself. She'd be much happier all round.

As Stella lay back and let the night breeze blow over her body, it occurred to her that the detective might not think it a wise thing for her to be doing under the circumstances. The thought of the perplexed policeman made her laugh.

'I'm not afraid of new ghosts, detective. I'm not even

afraid of old ones, and they're the worst,' she said, and dialled a number on her mobile phone.

'Michael?'

The hidden scanner picked up her call and duly taped it. Michael answered. He too had been staring with sleepless eyes at the night sky.

'Michael, Michael. Come now.'

'Now? Is it OK?'

'It's OK, I promise.'

'Is there something going on?'

'I want you, that's all.'

'Should I come up to the door?'

'To the pool.'

'You're outside? Are you crazy?'

'Of course, darling. I'm *absolutely* crazy.'

She disconnected the call.

'Are you watching, you fool?' she said as she lay back under the stars. 'Are you watching, my sick little fool, my sick little lover? I think you are. I do hope you are, because I'm so tired. *I'm so sick and tired.*'

Stella sang to herself until she slumbered in a silence which was broken only by the sea wind blowing through the palm trees, and the wings of night insects electrifying the air. It was a hand clamped firmly over her mouth that woke her, and her first instinct was to grab the knife.

Her eyes blinked open above his fingers with a look first of surprise, and then menace sufficient for Michael to move his other hand quickly and grab her wrist. He forced the knife away from his chest and removed his hand from her mouth.

'Oh, baby,' she whispered.

'Holy Jesus, Stella.'

'Come here.'

He lay beside her.

'You're freezing cold,' he said.

'Hold me.'

'You shouldn't be out here. What about security? That creep could be anywhere.'

'Steven's asleep.'

'I don't mean Steven.'

She laughed and whispered in his ear.

'I could have killed you with this.'

The sharp point of the blade pressing hard against his lips took him by surprise.

'Don't kid around. I mean it. I could have been him. You wouldn't have stood a chance.'

Stella smiled and snuggled against his warm body.

'You wouldn't,' she said.

'*You* wouldn't,' he replied.

She lifted her head off his chest and turned her face to look up into his.

'Idiot. Fuck me now. Fuck me until I see stars.'

He obeyed, rolling on top of her, and she held him tightly, looking over his shoulder at the vast sky. She contemplated the sprinkling of light across the blackness that stretched above her as his hand fumbled between her legs, and began to laugh.

'My, that *was* quick,' she said, and Michael turned away from her to look up too. They gazed up at the Milky Way and laughed together and then he kissed her and licked her, inside and out, watched by a masked face at the French windows, a comic expression of horror fixed in its crudely painted features.

Steven trembled with excitement as he watched his wife open her legs and scissor them around Michael. He took his penis in his hand and began to knead until he heard her groans carry unexpectedly across the water, joined almost at once by Michael's reluctant moan and his own stifled gasping.

Underneath the mask, Steven began to cry and he turned

away, wrapping himself in the drape by the window so that he couldn't see and couldn't hear them any more.

A quarter-inch of magnetic tape edged over the machine heads, and fragments of speech were topped and tailed with red and yellow film. Silence was plain yellow.

It took two hands to rub the tape backward and forward, and an attentive ear to hear the cycle of sounds that indicated the beginning of one voice and the end of another.

'He tried to kill me. He hurts me. He hurts me, all the time. I want him dead. I want to kill him. I want him dead.'

'Leave, Stella. Please leave him.'

'I can't.'

'Tell me.'

'I can't.'

'Why?'

Pause.

'You love me, don't you?'

'I love you, you know that. I love you.'

'Kill him for me.'

'That's crazy talk. Cool it,' Michael said.

'I can't breathe,' she said.

'I'll come and get you.'

'No.'

'I'll come and get you, Stella. Stella?'

The conversation was pulled back across the heads until the deep resonance of Michael's voice repeated, *'That's crazy talk. Cool it.'*

A yellow wax crayon marked the spot, and the tape was lifted across a splicer and sliced with the razor. The technician used the blade to lift a fresh piece of tape that was lightly attached to the desk and insert it where Michael's reply had been detached. The tape and its new repair were fitted back into the machine, the tape eased back, rewound and played.

'*He tried to kill me. He hurts me. He hurts me, all the time. I want him dead. I want to kill him. I want him dead.*'

'*Leave, Stella. Please leave him.*'

'*I can't.*'

'*Tell me.*'

'*I can't.*'

'*Why?*'

Pause.

'*You love me, don't you?*'

'*I love you, you know that. I love you.*'

'*Kill him for me.*'

One finger pressed the stop button, and two fingers gently eased the tape back and released it over and over, playing it again and again until the request brought an answer.

'*I'll kill him for you. I'll kill him for you.*'

The sound of silence was bracketed by the hiss of the machine and the rhythm of breathing. The technician paused the tape and rewound to the precise point where Michael's voice had disappeared and a new lover had arrived.

'*I'll kill him for you. I'll kill him for you.*'

In the dark room, a hundred repetitions later, a voice said '*Yes*', to no one in particular.

Chapter Ten

The next morning Steven was hung-over, but he was dressed in his jeans and sweatshirt and ready for work. He had to get down to the boat because good old George wanted a day out. Stella was up and dressed too, in another one of her chic suits. They sat opposite each other in silence until Stella said, 'You know? You're right, Steven.'

His shoulders dipped. The tone in her voice meant that he was going to have to raise himself for a little verbal snicker-snack.

'The jaws that bite, the claws that catch,' he said.

'You are, though.'

'About what?'

'About me. I need an audience. I do. You are absolutely right.'

'Oh, frabjous day! Calooh! Callay!' he muttered, spreading the marmalade thinly over a melting slab of butter.

'There was someone here last night.'

Steven didn't reply, but Stella continued.

'Do you think we should call the police, tell them there was someone here?'

'I checked when I came in,' he said. 'And later. There wasn't anyone about.'

He bit into the toast and stared at his wife. She was licking crumbs from her lips.

'But there was,' she said. 'There was. You could almost smell it, that *sickness* in the air.'

Steven finished eating and wiped his mouth. He took some tobacco from a tin and began to roll a cigarette. Stella took another piece of toast. She was hungry, he noticed.

'I wasn't afraid,' she said. 'My sick little lover played his part, bless him. He gave me the audience you say I need. I felt his presence. I knew he was there watching, and somehow I felt so much better. It was wonderful, just like old times. It was as perfect as perfect could be, but I didn't want to wake you.'

Steven spat out a stray tobacco leaf.

'I heard you all right.'

'Oh, no, Steven. You must have been dreaming. It wasn't you. It wasn't you watching. I could feel it was someone else.'

'What about him? Was *he* dreaming? Your dog. Your Mr House on the Prairie dog. I bet *he* thought he was dreaming. I should tell him how it works with you.'

'Pass the marmalade, Steven.'

He did as he was told and leaned forward, smoke pouring out of his mouth and nose.

'I should tell him.'

She bit into the toast and waved the tobacco fumes away from the table, and, like two sluggers when the bell sounds, they both took a little break from the blood and spit of battle. Steven gazed out at the pool and thought how cold the water looked despite the sunshine. A number of brown leaves floated on the surface, and he felt irritated that he wouldn't have time to clean them away that morning.

'He's a fake,' Steven said, eventually.

'Who?' she said.

'His art's a fake. You fake it for him, you do, his art. Even his sex life's a fake. He's your creature. Your dog. He does what you tell him. Woof, woof, bloody woof.'

'His baby isn't a fake,' she said, getting up and tugging her silken scarf from the back of the chair. He watched it float in the air behind her and fly up to her neck.

76

'You don't really want him down there, do you?'

She turned around.

'Down where?'

'Down among the dangerous rocks, down among the dead men.'

She flicked open her lipstick holder. He watched her grease her stretched lips with red and then check her closed mouth in the mirror. She looked over at him.

'You mean like you?' she said, and walked out.

He followed her outside and stood by his four-wheel drive, rolling another cigarette. Stella dropped her briefcase in the seat beside her and he glimpsed the tops of her thighs under her skirt as she eased into the car. Her hair was tied back so that it accentuated her cheekbones, and he couldn't see her eyes behind her expensive sunglasses. Her turned head looked like that of a snake.

'Deedes thinks I want you dead,' she said.

'Oh, yes?'

'And if I did, he'd do it for me. He knows how. He's been to 'Nam and everything. He thinks he can earn more out of me than taking my photo.'

'How much is he asking?' Steven enquired, inhaling the aromatic smoke deep into his lungs.

Stella laughed bitterly.

'If I told you, I'd save myself some money,' she said, 'because you'd die when you heard it. It's absolutely priceless.'

Steven slid his own sunglasses on to his face and got into the Ford. He already knew what she was going to say, but she called over to him anyway.

'Ten grand, Steven. Can you believe it? Ten grand.'

Her car screeched out of the carport and she re-engaged the gears roughly as she turned the vehicle round.

'Ten fucking grand,' she said to herself, and accelerated out of the drive and around an oncoming truck.

*

She bothered him. He'd spent maybe three-quarters of an hour in her company and he hadn't stopped thinking about her since he'd left. Johnson stood on the corner of the high street looking at the blue sea. He couldn't get her out of his mind. He should've handed the whole case over to the uniforms. Dandy had had them cruise past the house. It was all quiet up there. They'd talked to the neighbour in the one other house that was left standing in the street. He'd seen nothing. Saw him sometimes, saw her. Had never been into their home. Sometimes the music was a bit weird and loud.

'The neighbour's gay, not interested in her, for sure. He says they're not very community-minded. He's a member of Protect Laguna Coalition – you know, no more hillside development, no toll roads, keep Laguna the way it is – kept me there for a while talking about the Treasure Island resort down the coast,' Dandy had said.

Johnson breathed in the fresh sea breeze. There was a lot of kelp on the beach. Its long brown tubes had been uprooted from some deep marine forest, and it lay heaped on the sand like the tangled hair of a giant mermaid. The summer crowds had deserted the long crescent of sand, and the wild cliff with its formal municipal border of daisies and ornamental bushes that barely contained the impossible spheres of cacti and crowns of yucca that had colonized it. The ragged fronds of the palm trees stiffened in the breeze, and beyond the cliff on the flat rocks close to the shore, seals rested like old men on park benches while pelicans stood by them like sentries.

Johnson's eyes scanned the water in case a school of porpoises appeared, synchronizing their commute down the coast. It made him feel good to see something like that, disciplined and yet free. Yes, he liked working in Laguna Beach. Sure, it was boring and uneventful compared to Los Angeles, or San Diego, but it was a good-pay, low-risk job. He couldn't afford to live in the town itself, of course. He rented a house in Laguna Hills, six miles inland up near the Leisure World retirement complex. Seizure World, Dandy called it. It was close to the Y, but it was country. The wilderness came right up to the fence.

Before his divorce, he'd lived in Laguna Niguel, a sterile suburban tract that had hijacked the name of its coastal neighbour as if it might absorb the character by some sort of semantic osmosis. They'd been sold a good life in the suburbs, but he had never felt he had lived anywhere when he lived there. It was just a white sort of place with no history and no identity to shape it. It had been sold, built and hooked up to the mains. Ella had gotten so bored with the damned place that she'd slept with the gardener, a thickset Guatemalan with a sympathetic smile and capable hands, who had gone back to the old country when Johnson had reported him for being an illegal.

The residents of the old-money resort of Laguna Beach liked to think of themselves as a creative community. There were certainly more art galleries downtown than he'd seen in LA, but, even so, it was hard to see anything that hadn't been imported from somewhere else. There was a large but restrained gay scene and a relaxed, low-key nightlife. It was where, they said, old hippies came to die. The expat British liked it down here too, like they loved Santa Monica. Maybe it was the small-town atmosphere. Or maybe it was because there was somewhere to walk. The town had the feel of a wealthy village with its safe, narrow streets, its bookshops, its delicatessens, its pavement cafés, chic beachwear boutiques, fun souvenir shops and its banks with red-tiled roofs and Spanish arches. People walked down the sidewalks in the sunshine looking nice, relaxed, pleased with themselves. The most that happened to stir up the people around here was that some deadbeats hit the beach after dark, left their needles around and made a nuisance of themselves. There had been a few robberies up in the hills, and that was rare enough to be remarked upon. Laguna was quiet, a civilized enclave of humanity, upmarket and individual, and not rich enough to have developed the social paranoia that required security walls and patrols, nor aged enough, nor conservative enough, to want to exist in a walled retirement centre-cum-golf course carved into an appropriated hillside.

The fire had terrified the folks that lived on the hill, but it had brought them together like a common disaster usually does. Almost three hundred homes had been burned, but reconstruction was well on the way and people had begun to look around for external threats once again, like the pollution out at Aliso Creek, the disappearing green belt, the encroaching freeway and the condos and high-rise hotels clogging up the coast. Murder and mayhem happened elsewhere beyond the hills, where the freeways converged and were contaminated by the barrios and ghettos of Los Angeles. They wanted to pull up the drawbridge on all that. Stalkers went to the Hollywood Hills, not Laguna. They reached for the stars.

He gazed over at Stella's gallery by the beach and wondered about her.

'When I came here, to Southern California,' she had said, 'I never understood what it was *for*. I never learned about a city like Los Angeles at school. Cities start at some sort of nexus, a crossroads of trade or an industrial base. I couldn't work out what Los Angeles and Southern California was for, what was its base. I really couldn't. Steven did. The Dagenham of Dreams, he called it.'

Johnson hadn't understood the metaphor.

'Dagenham?'

'A place back home, a huge housing estate to the east of London, once said to be the biggest council estate – project – in Europe. It was built to service the Ford Motor Company.'

'Like Detroit?'

80

'No. Dagenham never existed. It was built only to service the firm, and the working classes were shipped out there from the East End. The same thing happened here. California is the Dagenham of Dreams. Hollywood and homesteads. That's what it's for.'

Johnson had stood with the coffee in his hand.

'Don't forget the military. Can't talk about this state without talking about the military,' he had offered.

'My husband was in the army,' she had replied. 'He'd served seven years when I met him. Northern Ireland, you know. Our little Vietnam.'

He was surprised. Johnson would never have had Steven Gates down as an army man, but he didn't share that opinion with her. He asked where they had met.

Stella had laughed.

'On a train. He followed me home,' she said.

Back in the office, Johnson lifted his eyes from the gallery catalogue and stared out of the window.

'See anything you like in there, sir?'

Ruth Dandy placed a coffee for him on his desk and walked back to her own and sat down.

'You didn't have to make me that,' he said.

'I know, sir. For the record, I was getting one for myself, and I don't feel in the least diminished by my own generosity.'

'Thank you,' he said, and stared down at the catalogue again.

'I'm trying to get a handle on this thing. Maybe it's got something to do with what she sells in the gallery.'

Dandy got up from her desk and walked over. She turned the catalogue round so she could see the photographs.

'Strikes me she sells tits and ass,' she said. 'Her tits and ass. It ain't art.'

'What do we know about art, detective?' Johnson replied, carefully placing his lips to the rim of the hot cup.

'*I* know about art,' she insisted.

'Oh?'

'Japanese art, as a matter of fact.'

Johnson was amused. He leaned back in his chair and swung his feet with their highly polished shoes on the desk.

'Japanese art?'

'That irony, sir?'

Johnson lost his mocking smile.

'No, detective.'

She pursed her lips and said, 'The Edo period, when the shoguns ruled. Everything from the seventeenth to the nineteenth century before the Meiji Restoration and the Westerners arrived. The Edo period, you know.'

Johnson didn't know, but he didn't say so.

'How'd you get into that?'

'I was channel-surfing one night and got hooked on sumo wrestling. You want to see these guys, sir . . .'

'The art, detective.'

'Well, sumo is . . . OK, I like the woodblock prints. They made them with line block in ink and separate colour blocks on *kozo* paper? The craftsmanship, the colours, the composition, I like all of it. The little pictures of people doing this and that, real things, everyday stuff, but the pictures still look kind of dreamy. There's something sad and kind of humorous about those little scenes from their lives, something really human. There's a whole collection devoted to their whorehouses and amusement arcades, you know? I like them. It's like looking at *Life* magazine.'

Johnson looked down at Michael Revere's work, the torn limbs and the broken stones.

'*Life* magazine,' he repeated.

That's when the call came in.

Chapter Eleven

The Ford Blazer four-wheel drive was on its side. Johnson walked around the vehicle and noticed that the brake cables had been cut. He was taken aback because it was so obvious, and for a moment he thought of the catalogue and the feeling he had of being directed by signs strategically placed about him. He crouched down to inspect the sabotage more closely, and looking past the truck he could see the shapely brown legs of Stella Gates. She was leaning against his car and smoking a cigarette with a shaky hand. The paramedics had already loaded her husband into the ambulance and left. The sound of the siren whooping reverberated around the canyon and united the squeals of drills and the slam of hammers.

A site worker waved his dusty hands up the road and told Ruth Dandy what he saw.

'I saw the sports car coming down fast, then there was a curve and it disappeared, then I saw the Blazer coming, real fast. Looked like he was after her, you know? They come past me over there, the Blazer's overtaking and it's too close to the next curve coming up down there. No way he'd make it, and he didn't seem to be slowing down none. That's when I saw her turn the wheel and push him into the side of the hill. The Blazer slowed up, but then it tips over and the guy gets thrown in front of her car. Man, he was lucky.'

The man looked down the hill towards the sound of the siren.

'Well, maybe he was lucky.'

'You see her brake?' Dandy asked.

'Both vehicles slowed up after she hit him, detective. Ask me, she probably saved the man's life.'

Johnson sighed, dusted off his hands and checked the pattern of the swerve marks before ambling over towards Stella.

'You OK, Mrs Gates?' he enquired.

She looked up and smiled.

'He couldn't seem to slow down,' she said.

'You want to tell me what happened out here?'

'We argued.'

'Uh-huh?'

'Nothing unusual in that; we argue a lot. This time he got mad and chased me down the road. He was overtaking me coming into the bend, but I don't think he meant to. I think he was trying to avoid running into the back of me. He seemed to be pumping at his brakes. He couldn't slow down. I swerved into him. I didn't know what to do.'

'The brake cables were cut.'

Stella put a hand over her face.

'I thought there was someone out at the house last night,' she said when she had recovered her composure.

'Why didn't you call us out?'

'It was just a feeling. I didn't hear anything. It was just a feeling.'

'You OK?'

'I'm OK. I'd like to go to the hospital now. I want to see him.'

'Detective Dandy'll take you,' he said, beckoning to Dandy and placing a hand around Stella without actually touching her.

Despite his injuries, Steven Gates discharged himself and was on the boat when Dr George Peyronie arrived with a company of three men and four women. The sight of Steven silenced their chatter. They looked at him, the swollen eye and the stitches above it and over his nose and the bandage on his hand, and wondered if the day was over before it had begun. George set down the large cooler that he was carrying and hurried up the steps. Steven had called him and told him what had happened, but he didn't expect the man to look so beat-up.

'You OK to do this today, Steve?'

'Yeah, sure, why not?'

George looked down at his party, who were staring anxiously up at them. He slapped Steven on the back.

'Women drivers, Steve, my man, women drivers. Who needs 'em?'

Steven ducked into the cabin.

'Someone cut the brake cable on the pick-up, George.'

The doctor was astounded.

'Jesus,' he said, his face a blank of disbelief. Then he leaned forward with a shrewd expression in his eyes. 'You been screwing someone's wife?'

Steven smiled as best he could.

'Only my own,' he said, at which George slapped him again, almost gratefully.

'Hey, stress biz, Steve. What do you say I fix you up? Special price. Come on, it's an unbeatable, unrepeatable offer.'

'Gimme a break, George. I'll pay top dollar otherwise, who knows? I might get my dick and a couple of pebbles for a nose.'

The doctor thought this was pretty good, and gave Steven another slap. The sound of women's laughter joined his own.

'Hey, George, we're missing you already,' one of the women piped up, and George raised his eyebrows.

He gave Steven a final squeeze before leaving him at

the bridge. As he welcomed his guests aboard, he called out, 'Let her rip, Stevie boy, let her rip. For this I went to college.'

Steven steered the boat out of the marina and into the bay. He felt sore about the head and his hand throbbed, but, all in all, he reckoned he'd got off lightly. He kept trying to remember what happened, and it was hard to do. He kept thinking that Stella had tried to save him, and wondering why. Mostly, he tried to remember what *he* had been doing, and that was the hardest of all.

Lee Johnson stood outside the gallery and stared through the window at the arrangement of work that the poster described as *Michael Revere: An Installation of Memories*. He didn't ask Ruth Dandy what she thought this time. He stared at the painting of the child. He couldn't see it very well, but the limpid blue of water all around the baby was clear enough.

'That reminds me of something,' he said.

'Everything in here should remind you of something,' Dandy replied.

He stopped and stepped back. Dandy pressed her face against the glass and cupped her hands around her head so as to cut out the glare.

'He doesn't want her charged, whatever happened. He says if it wasn't for her, for her quick thinking, he'd have hit the curve and gone over the cliff.'

'Why not her brakes? Why his?' he replied.

'Maybe the wacko isn't after her. Maybe he, or she, is after him. If the wacko exists.'

'The lover? You think it might be him?'

'Or her. She gave that pick-up one hell of a bump. She ran the guy over.'

Johnson stuffed his hands in his pockets and shook his head.

'My, oh my,' he said. 'You'd think these people had never heard of divorce.'

Dandy moved back from the window and put on her sunglasses.

'Maybe they're just old-fashioned, sir,' she said.

That afternoon Johnson returned to the gallery and asked Stella the same questions he'd asked himself, like, for instance, if she'd meant to run her husband over. She kept moving about, and he was forced to follow her around while she stuck *Sold* stickers on some of the more expensive items. She didn't break her stride.

'That is the most ridiculous thing I have ever heard,' she said.

'I doubt it, in your business.'

'You know as much about women as you know about art, detective?'

Johnson stopped walking and let her go.

'I know what I like,' he said.

Stella bent down over a body cast.

'That's quite unusual, actually. Most people are better able to tell you what they *don't* like.'

Johnson looked around and pointed at a painting of a female torso that hung on the far wall. The upper shoulders and head were obscured by a hooded crimson cape, the breasts were firm and exposed and the rounded pelvic area was wrapped in strips of white material.

'That you?' he asked.

Stella moved away and placed another sticker on another female nude.

'All these, are they you?' he said. 'They're pretty sexy. What does your husband think?'

'This is art, detective,' she said, 'not life.'

'He struck me as the kind of person who could take it or leave it.'

'Life?'

'I mean art.'

She looked down at the catalogue, the *Sold* stickers still glued to her fingers.

'He knows what he likes,' she replied without looking up, and this time Johnson turned his back on her and walked over to stand in front of the watercolour of the baby.

'The brakes were cut. You pushed him off the road and ran him over. You're having an affair,' he said. 'You have to admit, it looks bad.'

He heard Stella's heels tip-tapping across the marble floor closer to him.

'This guy that's been hanging around our place. What about him? Have you bothered to look?'

Johnson pointed at another depiction of a female body.

'Sure, we have. Is this you too? Thirty-five grand. Sheesh.'

'What would *you* pay for something that combined eroticism, emotion and intellectual ingenuity, detective?'

It was an interesting question, and the only comparison he could think to make was a movie ticket he'd bought to see *Last Tango in Paris* when he was eighteen. He didn't have the ticket, just the memory of Schneider being humped in that empty room. He pointed to a sheared torso of a man, one breast and the hips remaining, and turned to face her.

'I'd say there were a lot of damaged people in here, Mrs Gates,' he said.

Stella came and stood in front of him.

'Not damaged, focused, detective, focused. It's a matter of interpretation,' she said, and then stretched her arm out to make him take in all that was in the gallery.

'What would you choose, if you had the money?' she said. Her eyes were bright with prurient interest, her lips shiny with gloss, and he noticed a thread of saliva was stretched between her teeth like spider's silk. Johnson wanted to move in on her right there, but he played it cool. He reached his hand out to the female nude closest to him, drawing his hand down its thigh.

'I like this one,' he said. 'But then I've always been a leg man myself.'

She watched the detective go, and closed the gallery for the afternoon. It was the right thing to do. She realized she had appeared too cool for someone whose husband had almost been killed. The detective knew she was having an affair, so she couldn't appear too overwhelmed by the accident either. It was a fine judgement. She was English. That worked for her. They expected a certain emotional detachment.

The detective's fingers curled over the edge of the car door, and she had imagined the door slamming. She saw the fingers falling to the floor like sausages as the metal sliced them, and her memories engaged like teeth in a steel gear. She thought immediately of the boat. Steven was out on the boat. She would collect him. That would look right. It wouldn't take her long, and she would wait in a little café by the seafront for him. She would do that, she decided, after she had paid a visit to Ray Deedes.

He had an address somewhere in Santa Ana off the 55. Once she got out of the canyon, she could get to it via the surface streets or through the country, as the locals described it. Rather optimistically, she felt, as if the trip through Irvine would be a pleasant journey through leafy, picturesque orange groves. In reality, it was a trundle past a few flat oblongs of overworked farmland that linked dense patches of walled suburbia to complex commercial islands of banks and hotels, glinting above the haze of pollution like emerald cities in the sun. There was one surface road that stretched out between an avenue of sentinel cypresses, and for a few minutes as she drove along it, she remembered a landscape that she had visited a long time ago.

*

They were waiting for the meeting with Duran to happen and she was bored, so Steven took her for a drive. They left the greens and fairways and sand dunes of the golf courses and the white villa complexes by the listless sea, and wound inland across the plain away from the coastal pines, the palms and eucalyptus trees towards the arid cliffs. Beyond the violet drapes of bougainvillea, they found the old town by a river hollow. At its small bridge, they waited in a cloud of dust and manure left by a muleteer, who was crossing laden with heavy sacks and panniers. They followed him into the town and through the narrow Andalusian streets, which were lined with antique shops and cafés that had tin tables set outside under the orange trees. Through the black ironwork grilles of the whitewashed houses, the paved patios were lush with scarlet geraniums and white jasmine, the smell of which mingled with an aroma of fresh bread, spiced sausages and rosemary. A white-hatted policeman waved them into a whitewashed square with a central ornate fountain.

Steven wanted to find a bank and left her sitting in the shade, twirling a straw in a long glass of iced coffee. The square was quiet and peaceful but for the sound of the fountain and the clack of dominoes being slapped down by some old gamblers inside the café. Steven had been gone just twenty minutes when the boy approached her. She didn't understand what he had said, but she was attracted by the seductive smile on his lips and the direct look in his eyes. He was so brown and dark, he could easily have been mistaken for an Arab. He was about nineteen years old, she guessed.

She smiled and looked away, but he spoke to her again. His hand was outstretched and his fingers held what at first she thought was a small, mottled orange. It was only when she took it and held it in her hand that she realized what it was: the round fruit of a prickly pear, the cactus that had been brought back from the Americas by the conquistadors and was now rampant along every dusty roadside. She smiled and rubbed her finger over it, and he smiled too and indicated that she should dig her thumbnails in to split the skin and taste it.

The boy sat down at the next table and drummed his brown fingers gently on the table top while she ate. He wore crisp blue jeans and a clean white T-shirt with a pair of sunglasses tucked into the collar. She sucked at the fruit and left her coffee. They didn't speak again but the flavour, reminiscent of oriental lychees, lingered in her mouth.

By lunchtime, Steven had still not returned and she decided to look for him. The sun had risen higher in the sky and the subtropical heat was making her perspire as she climbed the steep cobbled streets in the direction of where the boy had said the bank was. She found the bank but not Steven, and she returned to the square to find it deserted, the car gone and the boy waiting under the orange trees.

Steven had left a note. He had called Charlie and there was some business to arrange. He'd be back for her if she couldn't get a taxi. He'd be a couple of hours maybe.

The boy stood with his thumbs tucked into his pockets while she read. He told her in halting English that he had told Steven where she had gone, but with quick hand movements he explained that her man had been anxious to leave.

'Un taxi?' she enquired, but the boy shook his head.

She had to wait, the boy said. He pointed downwards, right here in the square. Stella thanked him and sat down at a table, exhausted by the heat and thankful for some shade. She resigned herself to sitting in the empty square and listening while the sound of distant transistors and motorbikes faded into the quiet slumber of siesta. He waited a few minutes in the harsh sunlight before approaching her.

'Raphael,' he said, his hand outstretched.

She looked up at him and smiled. He went inside the café and brought her a glass of iced water. The condensation streamed down the sides and soaked her hand as she grasped it.

'Gracias, *Raphael*,' she said, taking care to pronounce his name correctly. He gestured to his mouth, his hands curved like the neck of a pecking hen.

'Comida. Mia casa. *Eat.*'

She raised her hands to thank him and politely refuse his invitation to lunch at his house. She pointed.

'Un taxi?'

It was his turn to raise his hands. No. Then he rolled his hands into fists and mimed an accelerating motorbike before jabbing a finger at his chest. She laughed and nodded. He was delighted. He indicated that she should wait for him, and ten minutes later she heard the rumble of his machine. He kept the engine running as he sat astride the bike and his sunglasses covered his eyes as he watched her walk towards him. She swung one leg behind him, slipped her hands around his waist and enjoyed the ride through the dust clouds down to the sea. She'd kept her hands around his waist most of the way, but occasionally she'd let one hand slip on to his thigh under the pretext that she was trying to lean back a little and ride without holding on.

He was impressed by the boat, and she invited him aboard. He had a good look around. He loved being up in the cockpit with the steering wheel and the electronics. He looked out and nodded with happiness. She left him to it and went down to the cabin. Steven had planned it this way, she knew it. She wanted to scream with delight. It was his idea of a joke. He'd seen the boy standing by the fountain and he'd decided then that she could have him if she wanted. He always said that. She could have anyone she wanted, it didn't have to be him all the time. She'd liked that. She'd liked the independence it gave her, not the freedom. It wasn't freedom. Independence is not the same thing.

'Don't you get jealous?' she'd asked him once.

'Why should I be jealous when you always come back to me? I know there isn't anyone else inside you, not in there,' he had said, and he had pointed his fingers at her heart.

So she sat on the bunk and waited for Raphael to finish dreaming about owning a boat as sleek and expensive as this one. He came down and peered into the cabin. She didn't speak but he came and sat beside her, looking coy and vulpine at one and the same time. When he leaned forward to kiss her, she took his hand and pushed it between her legs.

He was taking her excitedly from behind when they heard footsteps. They both stopped for a moment and listened, but no one appeared to be moving outside. They could hear nothing but the lap of water against the boat and the sound of distant laughter from the harbour cafés. Raphael rubbed her buttocks reassuringly and bent over her once again, sliding his hands up her body towards her dangling breasts. The back of her loose summer dress was up over her shoulders and the front hung down. She could see herself being kneaded by his tanned fingers. He was whispering something to her as he banged at her backside, and she listened for Steven. This was for Steven. This was for Steven, she repeated to herself, her thighs pressing wetly against the boy's. She imagined that the boy was going to come quickly, but Raphael was not about to throw away the luscious moment he had been handed by chance. He pulled away, bent his face underneath her and began to suck at her like a calf at a cow until her legs collapsed and she cried out, and he returned to pound away at her to the finish. As he lay on top of her and held her tightly and lovingly to him, it was Steven's applause that brought them back to their senses.

'How was it for you?' Steven had asked later, after Raphael had launched himself out of her, hauled up his jeans and got out of the cabin and off the boat.

93

'Pretty good, thank you,' she had replied.

'It looked fantastic.'

'It was. I was thinking of you.'

'That's good. That's nice. No, really, I appreciate that. I'm glad it was good for you. It looked great.'

'Did I look good?'

'You looked fantastic.'

'You want to do it now?'

They'd made love and drank some wine before going down to the café, where some guitarists were playing soft love songs. Steven told her years later that he had killed the boy, cut his throat, but she had never believed him. He was just saying it, trying to hurt her.

Chapter Twelve

Deedes's office was situated in a low-rent brown and cream building, a featureless block of functional architecture in a quiet business district with too much parking space. Stella glanced at the business card as she pulled into the lot, and got out to identify the numbers that were listed on the sign outside. Deedes Detective Agency was in Suite 1115.

Suite 1115 was behind a dull door down a long, airless corridor that Deedes shared with a dentist and a couple of attorneys. It smelled of antiseptic mouthwash and old carpeting. She pressed the buzzer and Deedes's voice crackled on the intercom.

'Yeah. Who is it?'

He made her wait for a good minute after she told him, and when he opened the door, he stood there grinning and waved her in like she might think she was important but he knew better.

Stella looked around. The office had a bland exterior typical of late twentieth-century commercial infill. Inside, a visitor seemed to step back fifty years. The place smelled of dust and the carpet was just something on the floor. There were six green filing cabinets, three of them probably full of nothing, three hard chairs and a swivel chair, a flat table with a glass top, a phone and a framed licence on the wall. The net curtains at the two windows sucked in and out with the breeze, and, if it wasn't for the computer screen, the printer, disk holders and the lengths of cable that spewed off the desk and down to an adaptor tucked underneath, anyone entering would expect to see a Homburg perched above the overcoat that hung from the wooden stand. There was even a communicating door, with a frosted glass panel, to a room beyond.

'My,' said Stella, looking around. 'What's through there? Casablanca?'

'I shut at five-thirty,' Deedes replied.

While his wife sat in Deedes's office, Steven looked down and watched one of George's friends run his hairy fingers around the oiled nipples of his lady friend. His other hand had slipped under the colourful Lycra material of her bikini bottom and was working hard. The woman's eyes were closed and she wore a slightly amused smile. Steven wondered if he could work Stella's face into the picture. But he didn't want to see her eyes open, those incredulous eyes searching for him. He hoped the woman would keep her eyes shut so he could dream in peace. As he felt his jaw tighten, he knew it was coming and he gripped the rail.

Duran had thought Steven was asleep but he was not. He had heard Duran move and had opened his eyes. He could see everything. He saw the shadow of the man over her, the belt unbuckle and heard her grunt a little as Duran pushed his fingers into her. It was hard to see at first, but when he started with his cock, the union was so much darker than the separation that it was easy to see what was going on when it was buried, and when it was slick and white as a moonbeam. She had come round pretty quickly, and began to shout, 'Steven! Steven!' Her screams made the hair on his skin march up his body, but he slumped motionless in the chair.

The world had turned and the stars in the endless sky had

glimmered above him, and he could only watch. He watched as Duran's hands moved under her dress and over her flesh and the bulk of the man pinned her down. His heart pounded, his cock swelled and his mouth grew dry as he watched and felt an indefinable longing within himself released. From somewhere in the starlit night above, he could see himself blurring into her, her black hair against his chest and against his groin. She was something to see, with her legs spread under his hips and her arms and her breasts and her hair.

Stella. His tongue flicked inside his mouth. He was almost coming. He was almost coming when he saw the silver blade of the fishing knife arc in her free hand, and he recoiled as if the blade had penetrated his own flesh. Time stalled for one endless moment before the pain of consciousness pierced his brain and forced him to spring from his chair and haul the wounded man off his wife.

'The little whore came on to me, I swear, Mother of God,' Duran had blubbered as Steven manhandled him to the deck. He looked down at the struggling man and a sudden and terrible rage had boiled inside him. He threw Duran over on to his back and stamped repeatedly down upon his screaming face until it was a bloody, formless mess. He couldn't remember ever stopping or sleeping, but he had woken first, dry-lipped and hung-over. It was late morning, the boat was anchored and Duran's dead body was out on deck, baking in the hot sun.

Steven drank from a water bottle to quench his torturing thirst and still the pain in his head. The boat's engine was dead but he could barely remember cutting it. The gentle swell of the sea lapped against the sides. Stella was sleeping inside the cabin. He remembered then that he had covered her with a blanket, and as he pulled it from her face, she awoke and grasped the bottle from his hand. She drank deeply from it to slake her own aching thirst.

'Take your clothes off, everything, take them off,' he said.
'Leave me alone.'

She let the empty bottle roll on to the deck and pulled the blanket over herself once again. He tugged it off.

'You have to help me with this.'

'With what?'

He pulled at her this time.

'Get up. Help me with this.'

She had shrunk away from him when she realized that everything she had thought had been a booze-fuelled nightmare was, in fact, reality.

'I don't want to.'

He had hauled her off the bunk and her dress had remained creased and folded, stiff with dried blood. She had begun to scream and he had slapped her a little until she stopped and stared at him like a cowed animal. They had both stripped and walked naked out towards the corpse.

They had stared at it: at the man's bloodied shirt and thick mat of hair that poked through, at his soiled trousers, his flaccid, pointless cock and the monstrous sac of blackened flesh that was attached to his neck and that still retained some element of Duran's identity. They had stood motionless until Stella, filled with bitterness and spite, had stepped forward and spat on the body and then at her husband.

With the back of the hand that held the fishing knife, Steven wiped the spittle from his face. The blade glinted in the sun and blinded Stella with a burning light that seared the sky and obliterated the blue and the circling gulls. She blinked and when her sight returned, Steven had apparently disappeared and she panicked, stumbling over him, as he crouched over the body. He was hacking at Duran's hands.

'Don't. What are you doing? Don't,' she said, pulling at him. Steven ignored her even while she stood back and shrieked, 'His fingers? Cut off his fucking balls for what he did to me, you sick bastard, cut off his dick, his fucking balls. His fingers?'

'Get a rope,' Steven said, 'come on. Help me. I want him to stay down. We've got his blood on us, on our clothes. Come on.'

He had piled Duran's fingers neatly on deck and Stella had helped him tie the body and weight it with bales of cannabis at the head, the feet and the trunk. They threw the bales overboard and as the corpse rolled with the tug of the ropes, they lifted it and dropped it over the side. They saw it bump against the boat and sink, and Stella walked dumbly to the stern to watch the whirlpool it left behind. She stared into the water, expecting the dead man to bubble and bob up like a half-submerged buoy.

Steven had dipped a bucket into the sea, poured it over himself to wash the organic debris of dismemberment from his own living skin and hair. Then he had cleaned the deck while she washed herself in the same way.

'Don't look at me,' she had said as they dried themselves silently in the cabin.

'Oh, *l'amour*,' the doctor sighed as he stepped up beside Steven and gazed down on the blissful couple below. Steven didn't reply, and after a minute or two of silent observation, George sighed disconsolately and said: 'You know, Steve, I sometimes wonder if romance wouldn't be more my thing.'

He smelled of beer and perspiration.

'You end up doing the same thing, George.'

The doctor nodded ruefully and sucked on his beer can before wiping his mouth with the back of his hand. Steven noticed that it was streaked with dried blood, and he looked away. The woman below had begun to bite her lip.

'Yeah, I know. Don't get me wrong,' George said. 'Most days this consenting adults stuff is just what I need and more than I deserve. But y'know, sometimes, just sometimes, I want something gentler, hearts and flowers, some goddamned *romance*, you know what I mean?'

Steven was struggling to concentrate.

'No, not really,' he replied.

The woman began to sigh and spread her legs apart. The man placed his mouth over hers and seemed to gnaw at her. There was laughter from elsewhere on the boat, but George and Steven stood together in silence and watched until the two bodies below them stopped twitching. The spent couple lay clumped together, and George straightened up with the rueful expression of a man whose horse had just come in second. He looked out at the white ruffles of foam on the little blue waves and took a deep breath of sea air.

'Jesus, you're right. What the hell's the matter with me, Steve? You'd think I was just about to get a period.'

Blood had started seeping through the bandage on Steven's hand. He gazed down at it, and as he turned to move away from the railing, he staggered backwards. George made a grab for him.

'You feeling OK, Steve? Steve?'

'I'm perfectly all right.'

The doctor pointed to Steven's hand.

'If I hadn't been handling bait, I'd fix that up for you right now.'

Steven stared at George's hands, always the cleanest and most immaculate part of the man. They were as bloody as a butcher's. There seemed to be so much blood.

The sharks had already begun to track the boat. Steven dug the rods out of the cabin and checked the instruments. He had to turn the boat around and go somewhere different. He told her to set up the rod and line, and she did as she was told without a word. She'd almost done when he came out on the deck, sweating with the terrible heat, and she looked up at him, her face sharp and vicious. He was too slow. His mind had been occupied with his plan when she had attacked him, whipping at his arms and face with the fishing rod. He put his hands up to protect his eyes and the flying hook in the line caught his finger. The blood began to flow from the rip in his flesh and as the fresh, red, living blood splashed down by the dead man's fingers, she understood.

'Get me a bandage,' he said and she did, wrapping his wound quickly and efficiently.

'Do it,' she had said.

He stuck the hook into one of Duran's severed index fingers and cast the line out among the sharks. He had to catch one. He had to catch one to cut it up. He had to have blood on the boat and on their clothes that was not Duran's.

'There seems to be so much blood,' he said as the doctor grabbed his shoulder and held him up.

'Turn her round, Steve. You think you can? Come on. That's it. My man,' he said.

Chapter Thirteen

Ray Deedes offered Stella a cigarette which she refused.

'I don't smoke,' she said.

Deedes lit one for himself and offered her a seat on the other side of the desk.

'You look as if you might,' he said.

The smoke drifted over her, and she waited while he eased out his belt around his thick waist and made himself comfortable in the old swivel chair that seemed to lean back permanently even when he wasn't in it. She sometimes wished she were stronger, not a man, just stronger. Strong enough to punch a man like Deedes in the guts and make an impact, some internal haemorrhaging, something like that, or flatten his nose, watch it spread across his face, black and blue and bloody like a busted toe.

She'd employed him because he was low-down and stupid. He'd turned out to be low-down, but stupid? Like a *fox*. She knew about the photographs. She'd paid Deedes to take them for him. It was the least she could do, since she was the one best able to afford it. She knew for a fact that Deedes wasn't the mysterious misappropriator of her ignition keys. She'd given him the extra job of finding who it was. She opened her handbag, took out her chequebook and a fountain pen. She wrote quickly and pushed the cheque across the glass-topped table.

'This is what I owe you, including the cost of the camera. I want the file, please, and the tapes,' she said.

Deedes didn't bother to pick up the cheque. He leaned back at a seemingly unstable angle in his chair and smoked his cigarette.

'My job takes me up to the police headquarters once in a while. It sure was buzzing today.'

Stella clicked her handbag shut.

'My husband had a car accident this morning,' she said.

Deedes continued to enjoy his cigarette.

'Oh,' he said, with a smile.

'The police say the brakes on his car were cut. Any ideas?'

The gumshoe chewed the inside of his lips with exaggerated concentration.

'Might have been the spaceman you got me following for a while.'

'It might well have been.'

Deedes leaned forward and moved the cheque around so that he could see the figure Stella had written.

'Funny, I never saw him, excuse me, or *her*,' he said. 'You got to be so careful not to offend anyone nowadays.'

'I can see you take endless pains not to,' she replied.

Deedes pulled a tin ashtray over so that he could flick the ash into it instead of on to the carpet.

'I never saw *him*, but I did see your old man a couple of times, going to the joints downtown where he could look up some broad's dress. I saw pretty boy, too, coming for a swim, I guess.'

'What's your point?'

'I ain't got a point.'

'To make.'

'I ain't got a point to make, is what I meant. You think there's no point to me, Mrs Gates? Very funny.'

'You weren't perhaps showing me a sample of your

professional expertise, were you, Mr Deedes? Something you learned in 'Nam? You weren't making a point about that?'

Deedes made a big show of trying to remember. His index finger pointed to his temple like a .45; his expression barely made that number his IQ.

'Did you pay me ten grand, five down, five when it's over? Or did I miss that? The part when you handed over the money. Did I miss that? That ain't like me at all, Mrs Gates. Really. It ain't. I pay real close attention to that part, as a rule.'

Stella pushed her chair back and stood up. She straightened her skirt and made sure her jacket was buttoned.

'Just as long as we understand each other,' she said, and turned to go.

'Sit down, Mrs Gates.'

Stella turned back to the man who was smoothing the cheque with his fingers. He didn't look at her but he was waiting. She wanted to take a swing at him right then, catch his jaw with her handbag, set him off balance. She'd have her shoe off and he'd be getting it in the face with the sharp tip of her heel. He'd have a gun, of course, in the drawer under his desk, the one that was slightly open. *What satisfaction was there in a gun?* she thought as she sat down. It was all over so quickly with a gun.

'I like those pictures and statues of you in your fancy gallery,' Deedes said, rolling his tongue up like a taco. 'You got a fine and highly desirable body, Mrs Gates. It sure is a work of art. I bet that painter friend of yours gets a real treat, don't he?'

Stella ground the heel of one shoe into the threadbare carpet and kept her eye on him. His doughy fingers kept smoothing the cheque.

'What do you say to giving me a chance? I could do a good job for you. I can hold my pencil in one hand like the best of them. You could hang my stuff up there next to the real expensive wall hangings because you know what? I'm not cheap either, so who's going to notice?' he said, and pushed the cheque across the desk to her.

'Think of a number, Mrs Gates.'

Stella tore the cheque into pieces and wrote him another. Deedes liked the new one much more. He pressed down on the glass to ease his bulk out of the chair and walked over to one of the green filing cabinets and took out a folder. He took a Jiffy bag out of another and slipped the folder into it. He took a tape cassette from the drawer under his desk and slipped that into the envelope with the folder. He handed it to her and she checked it.

'It's all there,' he said.

She got up to leave once again.

'You're from England, aren't you, Mrs Gates?'

Deedes tapped the computer on his desk.

'You know something? You can send and receive messages back home for the price of a local call if you got the right equipment. Even stupid people like me can learn how to do that.'

The afternoon heat in the office seemed oppressive to her now, even with the breeze that was moving the nylon net curtains. It was impossible yet, she knew it was too soon, but it was as if the child had turned inside her. She felt it move and heard the loud, syncopated hammer of two heart-beats as Deedes ground his cigarette into the ashtray so that the charred tobacco and ash stuck and blackened his nails. She felt some pressure behind her eyes as he walked over to the corner of the room and washed his hands. She hadn't noticed the basin before. She looked again. Deedes hadn't moved. He was still grinding the cigarette into the tin and messing up his fingers. She glanced again into the corner. There was no handbasin. She controlled a shiver that began from the top of her head and threatened to shudder through her entire body.

'I don't have any interest in hearing from anyone back home,' she said, and left.

Detective Ruth Dandy sat across the street and watched Stella Gates light a cigarette and walk back and forth for a few seconds before getting into her car and driving out of the parking lot too fast for her or anyone else's safety.

The boat was tied up in the marina and George's party was preparing to disembark. Steven was sitting it out while the women and men ambled down the gangway. George picked up the cooler and handed it to the man who had entertained them earlier.

'Here, Charlie, take this,' he said, and as Charlie reached for it, his lady friend twanged the elastic of his shorts.

'She's insatiable, George,' he said with a grin.

'Sure,' George replied, looking down at the two bloody buckets of disembowelled fish he'd prepared as bait.

'Fucking fish. Fishing and fucking. My God,' he muttered, and called out, 'Hey Steve, leave this today. Tomorrow. Clean it up tomorrow, if you feel up to it, or I'll send someone to do it.'

'You look as if you need a drink,' a tall, good-looking brunette said as she stood in the doorway of the cabin.

Steven wanted to roll a cigarette for himself but he was having trouble.

'I don't think so. I'm just the hired help.'

'You look as if you need a drink, *real* bad,' she said, stepping closer so he could smell the liquor on her breath. She took the tobacco tin and the papers gently from his hands and rolled him a cigarette, licking the fine paper carefully and smoothing the roll-up expertly into an acceptable shape, which she placed between his lips and lit with a match. She waited as he took a first, grateful drag.

'I have things to do, sorry,' he said.

'I love your accent.'

'You're very sweet.'

'You're very sweet too,' she said before she turned away.

George was waiting for him.

'Come on, let me buy you a drink,' he offered, and then followed Steven's gaze to where Stella was walking towards them along the quay. The doctor hurried towards her and kissed her lightly on each side of her face.

'You gorgeous piece of ass,' he whispered, and she smiled and squeezed his plump arms.

'He insisted on coming. How'd he do?'

'He did OK, but he shouldn't have been doing a damn thing. Tonight I'd prescribe some TLC.'

'I'm good at that,' she said.

'Sure you are, Stella.'

'The police think I did it.'

The doctor turned around. Steven was walking towards them now, and Stella recognized the woman and the man who were walking in front of him. The woman had wanted to buy the lion mask and the man had lent her the money. They didn't recognize her.

'You're kidding me,' George said, waving to them to hurry along. 'You're kidding me,' he whispered. 'Steve told me you saved his life.'

'I did. I also ran him over. Could have killed him.'

'Holy shit.'

'George, you have to be cruel to be kind sometimes.'

By the time George had worked out whether or not she was joking, Steven had reached them and was standing next to him. As Stella reached up and kissed her husband's cheek, he looked over her head at the doctor and winked.

'I must have been hurt worse than I thought,' he said.

George laughed.

'You guys,' he said, waving as he walked away.

*

Steven and Stella left the party and drove in the evening traffic down the Pacific Coast Highway through the strips of seaside suburbia that straggled along it. The shock of the trip was always the sight of undeveloped land, the wilderness, and then a brown hill, roped like a wild mustang and duly fenced off, with the white earth exposed in an unpaved road for some future access.

The unpopulated, unlit stretch of highway by the sea was difficult to gauge at night. The blackness of the sky and the land and the sea below required caution and concentration. No rules had been written up yet on signs by the side of the road, and no identifying marks clarified the dream that had yet to be built there. Steven liked to make up names for the potential conurbations, the faux pueblos with red-tiled roofs and white walls, homesteads that would spread over the hills and wall themselves in facing the west, the ocean and the setting sun.

'*Lista de Vinos. Cinturón de Sequridad. Prohibido Fumar,*' Steven repeated like a mantra.

They had taken a trip to Mexico the previous year. The San Diego freeway had been jammed with weekenders travelling south to purchase cheap, counterfeit antibiotics and designer products that were available at the border towns. The sterility of the McDonald's deteriorated the closer they got to the border, and finally the effort to conform to franchise values collapsed as one approached Mexico, where the litter regulations were no longer rigorously enforced by linking the fines to an annual car licence renewal. On both sides of the floodlit line, small signs depicted a family group on the run. They were identical to those cautioning North American drivers of the traffic hazards caused by wildlife or livestock or a school in the vicinity, except that these depicted Mexican illegals running furtively northwards, risking their lives in the dash across the Interstate 5.

Steven and Stella drove through the imaginary line, across

the pseudo-frontier from the north to the south, as if through an invisible membrane. The deodorized smell of the air evaporated and the freeway ceased to be lit. It was darker and wider than the one on which they drove now but the hills were the same, untouched. Stella had been driving then, as usual, and she had had to brake hard to avoid a traffic cop waving a lamp in one of the lanes where his car was parked. Another had sectioned off the area with red tape. A horse had been struck and killed on the road. This was still horse country. Steven saw them tethered behind the super-markets that appeared to be like any other across the border, only in these the packers who ran up and down the littered aisles were small brown children in uniform.

On that weekend trip to Mexico, they had met a man in a restaurant. Stella had been very attracted to him and Steven had bought a bottle of wine for the three of them to share. It was an evening full of promise until the man told them he was looking for an abducted child. Child snatchers ran babies-for-sale rackets in Mexico and the kids taken across the border, even if they were found, were doubly trapped, by their abductors and a bureaucratic quagmire. The man's eyes mirrored his agony. The child, his child, was in this town, he'd seen him. The man's hands trembled. He had a gun, he said. Could they help him? Stella and Steven had got into their car and headed straight back to California. She drove, without speaking, all the way back to Laguna.

She was silent now. The orange sun began to dissolve into the dark ocean and Steven turned to watch her profile against the red sky.

'Remember the Road of Death?' he said.

She didn't answer.

'This could be the Road of Death,' he said. 'The bill-boards. Remember? The construction work all along the road and over the hills? The unfinished hotels and apart-ments? The ones that ran out of money?'

109

Stella concentrated on the road ahead. It was not yet dark but the light had faded enough for there to be a stream of tail lights to follow. She remembered the Road of Death, the part of the Spanish coastal highway that twisted and fell away to the sea. The locals had given it its apocalyptic name because of the many lives it had claimed. She remembered the millionaires' marina, Puerto Banus, south of Marbella, to where they had sailed the forty-foot sea cruiser. The area had been a haven for expatriate British gangsters, who controlled the drug trade, safe from extradition. The coastguard had handed them over to the police at Puerto Banus. Steven did a deal. He went to jail and she went free.

Steven interrupted her memories.

'I don't think it was you that cut the brakes. You didn't do it,' he said. 'I don't think it was Deedes either. No, I don't think so.'

He took her cigarettes from her handbag and lit one for her and one for himself. She looked across at him and pulled at his seat belt.

Steven tugged at it, and with a little difficulty secured himself in the passenger seat.

'It's the law,' he said, and her mobile phone began to ring. He picked it up and passed it to her.

'You can't call me on this any more. I'll call you,' she said into the mouthpiece, and cut the caller off.

'Bit abrupt, weren't we?' Steven remarked.

She ignored him and moved into another lane. There was much more traffic as they approached Laguna, and she was searching for quicker routes through. Steven was quite content to be held up in the evening congestion. He didn't have anything to do. He was smoking a cigarette and sitting down. Stella was the one who was agitated.

'Had a little falling-out?' he enquired at last.

'Someone's been taping our calls,' she replied.

Steven absorbed the information. He felt a frisson of anticipation.

'Who?'

'Deedes.'

Steven mulled it over. Deedes had mentioned audiotapes.

'And you've been indiscreet?'

Stella flung her cigarette from the car.

'As indiscreet as you can be in a private telephone call,' she said, and gunned the car through a space in front.

Steven reached down and lifted up the envelope that was on the floor between his legs. He peeled open the seal and dug his good hand inside. There was a tape. Stella placed her hand over the mouth of the car's tape machine, but Steven bent her fingers back and slid the tape in. He pressed play.

There was silence.

Stella's hand reached for the machine and turned the volume up high. There was nothing until the voice of Jerry Lee Lewis blasted from the speakers and Steven began to laugh and move his body to the rockabilly rhythm of 'Chantilly Lace'.

'I'll kill him,' Stella said, 'I will. I'll kill him.'

'Careful,' Steven replied. 'Someone might be listening.'

Chapter Fourteen

'The policewoman thinks you did it,' Michael said. He was edgy and he'd been drinking.

Stella sat naked astride a chair with her back to him. She wore a red cape which was lifted up to form a hood over her head, and its folds covered her breasts and belly. Her hands clasped a mug of coffee.

'Have you ever had a child, Michael?' she asked.

He rubbed his stained hands on a cloth.

'Not to my knowledge.'

'Not to my knowledge,' Stella repeated after a while. 'A woman can never say that. Not to my knowledge. Adam was ever innocent, and ignorant.'

He walked over to her and placed his hands on her shoulders.

'The policewoman thinks you did it,' he said, as if she hadn't heard him the first time.

'Did she actually say that?'

Stella felt Michael's hands release her, but her shoulders continued to ache from the pressure of his fingertips. She listened to his angry footsteps walking away. She heard the metallic twist of a bottle top and the splash of liquid in a glass.

'She told me the brakes had been cut at the house. She mentioned the quantity of brake fluid on the ground. She asked me where I had been last night.'

'And you told her the truth?'

'I told her the truth, goddammit.'

Stella got up from the chair and the cape fell down to the floor, covering her entirely.

'That's OK then. If you can't say nothing, it's better to tell the truth.'

He turned and slung the empty glass against the white-painted brick of the back wall. She didn't flinch as the glass cracked and splinters shot out, nor when he lifted a wooden chair and flung it across the room. The sound still reverberated as he put his hands to his head, as if he wanted to crush his skull with rage.

'I don't know the fucking truth. What is it? What is the truth? Do I ever hear it, Stella? Do I ever fucking hear it?'

She walked towards the window where the fire escape was and pulled the curtains back. As she looked down, she seemed to disappear in the shaft of yellow dust-filled light that penetrated the room. Michael's eyes ached.

'I told you the truth. You just don't believe me.'

He peered at her.

'That there was someone there last night?' he said.

'There must have been.'

'How do you know?'

'What other explanation is there?'

'I can think of at least one.'

'Oh?'

'Why did you ask me to come to you last night? What was I, an alibi?'

'I told you, I felt dangerous.'

'How dangerous?'

'Dangerous. Were you disappointed?'

She turned away from the window to face him. With her thick hair piled on top of her head and her neck rising out of the deep red material that covered her shoulders, she looked like a queen. Michael felt afraid. He didn't know this woman. He took her body time after time and didn't know her. She had secrets. He had gone home last night like a man who had conquered the world simply because, for the first time, she had allowed him to push her up to a state of ecstasy. She was carrying his child but he was being strangled by doubts. What was the truth? Why did that policewoman want to know if he'd been hanging around the property? Why couldn't he believe that Stella might do something spontaneous? Was she his? Was even the child his?'

'No, no one was disappointed,' she said. 'Everyone was satisfied. Isn't that nice?'

'I know you hate him enough to want him dead. What about me? Do you hate me too?'

She walked towards him and he felt afraid. He almost flinched as her hand reached up to touch his cheek.

'I love you, Michael,' she said, 'but I'm in trouble.'

She told him about the tape that Deedes had of their conversation. Michael assumed at first that what she had said to him was going to be used against her, but his outrage turned to horror when she told him that Deedes had come to her and offered to kill Steven for ten thousand dollars.

'You turned him down, I hope. You turned him down.'

Michael was desperately trying to think where this new information placed him. His head cleared as the effect of his raised blood-alcohol level was temporarily swamped by a surge of adrenalin. His need for truth, his need to know her feelings for him, were overwhelmed and flattened by a powerful instinct for self-preservation.

'You asked me to kill him. I said no. Clearly. No.'

'I know,' she said.

'You asked. I said no. He *taped* our *calls*? How?'

'He must have a scanner.'

'Why? Why did he tape our calls? He was supposed to be tracking the stalker, not us. You said you employed him to see if Steven had a detective on to us.'

'He hasn't.'

Michael thought he was going to have a heart attack. He was hyperventilating. He tried to remember the exercise his yoga teacher had taught him, and held one nostril and then another. He breathed in for a count of four and out for a count of four. He had to reach some sort of inner calm so that he could think.

'I paid him off,' she said.

Michael sat down and she lit a cigarette. He wanted to tell her to put it out. She had a baby inside her. She shouldn't be smoking at all, but he kept his mouth shut about it. She had a plan. If she had a plan, it would work.

'How much?'

'Ten grand.'

It should have been enough, but Michael began to feel a pain of anxiety in his chest again.

'You know what that looks like?' he said carefully, before inhaling through his nose and exhaling through his mouth. 'Don't you think it looks like you paid him to do it?'

Stella began to dress.

'I paid him to keep his mouth shut. Even if it looks like I paid him to do it, he didn't do it,' she said. 'If I'd asked him to do it and he didn't, I wouldn't be paying him the full price, now would I? I wouldn't be paying him at all. I paid for his silence. He's blackmailing *me* anyway, not you.'

'OK. OK. So you have the tape. He's been paid. That's it?'

She sat down. She wore her bra and her skirt and smoked her cigarette as if she had neither the energy nor the inclination to present him with the truth. Michael hauled her up off the chair.

'That's it?' he shouted in her face.

Stella knew he was going to hit her whether she said it or not.

'No.'

'No?' he bellowed.

He started to shake her.

'No,' she screamed. 'He didn't give me the tape back. He didn't give it to me back. Not the original.'

She got it then. A smack across the face. He apologized, of course, almost immediately. The force had brought her to her knees and he was there too, on his knees in an instant, cuddling her, squeezing her, begging her forgiveness. She allowed him to mumble and cry in her ear. She didn't allow the repugnance she felt to show. He was not to know that forgiveness was a tender virtue she had lost a long time ago.

The cold night breeze coming in off the Pacific made it too chilly to eat out on the balcony, so the police officers moved their drinks inside the hotel bar to be close to the warm glow of its synthetic log fire. The night was black and there was no moon. The murky sea rollers were lit by the lights of the half-empty bars along the cliff.

'What's the interest in Famalaro?' Johnson mused as he dug his hands into the dish of pretzels. Ruth Dandy had got there first, but there were a few left.

'You mean, why does he keep bringing it up, sir?'

Johnson glanced at his colleague on the bar stool next to him.

'You think he might be starting a fanzine or something, detective? Yes, *of course* why does he keep bringing it up? Why Famalaro? If he was just passing the time, he'd have mentioned O.J., wouldn't he? O.J. makes more sense. No one's talking about Famalaro. Everyone's talking about O.J.'

Sergeant Dandy took a few more pretzels for herself and the two police officers sat silently munching and staring at their reflections in the mirror that formed the back of the bar. Johnson's skin looked darker than in real life and his shirt whiter than it was. Ruth Dandy's hair shone redly in the flattering lighting. She looked less wholesome, Johnson thought, and a lot more attractive.

'My guess is Famalaro is your typical geek serial killer. No empathy. Either doesn't have the mental connections to perform that trick, or never had the correct models to learn from. The victim is an object that plays a central part in his obsession,' she said.

Johnson nibbled at a biscuit.

'And what about O.J.?' he said.

Dandy contemplated the question that seemed to have been on everyone's lips every single day since June the thirteenth, and then articulated it. 'Think he killed her, sir?'

'Why did he beat his wife?'

'He'd say because she damned deserved it. She made him.'

'He said he loved her.'

'He said he *hit* her because he loved her.'

Johnson moved on the bar stool and drew his fingers down the condensation that clung to his cold glass of beer.

'Stella Gates. Did she hit her husband because she loved him?' he said.

'It's an interesting thought, isn't it?' Dandy replied, and after a few considered munches, added, 'I read somewhere that violence is a function of a distorted search for intimacy and an unsympathetic desire for control.'

'Is that so? Well, I'd agree with "unsympathetic" all right. You want to be in their face and on top, that it? That the control bit? Come on, you really go in for all that fed stuff, sergeant?'

'Sir?'

'She said they argued. They were mad at each other. You never thrown a plate at someone?'

Dandy looked at her senior officer with a blank and uncomprehending look. Johnson smiled ruefully. He wondered what the sergeant's definition of passion, of love, of betrayal might be. She'd probably have read something about it somewhere.

'Ella threw a whole plate of rice at me once. She got so

mad at me for being late *again*, she picked up the plate and let me have it,' he said.

'Proves my point, doesn't it, sir?' Dandy replied.

'How so?'

'She wanted to connect with you one way or another.'

'She missed.'

'Doesn't matter. Her desire was to connect. Violence is the product of the form of control. Question you have to ask then is, what *function* does the victim have for the assailant, the rapist, or the killer?'

Johnson pressed his long fingers against his temples. His mind kept returning to the bodies, or parts of them, that were displayed in the gallery. They were parts of her body mostly, her beautiful, beautiful body, some paintings, some clay, some bronzes, some simple body casts, which meant she'd been smeared in petroleum jelly and intimately sealed in warm plaster of Paris, and then there was the watercolour of the child. *Michael Revere: An Installation of Memories.* It was his gig. What was he up to?

'What function does the victim have for the killer?' he whispered to himself wearily. 'I don't know. I guess we just got to find out a whole lot more about these people.'

Dandy ordered another round of beers. Johnson thought she seemed pretty upbeat about the whole case. In fact, she looked real pleased with herself.

'I spoke with the private detective. Sleazeball, name of Ray Deedes? We ain't talking the Nick Harris Academy here, but he is licensed.'

The barkeep laid two paper doilies on the bar and rested the shining glasses on them. He moved a bowl of nuts nearer to Dandy and she left him a tip.

'She was paying a bill,' she said.

'Why not post it?'

'And collecting her file.'

'He couldn't post that, either? OK, what'd you get?'

Dandy smiled.

'Said she hired him to see if her husband had hired someone to follow *her*. She came to pay him and he gave her the files. End of beautiful relationship.'

'Did he find anyone?'

'No.'

Johnson took a handful of peanuts, made a fist and popped a single nut into his mouth.

'That Mrs Gates.'

'Well, you've been talking to her, sir.'

He looked at Dandy through the reflection of the mirror. Yeah, he had been talking to her. It was hard work *just* talking to her. What did Ruth Dandy know? Someone who never threw a plate in her life.

'So what's your take?' she said.

'What?'

'That Mrs Gates.'

'He must have had *something* on her for her to drive all the way out there to get it, personally.'

'I'd stake my life on it,' Dandy replied. 'Why'd a high-rent woman like her take the trouble to drive to a low-rent place like that to pick up an envelope? She was paying. He could have delivered it. Hell, like you said, sir, she could have asked him to post it. The US mail could have saved her the time, the trouble and the experience of smelling his breath one more time.'

Johnson drank some beer.

'I checked Deedes out. He's pretty busy. He takes nice pictures of people having a little bad fun in motel rooms,' she said.

'Pictures. Photographs. Maybe that's it,' Johnson replied.

'Blackmail? I thought about that. But what's Deedes got to blackmail her about? Her husband knows everything.'

The two officers stared at their reflections and said nothing.

'Steven Gates reported the stalker, she didn't,' Johnson said at last. 'What if the gumshoe got him on camera?'

'So why wouldn't she want anyone to know who it was?'

They stared at themselves again and together they agreed.

'Because she recognized him?' they said, their hands colliding in the bowl of nuts. Johnson did the decent thing and let her go first.

Dandy nibbled and chewed and drank her beer.

'She's pregnant. You know that, don't you? Revere confirmed he's the father,' she said. Johnson took a slow swallow of his drink and kept his thoughts to himself. Like Revere'd know, like the man could ever be sure.

'She smokes too. She's harming that child before it's ever born,' Dandy said. 'And the picture of the kid in there?'

'Yes?' Johnson said.

'Nirvana's *Nevermind* without the dollar bill. *So* derivative.'

Johnson could have kicked himself.

Chapter Fifteen

Ray Deedes charged a flat fee of $558 dollars to dig the dirt on any individual, any company, on any topic or subject. More often than not, he never had to leave the office. With a telephone, he could violate certain federal, state and local laws and gain access to a great variety of telephone records: bills, calls and unlisted numbers. With an online computer, he could legitimately search more than one thousand databases that held collectively a hundred billion – a hundred thousand million – records in the United States alone. He could access electoral registers and Motor Vehicle Department files. He could find out a name and address from a telephone number. He could list lottery winners by state, or insurance annuity recipients and the amounts they were awarded. He could access newspaper and magazine databases. He could search social security numbers and mortgages. He could list all the American soldiers who were casualties in the Vietnam War. He could determine past weather conditions for any day, or time, anywhere in the USA in case these circumstances proved important for whatever reason. Outside of the USA, things got much harder, but he could still access the UK Court Directory, the UK Public Record Office and the main credit reference bureaux. None of it took long, but images took an age. Images took time and bandwidth. And video? Forget it.

It was interesting to find out when Stella Gates had entered the country with her husband, but what was really fascinating was her highly unusual credit history. That had begun, Deedes discovered, just four years ago in the US. Before that, zip. Nothing. There were other Stella Gateses in the UK, but they had continuing credit histories and British addresses to match. Nothing matched the Stella Gates he had. Even if she had travelled most of her life, there would have been something, but the printout told him otherwise. Nothing. No Stella Gates. He pondered this awhile and then decided that if she had got married and moved immediately to the United States, he should be looking for a maiden name back home. Steven Gates's name would help him with that. He tried to track Steven Gates and got nothing. Steven Gates didn't exist in any credit reference bureau either.

It was a head-scratcher all right. In terms of living in Western society in the late twentieth century, people without a credit history are virtually dead. Or, to take another view, they had yet to be born again as consumers. Modern life truly begins with a loan.

Deedes had some luck. Steven Gates's name turned up on a database of certificates of marriage. He was aged thirty-six at the time. His new wife, Stella Gates née Wright, was twenty-six. Her occupation was listed as shop assistant, and he had been unemployed. There was the same London address for both of them. Deedes checked out the credit history of Stella Wright at that address. He was looking for a credit history that stopped four years ago. He found one. He checked for a credit history for Steven Gates, and found nothing. The possibilities the facts presented Deedes for his personal financial gain made his overtaxed heart flutter, and brought a broad smile to his lips.

Stella Gates's gynaecologist was in Newport Beach. He had an office on the fifth floor in a block opposite the hospital a little down the way from Fashion Island, a glistening shopping mall of spectacular proportions. She had gone to him for a scan, and as she lay back in the semi-darkness with her belly smeared with a clear gel, she thought of what Deedes would ask for next. She'd called him about the tape.

'I have been looking for that just about everywhere,' he had drawled. 'It's my favourite. Jerry Lee Lewis. My favourite.'

'Are you saying you gave it to me by mistake? That it was a mistake?'

'Sure was, lady, and as soon as your cheque clears, I'll make sure you get *your* tape right away. I just want you to know that next time, I'll be wanting cash.'

'Next time.'

'I know who you are, Mrs Gates. But just who is your husband, exactly?'

She thought how close he was getting. People knew about Steven's past, that he'd done time. If any of them had cared, they would have wondered how he had got into the US with an excludable offence on his visa. He'd lied, of course. He had acquired a copy of the birth certificate of a child with the same birthday and year of birth as his own. The child had died aged six months, and Steven had taken his name and details. They had married and got the passports. They had to. There was no way they would have been accepted with Steven's record. She had got her green card and she had wanted a new life. Steven had wanted their old one, but he came along anyway.

She felt the ultrasound scanner slide over her skin. Most women stretched up and peered at the monitor in an attempt to catch sight of the foetus. Stella didn't. She stared at the ceiling and waved the doctor away when he invited her to observe the shadows on the black and white screen.

'I can't tell. I would only be pretending,' she said, and the doctor asked if she wanted a printout. It was about twelve weeks old and would have a face. It would have a face, a recognizable face. It would resemble a human child and not a curious sort of lungfish. She said she did not want a printout, and the doctor had dropped the matter. He advised her on diet and vitamin supplements instead. He reassured her that she would probably stop feeling sick soon, and she complained that her clothes were starting not to fit.

'You shouldn't smoke,' the doctor told her, and she said she didn't as the nurse helped her up from the couch.

'The child would be underweight,' he advised her.

'That could be an advantage. I must buy twenty today.'

She smiled and the doctor patted her hand.

'Take care now, Mrs Gates,' he said, and when she had left, the nurse turned to him.

'Was that a joke?' she asked.

'I think so,' he said.

Stella noticed the man out of the corner of her eye as she crossed the car park. He had what she thought was a camera, but when she turned to face him he had gone. He had been there, she was sure, but she couldn't identify him. It was more of an awareness than a sighting. She wondered if it had been Deedes, but as she whirled around a full three hundred and sixty degrees, she could see no one. The sun sparkled on the roofs of the silent cars and she began to doubt herself until she heard an engine start. She began to run towards the sound, but it was on a lower level and impossible to see. The exit was too far away. Stella stopped and looked back, and realized that she couldn't remember where she had run from. She stood alone, lost in a quiet sea of hot metal that reflected the sky, her heart beating faster and faster. Someone was walking towards her out of the sun. He was tall and as black as a shadow. She shaded her eyes with her hand and took a step back.

'Mrs Gates?'

It was Johnson.

'Mrs Gates? I thought it was you.'

She leaned against a car and dug in her handbag for her sunglasses.

'I can't remember where I parked the car,' she said. 'Were you just passing?'

He looked at her, and at his own reflection in the smoke-coloured lenses that now shielded her expression from him, and smiled.

'That's right,' he said.

She smiled back at him.

'I'm getting paranoid,' she said. 'I thought . . . I think everyone's following me.'

The warm breeze took a strand of her hair and dragged it across her lips. She put her hand to her mouth.

'You look kind of shook up. Let me treat you to a cup of coffee. Or tea? Do you drink tea?' he said.

'I do, detective, but I am very particular about it.'

Their smiles were fixed on each other like their blank eyes. They were revealing nothing and everything in the curve of their lips and the angle of their bodies. He *had* followed her. He'd watched her make the call to Deedes and then come here to see her doctor. He liked watching her. It was part of the job, but he liked doing it. He liked the way her long hair had caught in the wind. He liked the easy sway she had when she walked. He watched where she'd gone to. There were only two reasons why a woman went to the doctor on the fifth floor: to make sure a baby was there and was going to make it, or to be sure it didn't.

'I don't know what to do,' she said.

'It's no big deal. I ain't forcing you to choose.'

She laughed and caught his hand.

'I'm pregnant,' she said. 'I was talking about my baby, not tea or coffee.'

They both laughed then. She still had hold of his hand.

He knew he shouldn't, and it would be crazy if he did, but he wanted to kiss her palm, somewhere near the wrist. He freed himself, tucking his hand into his pocket.

'Congratulations,' he said.

The drugstore café was a steel and Formica construction with a minimal wholefood menu and plastic disposable beakers. Johnson bought the coffees and they took a table in a corner.

'I thought I saw someone in the car park.'

'Parking lot.'

She smiled wryly.

'Some things are just too hard,' she said. 'I just can't bring myself to say 'erb, either.'

'What do you say?'

'Herb.'

Her lips pushed outwards to make the sound. He noticed a red smudge of lipstick on her teeth. If he cupped her chin in his hand, he could press his thumb between her wet lips and rub the mark away.

'Herb. 'erb. Whatever.'

'It would mean dropping one's aitches.'

Johnson shrugged and grinned. He didn't know what the hell she was talking about. Her finger circled the white plastic cup.

'I do think there was someone following me. There was someone here.'

Johnson gazed at her. She had kept her sunglasses on and that made it more difficult. He wanted to look into her eyes and see what was behind, but he couldn't. He watched her lips, her uneven teeth. She smiled lazily, and, reaching over, stroked his middle finger. Johnson's balls began to ache. He was in trouble. He wanted her and she knew it.

'Someone you might know, Mrs Gates?'

Her finger still circled the lip of the cup. She didn't seem to want the drink. Johnson remembered how his wife had hated the taste of coffee when she had been pregnant. This woman was pregnant too, but by whom? He remembered asking his wife that question. She'd slapped his face.

'Someone you might know, Mrs Gates?' he repeated, but she still didn't answer.

'We know you employed a detective by the name of Ray Deedes. Did he come up with anything? Any photographs? Did you see anyone in those photographs?'

'He came up with photographs of me, and Michael.'

Johnson's uncomprehending expression made her smile again. She patted his hand this time.

'My husband is a voyeur, detective. Isn't that obvious?'

'Now that you've mentioned it. Where does Deedes come into it?'

'He buys the photographs he likes from Deedes. He buys the videos he likes. I give him the money, of course, but I arrange it all. It has to be convincing, like I don't know. It's a charade, a farce. We both know that.'

'You have photographs of yourself taken with your lover?'

'Lovers.'

'Lovers.'

Johnson had to sit back against the metal chair to digest this information. Stella took a sip of her coffee. She licked a little of the froth from her lips.

Goddamn, he thought to himself.

'Michael doesn't know,' she said.

'Oh.'

He asked her if Michael was the father of her child and she said he was, but Johnson didn't know whether he believed her. He wondered what difference it would make if Steven Gates was, if it was possible, if she cared *who* the father was.

'Are you going to keep it?'

'Yes.'

'Are you going to leave your husband?'

Stella bit her lip.

'I don't know.'

'What's the problem?'

'History.'

They sat in silence. Johnson finished his coffee but Stella didn't want any more. She got up to leave and Johnson escorted her to his car. They drove around for twenty minutes looking for hers, until they found it pretty close to where he had walked out of the sun towards her. He leaned over her to open the passenger door. She let him touch her and then stepped out of the car. He watched as she bent to unlock her vehicle. He imagined her against it and him against her, his hands holding her breasts and his thighs between hers. The thought of it made him grip the steering wheel a little harder. She turned to face him and raised her hand to give him a little wave, and he smiled back at her. He waited while the car moved in front and followed it out of the lot.

While Johnson tracked Stella back to Laguna, Steven was working on the boat. George had told him to stay home, but he hadn't felt like it. He couldn't go in the pool with his hand like it was, so he decided he might as well make himself useful. He'd noticed that there was something not quite right about the engine, and he wanted to check it out. It needed a little maintenance. He'd been working there non-stop for more than an hour when he took a break for a smoke. It had been hot down in the hole and he was feeling a little dizzy. He'd only just lit up when he saw Geroge walking down the quayside with a Latino slightly taller than him. The men were both wearing baggy shorts, and the doctor's polo shirt was the original of the Latino's counterfeit Lacoste. He was, however, wearing a phoney captain's hat with braid around it, while the Latino wore an official Lakers cap. Steven hadn't been expecting them, and George had not expected to see Steven either. He called out to him as he hurried towards the boat.

'Hey, Steve! Steve! Leave that, for Chrissakes! What are you doing? I got help today.'

Steve disembarked and ambled towards the two men. His face was smeared with grease and perspiration.

'What the hell are you doing, man?' the doctor remonstrated with him. 'I told you. You're not to be doing this stuff. I got Raul today. Hey Raul, Steve.'

Steven stretched out his right hand and the Latino looked down at it, his own broad-knuckled brown fist hovering in mid-air. Steven waited for the handshake and when it didn't come, he looked down at what might be bothering the man and saw the bandage. There was stuff oozing through and muck all over it. It looked messy. It was a shock to him, and he gazed at it as if it didn't belong to him. He kept staring at it as George took hold of him with experienced gentleness.

'Steve, my friend, this is no good. Come on. Let's see to this. Come on.'

Steven felt disorientated. On the boat he'd felt secure, but back on land, it seemed that the tables and chairs over by the restaurant were moving in a shimmer of hot air. He could barely stand. His mouth was parched and he could hardly swallow.

'I need a beer,' he said.

'You need an antibiotic shot and a hot nurse. Come on. Let's go. Raul?'

George beckoned to his companion to take one of Steven's arms and the two men began to guide him away from the boat. Steven shivered suddenly.

'I need my jacket,' he said, 'I've forgotten my jacket.'

'Come on, Steve. Raul'll get it,' the doctor reasoned, but Steven pulled away from the two men and started to walk and then jog back to the boat. The Latino shrugged at George, who called after Steven.

'Take it easy, Steve. We're here, we're waiting for you. No hurry. Steve?'

He carried on jogging past the sea cruisers and yachts moored to the side and lifted his hand in acknowledgement. He was so damned cold, and the back of his eyes hurt. He was going as fast as he could when he felt a sudden pressure against his chest and he seemed to fly backwards. The air bent in front of him and fumes poured up from the boiling land. The sudden detonation threw him fifteen feet backwards in a firestorm of light and smoke and as he lost consciousness, he saw himself lying bleeding on the ground, spread out like a carcass.

At the moment of the explosion, Johnson's car was parked outside the house on the hill. He was inside, all the way inside. The sweat was pouring down his naked body, but Stella wasn't perspiring at all. She lay back with her arms and legs lazily spread and watched as he made love to her.

Chapter Sixteen

Johnson hovered a little sheepishly around Ruth Dandy. She'd finally managed to contact him up at the house. She had told him the news. The boat had a hole in it the size of a small car, and five people had been hospitalized.

'A timing device. What do you say?' he said.

'He was the only one on the boat before it happened. We've got to hear what he has to say, but forensics should be able to give us a line on it pretty soon.'

Johnson bit his lip and looked at the million-dollar disaster in the marina. Three boats moored on one side had taken the force of the blast. Dr George Peyronie's pride and joy was half submerged in an oily slick of rainbow-coloured water. The air smelled of gasoline and smoke.

'You think she could organize something like this, is that what you're saying? Come on, Ruth.'

Dandy walked towards the police car wondering why men were such assholes. Anyone with a mind to could organize something like that. She stopped by the car and faced him, her legs well planted, her hands hooked around her hips like a gunslinger waiting to draw.

'If she had help, maybe. Or, she could have done it herself. What do we know? We know she has a motive,' she said, opening the car door abruptly. 'The blast should've taken his head off and whipped his brains to guacamole. He was lucky, once again.'

Dandy ducked into the vehicle and sirens wailed in the distance.

'Seems like luck's really running for him. Yeah, I can see that,' Johnson replied, walking around to the passenger side. Dandy waited while he strapped himself in before keying the ignition. She looked quickly into the rear-view mirror.

'You've been talking to her, sir,' she said, without turning to face him. 'What's your take?'

'Does a boat park in the same place all the time?' Johnson enquired. Dandy switched off the engine. She seemed unusually agitated.

'Dock sir. A car parks. A boat docks, sir.'

'Does the boat dock in the same place all the time?'

'We have to check that.'

Johnson patted his fingers on his knees.

'Did you know it's against the law to send something in a bubble pack by registered mail, detective?'

He looked across at her, but she continued to stare straight ahead.

'Yes, I did, sir. But what has that, excuse me, got to do with anything?'

'Nothing. It has nothing to do with anything, but I just had a feeling you'd know that.'

Dandy keyed the ignition and steered the car cautiously out of the bay and through the hubbub of police vehicles at the scene. Helicopters circled above the smouldering cruisers like wasps around a rotting catch. The satellite vans had already arrived. It was big news.

'So what are you saying?' she said.

'Nothing,' Johnson replied. 'I'm saying nothing. I'm saying you're efficient that's all. Damned efficient.'

'I'm efficient. Damned efficient. That's OK, isn't it, sir?'

'Sure, it's OK. I didn't mean anything by it.'

'But it's not sexy, right?'

Johnson turned and looked at the woman. She was concentrating on her driving, her profile straight and serious, her eyes flicking up to the rear-view mirror and across to the wings.

'Say what?'

Dandy repeated herself.

'It's not sexy. Being efficient. It's not sexy.'

Johnson could feel the hot water rising up towards his neck. This was the sort of conversation he'd had a million times with Ella. The sort of conversation he never won. He should have shut up there and then, but hell, Ruth Dandy wasn't his wife. He was going to make his point.

'Wait a minute. Wait a minute, now. I didn't say you weren't sexy. I said you . . .'

'You said I would know that it was against the law to send a bubble pack registered mail.'

Johnson shook his head and pushed a finger against his sunglasses.

'I must be missing something here.'

The automatic kicked and Johnson felt the small of his back press momentarily against the seat. Dandy was putting her foot down. He stared at the poisoned sky that blanketed the Santa Ana mountains. Oh, brother.

'What about her? Would she know? What do you think, sir?'

Johnson made a big deal of thinking about it. He had to take the temperature in the car down a notch or two.

'Yeah,' he replied, easily, 'she'd know something like that. What are you building here, a harassment suit? I was having a little fun with you.'

'So she's efficient.'

'Yeah. She's efficient.'

'And she's sexy, right?'

'Yeah. What of it?'

'So would you ask her what you asked me?'

Oh, man.

'About the bubble pack? Sure . . . aw, c'mon Ruth, gimme a break . . . Sure I'd ask her. In appropriate circumstances, yeah, I'd ask her.'

'But it would mean something else, wouldn't it? You'd say it different with her, right?' Dandy said, accelerating towards an off-ramp. Johnson wasn't thinking about bubble packs any more. His mind was on other things, like the shape of Stella Gates's breasts, the feel of her nipples in his mouth, the sandalwood smell of her pubic hair.

'You feel better now, don't you?' she had said, but she was wrong, he hadn't felt better. He had fallen on her body like an animal tearing meat. The smouldering lake of bad feeling seemed to pour out of him, out of his corrosive cock and into her soft, deep parts. She knew. She knew he was taking revenge, not on her, on someone. His wife, maybe. His wife and her baby, the one he was never sure was his. He had felt elated and evil at one and the same time. He was using her. She was letting him. He wanted her down, subjugated and it was *better* that she was pregnant, my God, it was better. He was in there. He didn't belong, but he was in there. He'd taken Ella the same way when she'd told him. He'd taken her so hard, as if, as if he could become the father of the bastard child by sheer force. It finished them. It finished them. He'd looked down on Stella's body with nothing in his mind but to give, give, give it to her.

'You feel better now, don't you?' Stella had said, with all the confidence of someone who knows just how not to please. He had apologized. He apologized and she stroked his back.

'So what's your take on her, sir?' Dandy said.

Johnson put a couple of fingers to his temple.

'Just drive, Ruth. Drive, will you?'

Steven Gates tried to smile.

'You think Famalaro did it?' he said as the two detectives stood by his bed.

Johnson laughed.

'Is that a joke?' Dandy enquired.

'How are you feeling?' Johnson asked. He couldn't quite bear to look the man in the eye.

'Fine and Dandy,' he replied, and Dandy glanced at Johnson. The lieutenant thought about the photographs for the first time and felt a niggle of concern. Steven and Stella Gates had both known that Deedes had taken photographs, yet thought someone else was following her. Deedes. Johnson should have been more careful. He hadn't been thinking straight. He was in a bit of a spot. He could see that now. He wanted to turn to Ruth Dandy, bend over and ask her to kick his ass.

'The photographs,' he said.

'The photographs? What photographs?' Steven replied.

His voice cracked as he spoke. His back hurt him where he had fallen and caught the base of his spine. The skin had been flayed off the backs of both arms and legs. The small injuries he'd sustained in the car accident all hurt a little more, especially his hand. The back of his head had cracked on the concrete, too. That ached. They told him he had concussion.

'The ones you have of your wife and Michael Revere. Did you recognize anyone in them?'

'I recognized my wife and Michael Revere.'

'Jesus,' Dandy said, almost spitting with frustration. Johnson glanced at her.

'Anyone else, Mr Gates? Anyone who might have a vendetta against you?'

Steven closed his eyes.

'Mr Gates, it's obviously not your wife this stalker is after,' Dandy said.

'Perhaps not. But whoever it was, they did take her keys,' he replied.

Johnson said nothing.

*

'Who took your keys?' he asked her.

'My husband, of course. I think it was him.'

'Why?'

'To get into Michael's studio. To give the key to someone to get into Michael's studio.'

'And?'

'And to video us having sex.'

Johnson had suddenly felt vulnerable lying naked next to her. He searched the spaces where the door stood ajar and the curtain moved against the bedroom windows.

'That's what I think. I just didn't understand why. I mean, I take care of that, as a rule.'

Johnson's eyes had checked the walls, the corners of the room.

'He'd like to have seen this,' she said, and he couldn't bring himself to ask because of the sick, insecure feeling in his stomach.

'Before, when you said your husband had hired a PI, I asked you why should he come to us with this story about someone following you around? So, why'd he come to me, if *he*'d taken the keys?'

'Because he's crazy,' she said.

Stella Gates had watched Johnson leave, and was not surprised to see Ray Deedes step out from behind the carport.

'I thought I'd better stay where I was, out there by the pool,' he had said. 'It sounded like you were having a lot of fun with the nigger.'

Stella stepped into her house and didn't bother to shut the door. Deedes followed her into the lounge. She lit a cigarette.

'What do you want? Be quick. There's been an accident. I have to get dressed and get down to the hospital.'

'Anyone we know?'

'My husband.'

'What happened this time?'

'There was an explosion on Dr Peyronie's boat at the marina.'

Deedes walked over to the French windows and looked out at the blue rectangular pool. It shone like shot silk.

'You took so long, I had to take a piss,' he said, nodding to the outside.

'Have you got the tape?' she asked.

The gumshoe ignored her. He sat down heavily on the sofa, spread his arms out and stretched his solid legs.

'I could do with a beer.'

Stella stood in her house robe, one arm held tight to her chest and gripping the elbow of the other that held the cigarette. Her fingers scissored the filter and pressed it hard against her lips.

'I said I could do with a beer.' The insincere grin had disappeared from his face. Stella did as she was told and brought him an ice-cold can from the fridge.

'Don't I get a glass?' he said, popping the tab.

She fetched him one.

'Gonna pour it?'

She did so without bothering to put her cigarette down. He took it from her and waved the smoke from his face. He pressed his fleshy lips against the glass and took a long swallow.

'I have to get dressed,' she said, and walked to the bedroom. He belched and followed her.

'Do you mind?' she said as he stood in the doorway.

He laughed.

'Aw, come on, Stella. I've seen you every which way.'

She didn't move.

'Give me the tape,' she said.

The detective stuck his hand in the inside pocket of his raincoat and waved a small envelope at her.

'I reckon it's worth a little more now.'

'How much?'

His gaze wandered up and down her body.

'I'd rather pay,' she said.

'The way it's going, I don't think you're calling the shots, lady. I could make big trouble for you. Big trouble. 'Course, with what I saw today, I could make big trouble for the cop, and big trouble between you and Michael.' He put on a little-girlie voice when he said Michael's name. 'And what you going to do? Go to the police? Go to Lieutenant Johnson? Stuff I know about you, *Miss Wright*?'

Stella's heart lurched like a hooked fish. Deedes could hardly contain his glee. He was on a roll. He handed her the envelope which, of course, didn't have a tape inside. It had copies of photographs, court records and newspaper reports. Before he left he asked her for a quarter of a million dollars.

Chapter Seventeen

'She said her *husband* took the keys to her car,' Johnson said as he and Dandy walked through the hospital lot.

'When?'

'It's documented. Came into my office that day and told me the keys had gone missing, that someone was stalking his wife.'

'When did *she* tell you?'

'I'm sorry. Up at the house.'

Dandy glanced at him but said nothing, though he could read her mind. He couldn't stop thinking about what had happened either, and Dandy was reading *his* mind pretty much.

'She told me he was crazy,' he said, opening the door to the car.

'Crazy enough to kill himself, sir?'

Johnson had thought about that. The Ford Blazer with the brakes cut, the explosion on the boat: Steven Gates could be as much in the frame as anyone else.

'I interviewed Michael Revere again,' Dandy said. 'He told me Steven Gates had called him the day he found out that she was pregnant. Revere says Gates asked him to kill him.'

'Why didn't Revere say something before?'

'He thought nothing of it.'

Johnson felt a jab of anger.

'Yeah, right, he's sleeping with the man's wife, that's

nothing. He plants a kid, that's nothing. Guy, naturally enough, gets a little distressed and calls him up to finish him off. That's nothing either.'

Dandy noted the tone in her boss's voice and laid off a little.

'Revere doesn't know about the photographs Deedes took,' she said.

'How'd you know he doesn't? Did you ask him? I just this minute told *you* about them.'

'He doesn't know. He's scared. He's scared about the stalker. If he knew about the photographs and video she arranged for her husband's entertainment, why would he be scared? He'd know that someone'd be hanging around for the show. He'd be in on it,' she replied, and then to herself as much as Johnson, said, 'How do people get *off* on that?'

Johnson got in the car. Dandy sat in the driver's seat, gripped the steering wheel and leaned her chin on it. They sat there for a while, just thinking, until Johnson tapped the dashboard.

'Steven Gates was in the army, Ruth. If he wanted to kill himself he'd take a gun and put it to his head. That's the army way.'

Stella got to the hospital a little while after Johnson and Dandy had left. She sat at her husband's bedside and told him how much Deedes knew. When she got to the bit about the money, Steven laughed.

'Deedes, the fuck. He doesn't know anything.'

'He knows that we're not who we say we are. He knows about me, and it won't be long before he knows about you.'

'He knows fuck all. He's getting fuck all. Start thinking about the police. They'll be checking up on us too. They'll find out what? That I lied and you didn't. I get deported. You colluded, mind you. They could stretch to that. They could deport the both of us. So what?'

'It matters to me.'

'Don't worry. You've got friends. You've got money. The one thing that could hurt us only you and I know. So, be nice to me.'

Stella didn't answer. She was bored by the hospital room with its bland marshmallow decor and wishy-washy watercolour on the far wall. She felt tired breathing its recycled air. She didn't want to be there beside him. She didn't want to talk about anything. She sat next to her injured husband and cast her mind back to that summer long ago when she'd gone with Steven to take the stolen boat down to Spain.

He didn't steal them. He was employed by those who did to get the boats down there, that's all. The syndicate he worked for would check boats out that were for sale and pay with worthless building society kites. People thought those cheques were as good as cash. They weren't. They took twelve days to clear in those days, by which time the boats had disappeared. Steven wasn't involved in any of that. He was for hire. He took legitimate charters to the Med and he took stolen boats. He didn't care as long as he got paid, but if you worked boats along the Spanish coast, you inevitably got asked to carry a load. Moroccan. That's what they'd got caught with. Ten grand was what he'd been paid to captain the boat, and as far as they were concerned it could have been anything. Ten grand was a lot of money then.

They'd killed Duran after he'd raped her. They'd cut off his dirty fingers and they'd fished for sharks with them, and it had worked. The smell of human blood dispersing around the boat had brought the black-eyed beasts circling pretty quickly. Stella had watched them skim the water and felt them bump the boat in their eagerness to feed. It was instinct, dumb, indifferent instinct because pretty soon they'd be consuming themselves. Steven had hacked at the first one he had caught and thrown it back in. The sea had boiled like hot soup.

They had been heading back up the coast when the Spanish coastguard stopped them. Fresh meat and cartilage littered the deck and fresh blood had covered their tainted clothes as the officers called out to them and pulled alongside in their gleaming launch.

The uniformed men had stood in silence. The boat must have smelled like a charnel house. Steven had stared up at them from where he was crouching and waved, but no one had waved back. Two young people, a man and a woman, with their faces bleached with salt water and raw with desperation, what grim picture of insanity had they presented? Steven had called out that there was something wrong with the boat. They were boarded and searched.

She didn't know how it had happened. They'd tied the crates of hash to the body to weigh it down and rolled the thing over. It had gone under. They'd stood and waited while the search went on. One of the coastguards shouted out that they'd found something. He was tugging at a rope. Another length of rope was tangled up in it. The couple watched as four men heaved. Something heavy was weighing down the other end. She had expected to see the stump of an arm, a half-eaten leg, or the torso, the legs and arms having been gnawed away. As they hauled the weight in, the coastguards pulled up not Duran's shredded cadaver but one polythene-wrapped crate of cannabis, and she had collapsed on the deck like a puppet whose strings had been cut.

They had screwed up. No one had known the boat had left or where it had been going. If anyone was waiting for Duran, it wasn't going to be the authorities. The two of them had had a dead body to get rid of and blood all over the deck. It was their bad luck that the coastguard had seen them. Steven had planned, in as much as he had planned anything in those twenty-four hours, to pull into a harbour somewhere along the coast and talk about the fishing to be had. She'd thought about it every day since. He had wanted to get rid of the blood, disguise it, but he could have just dumped the body, dumped everything, washed down the deck, washed the clothes and they could have sunbathed naked for a while before taking the boat anywhere they chose. He had the tickets for the plane. 'Let's take the plane,' she had said. My God. Let's take the plane. They would have been gone before Duran's friends had even begun to wonder. Instead, they had dreamed up a nightmare and lived it.

She sat beside Steven in the shadows of his hospital room and thought about what she wanted more than anything: the child she was carrying. It was her child. It was a child whose face would belong to Michael. A face she might love, a face that held kinder memories for her. She tried to focus on Michael and think good things about him. Her hand reached up to her cheek. He had struck her. She flushed at the thought of it. Steven had never touched her, not once. My princess, my rose, he called her, and she had loved him because he had never *made* her do anything. He made her *want* to, he made her want to please him. He'd been honest with her. 'This is the first time I've felt like this,' he said. 'I have to see you. I can't *see* you up close.'

They'd started with a mirror, and she liked it with a mirror. He'd sit and watch her in the mirror. She wouldn't look at herself. She'd look at him and feel her power. That's when it began. She'd look at him watching her and feel in control. She fed him. She fed and loved him like you would feed and love a dog, or a child. Only the best, only the best pieces of meat, only the very best was good enough. He got the leftovers now. She gave him everything he wanted, second-hand: photocopies, photographs, videos, art, simulacra of love, a second-hand view of his rose, his princess, interpreted by someone else's eyes. Deedes's snapshots and videos, Michael's sculptures and casts: pieces of her that she could tear off and give away. It was no more than he deserved.

But Michael had struck her. She hadn't spoken to him for a week, maybe more, because of it. He'd called and called. All that kneeling and begging. Ridiculous. She just wanted to make sure she got out of there without a fuss. It couldn't be Steven's, could it? Oh, if it was. If it was.

Steven started suddenly in his sleep and woke up. She gave him some iced water from a beaker which he sucked at gratefully before easing himself back on the pillows. She grabbed at her handbag and prepared to go.

'I need a cigarette,' she said, and as she got up to leave he gripped her arm.

'Do you think the dead can rise up?' he asked.

'Are you asking me if I believe?'

'Do you think it's them?'

'Who?'

'Raphael. Duran. You know. That baby.'

'I don't believe in ghosts, if that's what you mean,' she said.

'I do,' Steven whispered. 'I believe I am one. I believe I died years ago. I am a ghost. I'm living proof.'

He chuckled, and Stella, bored with his sick humour and self-pity, picked up the remote.

'What's on TV?' she said, pointing it.

'O.J. What else?'

She slung the controller on to the bed and Steven began again.

'Someone took those keys. Someone other than Deedes is following you around. It's not Famalaro.'

He began to laugh and choke. It amused him to see the look in the eyes of those police officers when he asked after him. The truth was, he was in awe of Famalaro, not because he was a murderer, necessarily, but because he could express himself so totally. His will was all. He couldn't repress it and didn't. He had accepted the freedom of being himself. Steven had killed people too. He'd killed people all right: a rioter in Northern Ireland, an Argentinian lad in the Falklands War. Both deaths were different because he hadn't wanted them. He was following orders. He was killing an enemy and defending himself and his mates. There was no desire for it. And Duran? Yes, he'd killed him because he had wanted to. She'd struck the first blow, but he'd definitely made sure that Duran was dead.

He'd killed Duran all right, but it wasn't perfect. It wasn't like the death of the boy, the nineteen-year-old who thought his luck had changed. He had wanted to kill him and had done so, though Stella never believed that he had. She'd let him watch the boy make love to her. She'd wanted that. Those were the rules. She had to want it. She had to be in control. It was important. She had to make a free choice, otherwise it didn't work for her. He needed her to think that so that she would do it. The truth was, there were no rules. He was just working within her limits. He'd got off on Duran as much if not more than he had with Raphael. He couldn't let them live afterwards, either of them, any of them, but she didn't know that. He just couldn't let them live. He had the right to self-expression. He just couldn't live with it.

For her part, she had never forgiven him for letting Duran touch her. She made him watch her with someone else a thousand times since, but never let him see her come. He was left feeling incomplete, half a man, half quenched, half fed. The Californians had a word for it. They had as many words to describe a state of mind as Eskimos have words for snow. They called it *closure*. He could not get closure. He couldn't complete the act and kill anyone because she never came, and she watched him and she could pull the rope on him any time she wanted. He couldn't express himself any more, not like Famalaro. He wanted to kill Michael Revere the other night but he knew she'd faked it, set it up for him. It couldn't be faked. The fake didn't work. She said she wasn't faking it, that she'd done it for him, but it was a lie.

Steven stopped and his brain retrod the logical path he had taken. No, she hadn't faked it. She just hadn't done it for him. She had done it for the other eyes that watched her. She had said so: for her *sick little lover*, not for him.

'It's someone from back then. Someone who knew Duran,' Steven explained, saying the name again. Outwardly Stella remained calm, but inwardly she was in turmoil. The name exploded inside her and she cupped her hands around her belly.

'You mean his gangster friends? His family?'

Steven nodded his head carefully as if it might crack like an egg.

'What if they found out about the child?'

'The relatives?'

'Yes, the relatives.'

'After all this time?'

'Yes.'

'And they come to America?'

'Yes.'

Stella sighed again and offered him another drink.

'Then why are you lying there and not me?'

'You must be next,' he said.

Chapter Eighteen

'I got to ask you if you think your husband's trying to kill himself,' Johnson said.

She was drinking a margarita by the pool. Sunbeams reflected off the ripples in the water and danced on her skin. He couldn't see her eyes behind the sunglasses. Those eyes that were dark and deep when she looked at him, made him think he was being sucked towards her, inside her. She made herself vulnerable with that look. It turned him on and she did it without seeming to try.

'He might be. He's said he'd do it. I told him I was pregnant. He said he'd do it then. He called Michael and asked *him* to do it for him. Poor Michael, it was quite a shock.'

Just like Dandy had said, Johnson thought. Stella was telling the truth. Steven Gates *had* asked Michael Revere to kill him. Stella leaned forward and took a packet of cigarettes from her handbag. Johnson noticed how much she smoked.

'I don't think he's serious.'

'Why not?'

She lit her cigarette and inhaled. He had to wait for his answer. He watched her breasts rise and fall.

'If you were trying to commit suicide, what would be your weapon of choice, lieutenant?'

'A gun, for sure.'

'Exactly. A gun. A careering Ford Blazer or an exploding boat? I don't think so. On the other hand . . .'

Her voice trailed away. Johnson nibbled the edge of his thumb. The breeze up here in the hills was nice. He hadn't expected the day to be so damned hot, and he'd been sweating under his coat. He felt a little guilty that he couldn't be straight with her about the trace they'd put on them both. He looked at her and thought to himself that if he came right out and asked her, she'd tell him the truth. She'd give it to him straight. She gave straight answers. She told him stuff most people would want to keep to themselves. When he'd arrived that day after following her from the clinic in Newport Beach, she'd shown him some of the pictures her husband kept.

'Does he ever take his own?' he'd said, making out the sight of her naked with Michael Revere was having absolutely no effect on him whatsoever.

'I don't allow that. It used to happen like that, but it just caused trouble.'

Johnson handed the pictures back.

'Did he get mad?'

'No, he never got mad.'

'The other guys? They knew, right?'

'Sometimes. Michael doesn't. He doesn't know.'

She'd put her hands up to hold his face then, and he couldn't help but kiss her with those damn photos pressed between them.

He was going to have to tread carefully. The routine police trace had come back with more information than Johnson, at least, had imagined existed or wanted to know, not now, anyway.

Her maiden name was Stella Wright, and her picture had matched an arrest photograph from the UK. The police record gave more details than her visa entry record, which was accurate but made out she'd been in less trouble than it would have amounted to in the USA. In the USA, she'd still have been in jail.

At the time of her arrest, she was married to Steven Fiennes, an ex-soldier. When they had wed, she had been seventeen and he, twenty-seven. Two years later, Fiennes had been convicted for drug smuggling. He did six years in a Spanish jail.

Her police record showed that one year after her husband's arrest and imprisonment, she had given birth to a baby boy whom she had killed while suffering from postnatal depression. She had divorced Fiennes the same year.

Johnson'd been more sympathetic than Dandy, but the policewoman held strong views about justice and law enforcement.

'It's nothing to be proud of, sir,' she had said.

He'd looked across the desk at her and wondered if she had any understanding at all for the human condition. She had looked back at him defiantly but her face was flushed under the freckles, and her jaw was clenched. She knew what he was thinking.

'You don't have kids, do you?' he said.

'I'm not married.'

He shook his head.

'Of course, yeah, that's right, it's just impossible to imagine having kids unless you're married,' he said.

'What's that supposed to mean?'

'Goddamn, Ruth. You don't understand. You won't let yourself understand. Things happen out of turn, and unless you experience even just one thing for yourself, you don't understand any of it. I've got kids but I never *had* them. You get what I'm saying?'

'Don't beat yourself up about it, sir. You're a man. People will understand.'

He told her to sit down and not stand over him that way, and she pulled up a chair and he pushed the reports over to her. He couldn't stop his voice from breaking, and that bothered him.

'My wife was as sick as a dog for months, every time. Sick, and then all that time in labour. Labour? Don't ask. Hard, hard labour. She was there for so long. This was before they booked you in and cut you open like they do now, so you and the medics don't get stuck working over the weekend. Labour is hard, and then all of a sudden it's over, it's time to go, they tell her she's done trying and haul her legs up and cut her. It sounds like a sail ripping in a storm. They hauled my first kid out like that, with metal forceps as big as soup spoons. I cried. Man. And it didn't get any better with the second.'

Dandy had blinked her feathery ginger eyelashes and pursed her lips.

'Or the third,' he added, quietly.

'You'd think someone would want to keep something they'd work that hard to produce, sir,' she had said.

Johnson sighed. He wasn't getting through to the woman.

'You think she's cold, don't you?' he said.

'I'd say cold. Hot looks, but cold for sure. I'd give her a temperature of absolute zero, sir.'

'Look at those pictures. Look at her.'

Dandy had looked at the mugshot strip. She had to agree, though she said nothing, that Stella Fiennes was awful thin and gaunt-looking. The folder included a newspaper report with a black and white photograph of her that was almost unrecognizable: she was distraught and unkempt and was being supported by a uniformed policewoman.

Dandy read the facts to herself. Fiennes had given birth in what they called a bed and breakfast hotel, and had drowned her child in the washbasin of her room. The baby was found two days later in a river with his mother's handprint on its face.

'The baby was found in a river. It looked at first like it

had drowned there, but they found piped water in its lungs. She left her prints in that greasy stuff that covers a baby at birth, the vernix caseosa. Interesting forensics.'

'Yeah.'

'She was tried, given a conditional discharge and committed to a psychiatric unit with post-partum depression. Nice. Did your wife get the blues, sir?'

'She did the last time.'

'No one died though, did they?'

'Something died, Dandy. Something died, and that's the truth.'

Dandy looked up from her notes and he thought he detected a glimmer of sympathy, but she had snapped the folder shut and said, 'She likes a man in uniform.'

'Say what?'

'Steven Gates. He was a soldier, wasn't he? That's what she told you, didn't she, sir?'

Looking at Stella Gates sitting by the pool, pregnant with another man's child, Johnson was thinking about how she must have felt. He wanted to ask her, but they were building a case and it would be darned unprofessional. Hell, and that wasn't it either. That's what he told himself. He wanted to ask her because he had to know for himself, but he was afraid to see the look in those eyes.

He heard her say, 'Something on your mind, lieutenant?'

He shook his head.

'I was just mulling stuff over, you know. It's nice up here, what with the breeze 'n all, and you looking so good.'

She smiled and lay back in the sunshine and pulled the straps of her swimming costume down. The black shadow of her swimsuit cut underneath her breasts and framed them like a piece that hung on the walls of her gallery. She glanced t her watch to time her exposure and settled back.

'I have something to tell you,' she said, and Johnson's

151

heart began to beat like it was trying to knock a hole through his chest.

She moved in front of him, trailing cigarette smoke, as they walked up from the pool to the house. He'd felt overdressed in his suit and tie, and self-conscious about whether or not he could touch her. She'd taken him through the lounge and into the kitchen diner where she peered into a Native American Hopi jar and retrieved a key. He followed her along the wide hall and past the main bedroom. The door to the room right next to it was locked, and she used the key to open the door.

'Steven works in here,' she said.

Johnson peered around the door into the office. The furniture and fittings were unremarkable, a desk with drawers, shelves, black venetian blinds at the window, pencils in a tin, a filing cabinet. The computer on the desk was switched on, its screen saver spinning a coloured triangle in dark space. To one side of the computer was a large, old-fashioned reel-to-reel German tape recorder, a splicer, some yellow and red coloured chalk, some clear tape and a razor blade. On the shelves, among the few books, were boxes and boxes of labelled tapes, photograph albums, negative holders and a collection of black and white photographs of Stella with Michael Revere.

'It's his listening post,' she said. 'He learned how to do it in the army. That's what he used to do. Listen.'

She walked past him into the room and leaned over the tape machine.

'See what you think of this,' she said.

Johnson heard a sound he didn't recognize. It was unfamiliar, and at first he wasn't sure what it could be until he heard himself speak. He was breathing heavily, telling her what to do and calling her his bitch, something like that, and then a whole lot more stuff that listening to now he felt ashamed of.

'Got it?' she said, stopping the tape. 'OK, now look at this.'

She moved across to the keyboard and touched the trackerball. The twisting triangle disappeared and a screen of coloured icons appeared. She clicked expertly around the system until a small window opened on the screen. It was Johnson, naked, with Stella's legs wrapped around him. He wanted to die of shame, but she watched the screen as if it didn't mean anything, as if it were some movie.

'He's got the whole place bugged,' she said. 'Look. See all this stuff?' She pointed to the boxes of tapes. 'All my calls. These here . . .' She pointed to a stack of videotapes. 'These I know about. I arranged some of those. The photographs here, all filed and dated? I know about. But he's got the whole place bugged.'

Johnson pointed to the tape machine.

'I need that tape,' he said.

'Is it evidence?' she enquired, and he felt a chill inside.

'I need that tape,' he repeated.

She took the tape from the machine and passed it to him.

'The shit in the computer. I need that.'

'OK,' she said. 'But I can delete it.'

'That's what I meant. Delete it.'

'Are you sure?' she said, in barely a whisper.

He nodded.

'I'm sure, OK?'

She looked around.

'I think these are the only ones. The ones in here.'

Johnson leaned his head back on the door frame and wished he'd never been born. He took a moment and then beckoned to her to follow him outside.

'Where the fuck are we safe?' he said.

She took his arm and led him back to the pool. Johnson held the tape in his hand and watched her sit on the edge and start to splash her feet.

'OK,' she said, looking up at him, 'talk.'

Johnson was angry.

'Did you know about this?'

'Of course not. Do you think I want him to spy on my every move? I give him enough. I told you, he's crazy,' she said. Neither of them spoke for a while, and she stopped kicking and let her feet dangle in the water.

'You know what this means, don't you?' she said at last, with a kick that threw a sparkling fountain of water into the air.

Johnson knew. Whoever had been around there was on those tapes, somewhere. She had fast-forwarded it to give it to him. It had been almost at the end. But what, he was asking himself, came before? He didn't want anyone else listening to it, because the tape would run on and he would be there panting and groaning and telling her stuff he didn't want to hear again himself.

'What else is on the tape, Stella?'

'You'd better rewind it and see for yourself.'

Stella stopped kicked her feet.

'The tapes are three hours long.'

He felt the heat of the sun on the back of his neck.

'What's on here, Stella?' he asked.

Her eyes filmed over but she didn't cry. She hung her head and looked away from him, and he could hardly bear to look at the dark hair pour over her bare shoulder.

'I was going to tell you but it got so complicated,' she said.

They went back up to the house and she played back parts of the tape. It was a recording of Stella, apparently in conversation with someone with a familiar and unsettling voice.

'*He tried to kill me. He hurts me. He hurts me, all the time. I want him dead. I want to kill him. I want him dead.*'

'*Leave, Stella. Please leave him.*'
'*I can't.*'
'*Tell me.*'
'*I can't.*'
'*Why?*'
Pause.
'*You love me, don't you?*'
'*I love you, you know that. I love you.*'
'*Kill him for me.*'
'*I'll kill him for you. I'll kill him for you.*'

'*What about me? Do I exist? Now. In you. Do I? Do you love me? Do I exist?*'
'Yes,' she said. '*You exist. Yes, you exist. You exist.*'
'*You sing the blues, ba . . . by?*'
'*I could murder you.*'
'*You sing the blues, baby?*'
'*I love you. I love you. I could murder you.*'
'*I'll do it. I'll do it. Say you love me.*'
'*I love you.*'

'He has a gun,' she said.
She pulled open the drawer of the desk and showed him the snub-nosed Smith and Wesson .38.
'He got a licence for that?'
'Yes. I think so.'
'I thought you didn't approve of guns.'
'I don't, but he was a soldier.'
'Do you want to take it?' she asked. He looked into her eyes, which were wide and dark and deep and seemed to draw him in like the sight of a cool mountain pool on a hot summer's day.
'Why?'
'Just in case.'

*

Johnson drove quickly down the hill taking no time, as he would on any other afternoon, to wonder at the wide, cold, ocean that seemed to half fill the pale sky. His mind focused not on the twists and turns in the steep gradient down to the town, but on the contents of the tape that Stella had offered him and the implications, the *implications* they presented for him. Halfway down, the speed of his heartbeat and the tumult in his brain made him pull up and get out of the car. He stepped out on to the gravel and walked quickly to the edge of the gully, where reptilian imprints had been left by the huge wheels of the construction trucks that swung around on their tortuous way up towards the razed properties above.

'Son of a bitch,' he said to himself over and over, as he kicked the ground with his shiny leather shoes. 'Son of a bitch, if I wasn't an officer of the law I'd kill him myself. Oh, man. The son of a bitch.'

If any of the yellow hard hats up on the hill had, at that moment, chosen to take a break from their toil, they would have seen an agitated detective in a dark suit pick up one stone after another and heft them one by one as hard as he could across the wide ravine until he fell back, exhausted, against his car.

Chapter Nineteen

Michael Revere's car drew up to the house not long after Johnson had left. Michael's happiness was such that it almost obliterated the small gnawing in his guts that for days had made him restless and kept him from sleeping.

'I want to go to Palm Springs,' she had said. 'It's too cold here.'

'What about Steven?'

'The hospital is keeping him in.'

'What about the PI?'

'His product has lost some value. The police think that Steven is trying to kill himself.'

'Oh, Jesus,' he said and closed his eyes. However much he had wished her husband would just go away, this piece of news was as unwelcome as everything else that had happened.

'Do you think that gets you off the hook?'

She spoke softly and soothingly, like he was a cat whose tail she had caught in the door.

'I didn't mean any of that, you know that. I was upset. He tried to drown me, remember?' she said, and then she told him about the new tape.

'It's really weird, Michael. You have to hear it.'

So he had driven up into the hills and she showed him what she had shown Lieutenant Johnson, a dirty room of wire taps, scanners and tapes. She had, however, taken precautions. She had duplicated the contents of the original that she had given to the detective lieutenant, taking good care not to re-record the episode that he had found so exquisitely shaming. All she played back for Michael was a telephone conversation, the effect upon him of which was as disconcerting as seeing a photograph of himself with someone else's eyes.

'*He tried to kill me. He hurts me. He hurts me, all the time. I want him dead. I want to kill him. I want him dead.*'

'*Leave, Stella. Please leave him.*'

'*I can't.*'

'*Tell me.*'

'*I can't.*'

'*Why?*'

Pause.

'*You love me, don't you?*'

'*I love you, you know that. I love you.*'

'*Kill him for me.*'

'*I'll kill him for you. I'll kill him for you.*'

Michael stared at the machine like a man watching a cabaret conjurer, as if on closer examination it would offer up the secrets of its devilish electromagnetic sorcery.

'Play it again,' he said, and Stella obliged.

'Didn't *we* have this conversation?' he said, pointing at the two of them.

'I could play you others. Do you want to hear them?' she replied.

Michael was too confused by what he had already heard to make a decision, so she loaded another reel and played him an extract of another telephone conversation.

'*What about me? Do I exist? Now. In you. Do I? Do you love me? Do I exist?*'

'*Yes,*' she said, '*you exist. Yes, you exist. You exist.*'

'*You sing the blues, ba . . . by?*'

'*I could murder you.*'

'*You sing the blues, baby?*'

'*I love you. I love you. I could murder you.*'

'*I'll do it. I'll do it. Say you love me.*'

'*I love you.*'

Michael finally understood.

'He tapes our calls?'

'More than that.'

'That's not my voice. Anyone could tell that.'

'Please don't panic, Michael. Of course anyone could tell. He pretends that the things I say to you, I say to him. I don't say them to him. Of course I don't. I don't love him like I love you.'

Stella ran the computerized sequence of stills of their lovemaking. After the initial shock of recognition, Michael stared at the strange scene with the critical detachment of a passive observer.

'He's crazy,' Michael said, his eyes on the screen.

'And the police know it.'

'They have this?'

'No. That lieutenant asked me if I thought Steven was trying to kill himself. He told me that the early indications from forensics are that the explosion was an accident, a cigarette stub and some spilt fuel.'

'An accident. An *accident*. It doesn't prove that he's trying to kill himself.'

'What about the car? He could have cut the brakes.'

'But why?'

'He's stalking me, watching me, Michael. Taping our calls, making them his. Watching *us*. Look at this stuff.' She pointed at the screen and the miniature image of their entwined bodies.

'You're looking at the ceiling,' he remarked.

'Michael, please.'

159

'You are. You're bored.'

'You're just seeing what you want to see. You don't want to believe in me.'

'There's what you say and what I feel, what I *see*,' he said, and walked out of the room. She followed him into the kitchen. He popped open a can of beer and took a long, thirsty swallow.

'He wants you to love him, that's it.'

'Yes.'

Michael looked at her and felt the gnawing that had plagued him for days begin just beneath his heart. It felt like hunger and fear, an indigestible form of punishment with sharp edges that pressed outwards, and a black interior that yawned to infinity. He was afraid of her, of what she might make him do: worse, that she might not really love him. He should have felt reassured by her. There were all the visible signs that she did love him. They danced around him in the shape of her random acts of kindness, her smiling lips, the touch of her fingertips, the moist pressure of her tongue and her vagina, the soft squeeze of her limbs around him, the gentle whisper of her voice and her kiss. All served to lead and guide him until he was so far down the track that there was no way back. He was bound. He had to pour himself into her because the way out was through her, through whatever kind of love she had buried inside. He never thought he had anything in common with Steven Gates, but at that moment, in that kitchen, drinking the man's beer, he knew that he had.

'OK,' he said, 'so he's crazy. He's taking pictures of us. He's faking conversations with you. That doesn't mean he wants to kill himself. Not seriously. It's fantasy stuff. It could be a cry for help. I OD'd once. It was the same thing. I realized that afterwards, when I came to in the hospital and was real glad to have people around me, paying attention for once. *Listening*, you know?'

Stella lit a cigarette.

'You heard those tapes. What do you think? He's taken your voice away and spliced in his own. He thinks *I* asked *him* whoever he thinks *he* is, my lover, you, to kill my husband. Kill himself. Don't you get it? He needs help.'

'*I* said no. *I* said I wouldn't do it.'

Stella smiled at that.

'Maybe he loves me more,' she said.

Michael caught her eye and finished the beer. He belched a little and took another from the refrigerator. He drank it a little slower than the first, but not much.

'Dissociation,' he said.

'Depersonalization. Derealization. Whatever, he's not really himself, is he?'

Michael rubbed at his stomach, which was uncomfortably distended with gas, and politely smothered another small, beery belch. Her sarcasm snagged at his raw nerves like a nylon thread on a hangnail.

'You gave the private dick ten thousand because he heard us talking. He heard you ask me. But this stuff shows that Steven could be trying to kill himself. It helps, doesn't it?'

'How? Deedes has a copy of our *original* conversation, and, on this one, I'm still doing the asking, aren't I?'

Stella came towards him and pressed her body against his, kissing his mouth. The aroma of tobacco and ash and suntan lotion drifted from her and into him. Michael held her shoulders. He was afraid of everything now. He was afraid of her, of what she might make him do, and afraid of losing her if he did not.

'Leave him. You have to tell him. But not now, don't tell him right now. I don't know, give the guy a break.'

'Michael, he's got a gun,' she said, pulling her mouth away from him.

*

Sergeant Ruth Dandy had made an appointment to see Dr George Peyronie. She sat in the same chair that Steven had occupied, and stared at the bronze on the shelf and the watercolour on the wall while the plastic surgeon detailed the nightmarish insurance situation in which he now found himself.

'I'm happy for it to be an accident, but I badly need Steven Gates to check out,' he said, and Dandy noticed how his eyes had automatically scanned her features as he spoke to her. It was interesting to her that someone could outline the complexities of insurance law while at the same time go over a series of potential medical procedures in his head. She wondered if it was her nose that bothered him. It was normal as far as she was concerned. She was pretty satisfied with her face and her features, and, what was more important, she thought, was that she was healthy, in mind and body. She had spent the few minutes she had had to wait in reception leafing through his 'before and after' show book, and she had come to the conclusion that it was people's minds that needed help, and not their bodies. A view that was reinforced by her experience of daily police work.

As far as she could see, there were a lot of normal-looking breasts in the 'before' section, and a lot of normal-looking noses, for that matter. She reckoned only about one per cent would have seemed at all remarkable to the average right-thinking person. She'd forgiven the doctor for what she saw as his outrageous commercial exploitation of human frailty, because of the section in the book that showed how he rebuilt breasts that had been mutilated by disease and amputated by mastectomies. Whatever his redeeming qualities, she hoped he wouldn't make the mistake of mentioning anything that might need 'fixing' on her.

The officer didn't want to tell the doctor about their suspicions concerning Steven Gates. She and Lieutenant Johnson had felt strongly that Gates was Fiennes, and if that were so, he was a convicted drug smuggler, who had lied on his visa entry form. He was a candidate for deportation, and what would surely affect Dr Peyronie's claims and counter-claims was that Gates's original qualifications might not match his new identity. If they didn't hold up, when everyone had finished suing the doctor he wouldn't be able to afford the price of entry to look around the Getty, let alone a work of art from that gallery by the sea.

Dr Peyronie noticed Dandy's interest in the watercolour.

'He said that was his wife.'

A flush crept up Dandy's neck and she was annoyed by this visible reaction to Peyronie's comment. She looked directly at the doctor and tried to compose herself.

'Is it?'

The doctor shrugged and clasped his pudgy hands together.

'I have no idea. It could be. I know she poses for a lot of this stuff. She poses for Michael Revere, that's for sure.'

The doctor made a point of lifting his eyebrows so that Dandy would get his drift. She cut to the matter in hand.

'What was Steven Gates like as an employee, doctor?'

George explained that Steven was pretty good with the boat, that he knew exactly what he was doing and kept it looking shipshape. George had no complaints about him as an employee.

'Did you advertise?'

The doctor said that he had not.

'I mentioned I needed someone. I can't remember the circumstances. Stella asked me to see him. It was a favour to her, but he did a real good job.'

'He made a complaint to us that he thought someone was stalking his wife. Did he say anything to you?'

George shook his head.

'What about their relationship?' Dandy enquired.

'What about it?'

'Was it good? Bad?'

George swung back in his chair and tucked his chubby arms behind his head.

'It seemed pretty good, considering.'

Dandy waited patiently for the knowing smile to fade from the doctor's face. He brought the reclining chair forward to a more formal position and his arms back down in front of him, when he realized the police officer was not about to nod and wink her way through the interview.

'As I understood it, it was an open marriage.'

'You mean they both slept around and they didn't care?'

'No, not exactly. That's not what I meant.'

'What exactly did you mean, doctor?'

'I meant he seemed pretty cool about her affairs. They had an understanding.'

'The two of them? Did he sleep around too?'

'I have no idea. I have no idea what he did.'

'But you knew about her affairs?'

'Yeah.'

'How were they with each other?'

'Well, they've got this British humour thing going on. It's OK, but you're never in on it, you get me? It's negative stuff but it's the way they are. She looks out for him. She worries about him. She begged me to get him the job.'

'Why'd she have to beg?'

George shifted uncomfortably in his seat.

'She told me he went for job interviews and no one'd take him. She has plenty of money, but she was supporting him and it was getting them both down. She told me he had a few problems but that he was great with boats, loved working with them. He used to sail charters down to the Med. I said I'd see how he worked out. She's a friend. I did her a favour.'

'What was he like, Dr Peyronie?'

George pressed a buzzer and asked his receptionist to bring him in some coffee. Dandy shook her head.

'Just the one, Diane,' he said, and sat for a few moments without saying anything.

'I liked the guy. I did. He was kind of weird in a Brit sort of way; I told you, the humour takes a while to kick in, but I liked him. He didn't get in the way. He didn't come on to the women that came on board. I kinda wished he would've. It was like he wasn't there half the time. He'd drawn a line and stood behind it. He knew he was the hired help. He was OK, but sometimes you could tell something was eating at him.'

The doctor paused. He wasn't about to admit to Dandy just exactly what might have been eating Steven. He didn't want to mention that he knew the man had a past. The insurers would love to hear about the Spanish prison.

'He should not have come to work after the auto accident. I told him not to, but he came anyway. He was sick that day. He nearly passed out on board and we turned back. I told him not to come until he was better, I had someone else, but he came anyway to fix up the boat.'

'Do you think he was suicidal, sir?'

'Oh, Lord, I hope not. I hope not,' George said, hiding his plump face in his hands.

The television was on and Steven watched the evening tabloid news. A woman from the Orange County Battered Wives Association held up the Hallowe'en mask of a smiling O. J. Simpson to the camera.

'This is tasteless,' she said. 'And, I shouldn't have to point this out, but so is this.'

She lifted up the costume that went with the mask, a NFL shirt with the number 32, and a plastic knife accessory.

'I believe there is also a Nicole Simpson severed head in circulation,' she added.

Steven's lips were dry. His back ached and his bandaged hand was sore.

'Carnival,' Steven whispered, rolling and lolling through the vowels and leaning on the consonants to produce a Spanish accent.

They lost the woman and cut to camera outside the Central Criminal Court building, which did indeed reflect a busy carnival atmosphere of public anticipation and tension. The street hawkers had set up their pitches among the tourists and Jesus freaks in a temporary bazaar, to sell their colourful disaster merchandise: T-shirts and buttons depicting simplified timelines of justice and slogans for those for and against, hand-beaded caps bearing the number 32 set jauntily on effigies of the accused, and wristwatches, the hands of which carried a white Ford Bronco pursued by a police car in an endlessly repeated twenty-four-hour race around the dial. Banks of press photographers and TV cameramen lined the steps, and the scaffolding of temporary television studios and satellite trucks had cornered an area that was dubbed Camp O.J. It was from there that bulletins were delivered on the hour, against the backdrop of a monumental skyscraper that featured in the popular television programme *LA Law*. The sun shone and the sky was blue in a place where something might happen, any time soon.

'Fucking bulimics,' Steven muttered. 'They're going to swallow it all up and spew it over their shoes. They're going to see what they cooked.'

He cast around for the controller and switched off the set. In the sudden hush of his private room, he relaxed for a second. The slight give in his body that came with a single moment of ease didn't last. The pain he had been controlling underlined its true nature. He felt the anxiety start just below his sternum and spread like fire around his heart until he thought it might explode. He struggled to sit up and lay clutching his abdomen, his eyes closed and his breathing laboured. The nightmare followed him around like a shadow. It crept out of his sleep and into his waking hours, so that his thoughts could not escape into the light. The dark undertow of murder tugged at his soul, and he fretted at his powerlessness to prevent it. He was excavating the past now. The sun that had once illuminated his life was dead, and he only had a little time left before eternal blackness caught up with him.

It was impossible, but he believed Duran could come back. Duran, or someone like him, who would not let it be. The question had been asked over and over. What happened to Duran? He went out and never came back. You and your wife came back, but Duran? What happened to Duran? His family is waiting, they said, his friends, his dangerous friends, but he'd said nothing at all. They had beaten him every day for more than a year. The authorities moved him, for his own protection, to a high-security establishment where the cells were colder and quieter. He had only just heard that she had had the child when the news came that she had killed it. He was the last to know, and when he did they had to beat him to get him out of his cell. If she had no reason to fear them, he did.

He pushed the covers off his body and swung his legs over so that his feet rested on the floor. It was an effort. He felt the taut skin on his back stretch painfully between the crusted plates of tentatively healing flesh. He reached out his hand to grasp the glass of iced water that had been placed on the pale veneered bedside table, and drank deeply.

He watched himself, a thin, greasy-haired invalid drinking water from a glass, and felt no pity. The man had tried to drown her, and he would have done it, had *he* not been there to stop him. What was the point of security when the danger is there on the inside? The violence was ever-present, contaminating the inner sanctum of the home with its spores of pain. *Kill him for me.* She had begged him. He had heard her. What could he do but answer?

Somewhere from outside the room, along the corridor perhaps, or maybe even in the corridor itself, he heard another television set and the crackle of a line. It was an emergency call and a woman's terrified voice spoke against a background of shouted obscenities.

'*He's fucking going nuts. He's going to beat the shit out of me.*'

He began to dress himself as quickly as he could. Stella. Stella. He'd kill whoever touched her, whoever raised a hand to hurt her. The feeling of panic overwhelmed whatever immobilizing pain his wounds transmitted, and one hour later, he had hired a car and discharged himself from the hospital.

Standing alone on the sidewalk, he gazed through the glass at the truncated casts and sculptures that lay inside the gallery. *Stella. Stella. Stella.* Her name was in his head. His mouth hissed, and the tip of his tongue flicked from top to bottom. Stella, la, la. His mantra of hair, skin, breast, belly and thigh. She was here, with all her secret messages for him, crucifying him with them like the beautiful butcher songbird of the desert that impales its prey on barbs and thorns before tearing and consuming its dying flesh.

He pushed his trembling hands into the baggy pockets of his chinos and was astonished to pull out a set of Stella's keys. He stared at them in confusion. He recognized them because he had memorized each serrated edge at one time or another. He fanned them out around the fob and ran his finger over them. One for the house and another for the garage, two more for the security alarms, and this one unlocked Michael Revere's studio and his alarm, and this one, the gallery, and this one, its alarms.

The conflict within him of what he knew and what he saw froze his feet to the sidewalk.

'If I have these, then who am I?' he said, and let himself in.

*

Inside the gallery, it was more comfortable and much quieter than the hospital. He eased himself into a corner and fell into the restless sleep of a nightwatchman. He awoke at about three a.m. The night traffic had stilled, and he could hear the rollers breaking against the sea wall. The surge of the tide and the hum of the air-conditioning mimicked the slap of water against a boat and the gentle chug of an engine.

Both the men looked over at her. Her arms were stretched above her head and her dress had edged up to show the triangle of her cotton underpants, like a little blue-white sail in the moonlight. The boat was on autopilot and the bales of cannabis were roped and on board. Steven struggled to keep his eyes open and his head from tipping backwards. He turned his face to the sky and saw two stars falling out of the black-and-diamond night. As the boat headed north-wards around the coast and beat against the slight swell, the urge to close his eyes became irresistible. Duran lit a cigarette and took another drink. He kept his eyes open.

Duran had thought Steven was asleep but he was not. He had heard Duran move. He could see everything and he was waiting. He thought Stella was waiting too, but he was wrong. He saw the shadow of the man over her, the belt unbuckle and heard her grunt a little as Duran put his fingers in. She began to struggle against the black shape of Duran's back. She screamed his name. 'Steven! Steven! Get him off me, get him out of me,' but he had not responded to her desperate, angry yelps. His body had locked into a parasym-pathetic program of guaranteed satisfaction. It was as if he could hear the soft-satisfying hum of desire sluicing through the channels of his flesh. There was no longer any purpose to her other than from his personal point of view. He had no need to communicate his love with a caress of his hand or twist of his tongue. He had elected the surrogate servant to her passion and could now please himself. It had to be her only, because she was perfection, in that the shape and spread of her limbs, the shudder of her breasts with their nipples like eyes, the warm deeps of her penetrated body tuned his senses.

The world had turned and the stars in the endless sky had glimmered above him, and he could only watch. He watched as Duran's hands moved under her dress and over her flesh and the bulk of the man pinned her down. It was difficult to grip her because she was fighting and kicking. Duran had his belt unbuckled and his hand between her legs. He thought Duran might manage it. His heart was pounding, his cock swelled and his mouth grew dry as he watched the two wrestle against each other. From somewhere in the starlit night above, he could see himself blurring into her, her black hair against his chest and against his groin. She was something to see, with her legs spread under his hips and her arms and her breasts and her hair.

Stella. His tongue flicked inside his mouth. He was almost coming. He was almost coming.

'Bastard,' she screamed, and stabbed Duran with the knife. He thought she'd killed him but the man was alive and screaming like a pig.

'The little whore came on to me, I swear, Mother of God.'

He sat among the pieces of people and parts of human anatomy that were picked out of the shadows by bright spotlights. He knew which ones were the clones of his wife. He knew every cavity, every wrinkle and swell of her form. He struggled to control the pain that he felt when her neck disappeared into nothing, or her arm sheared off at the elbow, her leg, mid-thigh. Nothing was complete except for the swollen delta between her legs and her round breasts dangling like fruit. She had no fingers, nor toes, nor mouth, nor eyes, nor hair to cover her shoulders. Every depiction of her on the plinths and the walls was a reminder, and Steven knew their meaning and wept.

It took a little time for him to regain a kind of composure, and it was the steady gaze of a man staring in at the window that brought him to his senses. Steven was certain that the man was looking at the sculptures and had not seen him. He kept low and still in the darkness until the stranger went away, and he slowly stood up and walked back through the gallery towards the office, through the exit at the back and into the alley by the sea wall.

The sea near the rocks and the beach was lit up by the lights of the hotels. The kelp floated on the surface of the breakers and arrived in tangled knots on the shore. White flecks covered the surface of the bulging rollers like an unravelling net, but as Steven looked beyond the swollen surges of water that came towards him, he saw that the sea was as black and deep as the sky. The concave blackness before him spread upwards until he was no longer sure whether his feet were on the ground and his head in the air. The scale of it was so vast and wide that the compulsion was to yield to it, to hurl himself from the edge and dive into the infinite silent darkness of the ocean and the sky.

It was the thought of the stranger and where he might be going that stalled him, and sent him hurrying down the alley into the street instead. He searched anxiously for his car and when he found it, he drove quickly up the hill to where he knew there was a gun.

Chapter Twenty

Johnson's head ached from Chivas Regal. The white morning light streaming in through the blinds blasted his bleary eyes and forced them shut.

'It *is* him. Fiennes *is* Gates,' Dandy said.

Her voice jarred the delicate, desiccated membranes in his skull and they seemed to vibrate like brass cymbals on a metal stand. Johnson squeezed the bridge of his nose between his thumb and forefinger in a vain attempt to ease his discomfort. The pain was exquisite. He hadn't had a hangover like this in ten years.

The Spanish authorities had forwarded an old photograph of a young, skinny, unshaven man with long blond hair. His skin was burned and his lips torn, but the indifferent look in those blue eyes had hardly changed. Johnson didn't have the will to open his mouth and tell her that he had known that would be the case before he'd seen the mugshot. When he had seen it, that precise moment of recognition had given him a kind of hope, a way out.

'What do you think?' Dandy enquired, glancing across at him, the fresh excitement bubbling in her voice. He was leaning back in his chair now, his eyes shut tight. 'He's kind of good-looking.'

'Yeah?'

'Mmmm, but check out the eyes. They're a dead zone. He'd never tell you anything he didn't want to.'

Johnson could feel the beads of perspiration on his upper lip. He had yet to tell Dandy about the tape, and he wasn't sure how he was going to, or if he was going to. The possible choices had kept him pouring whisky into a tumbler all night long and he still couldn't make up his mind what to do about it. In particular, what to do with the final length of tape that included his matinée performance with Stella. He'd thought of cutting it out completely. The tape was a mess of splices, he reasoned, so who'd notice, or care? Gates wouldn't be expecting it to be there, so if he was faced with the evidence, he wouldn't necessarily know that there was anything missing. Even if he did notice a slight tell-tale fraying, and Johnson bet that, being a professional, he might, and forensics would in any case, why would anyone think it had anything to do with him? Who'd know, except her?

Stella. The thought made his head ache more. He had to trust her, and he didn't know if he could. She'd been open with him but he felt compromised. He'd eased his nagging doubts with the safe reasoning that what had happened that afternoon had been spontaneous. She couldn't have planned it. She couldn't have known it would happen, that they would meet in a car park and drive up into the hills to make love. It was a heat of the moment thing. Some heat, he thought, licking his dehydrated lips while his mind hit a still zone and becalmed him with the hypnotic memory of her body and his, their groins intimately and fervently fused.

The throbbing of his temples hammered his thoughts back on track. Was she that much of an opportunist? Maybe, maybe not, but she *knew*, that was the important thing. He might just have to play it straight for that very reason. And it wasn't just her knowing. He had other things to motivate him towards honesty. One, an unblemished sixteen-year police career; two, the fact that he knew the difference between right and wrong. There was also a third possibility that served to concentrate his mind: that the sleazeball

Deedes, who was keeping a video and who knows what other sort of diary of her life, might have a double of that tape, and more. Who was to say the guy hadn't been working that day? Johnson just didn't know one way or another, and the only way to find out was to meet the man and see what he had to say about what exactly he did for Stella. If Deedes had something on *him*, Johnson felt sure that the PI wouldn't keep it from him. Meanwhile, his head felt as if he'd smashed it up against a wall. He felt around in his pocket for some pills. He never kept any. He'd have to ask Dandy.

She watched as he threw the painkillers into his mouth and gulped down the iced water.

'So, what we got?' he said.

'Like we said, either he's trying to kill himself, the hard way, or *she*'s trying to make it look like an accident. We have no evidence that a stalker exists.'

'We have no evidence, period, but that doesn't mean he doesn't exist. What we do know is that he came to us expressing concern for his wife's safety, and that his safety has been in jeopardy ever since.'

'I don't think he's trying to kill himself. So, that leaves the mystery stalker – or his wife. My money's on the wife.'

Johnson reached over for the police report and checked the details.

'OK, it goes like this,' he said. 'They hauled the two of them off a boat. They claim they're on a fishing trip but the coastguard finds dope. Fiennes cops, does time, she goes home . . .'

'. . . And murders her kid. I don't know how it works over there, but over here she'd still be doing time.'

'Nine months later she kills her baby. *Their* kid. *Their* child. Why?'

'You're implying it was his. Maybe it wasn't his. It happens.'

Johnson didn't look at her. He took another sheaf of papers from Dandy's hand and concentrated on the paperwork. Dandy blushed.

'Maybe she just couldn't cope alone,' she added, a little too late for tact. Johnson, sensing her embarrassment, wanted to reassure her, but he couldn't bring himself to. There was no damn reason why the detective should have to, Johnson reminded himself, but why the hell did she *feel* she had to? It was his fault.

He took a few minutes to read the report, translating easily from the Spanish. It wasn't as familiar as the Mexican slang he was used to, but it was still easy enough to understand. He'd learned the language from his time as a probationer in the San Diego Police Department. He had provided back-up for the legendary undercover cops who patrolled the border looking out for illegals trekking north, and the junkie bandit gangs that preyed upon them with machetes and knives, raping and robbing them. He couldn't be anything but back-up because he couldn't pass for Mexican. He was too big and too black. He just had to listen out for sudden gunfire in the night, never getting a break from the anxiety of not knowing if his partners were getting smoked, or the bandits. He used to drink then because he felt kind of *unexploded* all the time. He had drunk enough to give himself a problem. It was nothing to be proud of. He hadn't actually been in danger himself, not like the other guys. But he had hauled his ass through the cactus up and down those canyons, and he never forgot what he had seen or how he'd felt. Some nights, he'd drive up into the hills of Laguna and watch the lights of rich people's houses and the dark valleys beyond, and remember those canyons outside the city of San Diego and how when dusk came, hundreds of people would just appear, rising up from their hiding places behind the rocks and the mesquite. Night would fall, smothering all that was light, and the mass of silent people would stream northwards over those hills like a flow of blackened lava. Those that made it got to work the fields, clean house and wash cars for less than the minimum wage, while their employers whined about paying taxes for schools and hospitals for them.

There was a snitch's statement in among the others. The informer had told the Spanish police that an Eduardo Duran, a known trafficker, had paid Steven Fiennes for the boat and had employed the Englishman to crew for him. The note attached indicated that Duran had disappeared at about the same time as their arrest and had never been seen since, nor his body ever found.

Johnson rested the folder down on the desk.

'The two of them said they went out to sea alone. It was his deal, and she knew nothing about it. She just went along for the ride. They don't mention any Duran.'

'Snitch said he went. He just fell off the boat? Oh, *right*,' Dandy said.

'Could've fallen. You think they killed him?'

'I'd say it's a strong possibility.'

'Why?'

'To steal the dope.'

Johnson shook his head. He didn't buy that. The outcome was too disorganized. If Fiennes had stolen the load, he would have connected with another boat to offload it or arranged for an inland drop. He'd have had to have had a buyer with a distribution network on the Spanish coast where he was headed. He'd have had to make sure Duran's partners wouldn't come after him.

'It could have been a double-cross,' Johnson said, flicking back through the papers to Fiennes's statement. He reread it and ran his finger over the part where Fiennes admitted to dumping the bales of cannabis overboard when he saw the coastguard. The statement said the area had been searched, but nothing had been found in the vicinity.

'He could've done a deal with Duran's outfit, eliminated Duran,' Dandy said.

'Maybe. Whatever happened, Steven Fiennes screwed up. He said nothing, probably enough to buy his wife a ticket home. He did hard time. She went home to have her baby.'

'And killed it. Why?'

'If it ain't yours . . .'

'The child is *always* going to be the woman's.'

'Women have terminations, don't they? Give me some reasons for a termination, Dandy. I can think of a few.'

Dandy went to the water cooler and poured two cups for herself and a grateful Johnson. His hand shook as he held the cup to his lips.

'I'll get you another,' she said.

'I'm OK,' he replied.

She ignored him and fetched two more plastic beakers, full.

'You have to drink lots of water because the hangover effect is due to your brain being dehydrated from the alcohol. That's why they recommend you eat pretzels because they are salty, and the salt will help your body retain water.'

'For a queasy stomach?'

'Drink tomato juice. That way, the vitamin C that the alcohol destroys gets replaced real quick.'

'Water. Pretzels. Tomato juice.'

'That's right. It works, believe me.'

It took Johnson a couple of moments to recover from the shock of the iced water numbing his throat and assaulting his brain with a fresh jabbing ache of its own.

'Let's go,' he said.

The two police officers sat in the bar drinking iced tomato juice, and this time Dandy gave Johnson a little time to graze the pretzels and peanuts in the bowl that the barkeep had left beside them on the counter.

177

'Water, pretzels, tomato juice *and* reduced lighting. I'm feeling better already,' Johnson said, taking off his sunglasses and blinking carefully just in case a chink of sunshine might have penetrated the cool shade of the bar and taken him unawares.

'Here we are again,' Dandy said.

'Hey, don't make it sound like this is my regular condition.'

'Here we are again, discussing the purpose a victim serves. This time for her, for Mommie Dearest.'

For me, Johnson heard the guilty voice inside himself say. He wanted to put his shades back on and cover his eyes, not from the light, but from what she might see in the mirrored reflection on the far wall.

'Hit me,' he said.

Dandy sighed and began.

'If the kid was a "mistake", or if it was one child too many, or if the mother knows it's not quite right, if the woman is just not ready for the responsibility, or too young, under age.'

'She wasn't any of those things. She was married. The child was hers and her husband's. Their first child.'

'Or if she hates the father.'

Johnson thought for a moment.

'I accept that. It doesn't always happen, but I can accept that. But once a kid is born and she sees its face. There's the pain of giving birth, the child is there, helpless, alive. She gets to hold it.'

'Hold it and see the face of a man she hates,' Dandy said.

'Or her own,' Johnson replied. 'Or the face of a stranger.'

Dandy caught the change in his tone of voice.

'Duran? You think it was his?' she said.

'He could have raped her. Maybe that's what happened on the boat. Eduardo Duran raped her.'

Johnson took some time to think about what he had just

said. It made sense. Steven Gates was a soldier. He knew how to kill a man. He went to prison without implicating her in anything. He protected her, like he wanted to now, no matter what.

'She went home, found out she was pregnant and never knew who the father of her child was until she held it in her hands. The father might well have been Duran.'

'Couldn't he have just stopped what happened?' Dandy said, and almost immediately her face reddened with embarrassment. 'Oh, right. I forgot. God, how could he get off on *that*?'

'Let's assume he didn't. He could have been asleep, or drunk, anything. It happened. He didn't like it. He killed the man. All right, let's think,' Johnson said. 'Someone is hanging around them and their property. Steven Gates has two accidents. The first was definitely sabotage. The second could be. Is this revenge? For the kid? How would they know about the kid? No. For the father. For Duran.'

Dandy spun the plastic stick around the blood-red mix in her glass.

'I don't buy it.'

'You don't think she was raped?'

'No. She might have been. I think that could explain why she could've murdered her own child. I think the two of them know how and why this guy Duran disappeared too, but I don't buy the idea that someone from the past has tracked them down. We've seen no one. No one who hasn't got an excuse to be around them. We've questioned everyone who has. I think we look to her. How are you feeling now?'

Johnson had finished his drink and was worrying the ice cubes at the bottom of his glass. He was thinking that Gates must have lied on his visa entry record. He was a convicted drug trafficker. If he did, she did too. Husband and wife were candidates for deportation. He could lose this problem and get back to enjoying the peace and quiet of Laguna. He would have loved to lose the problem, but not her. He didn't want that, and he needed to be sure that Deedes had nothing on him if he had to.

'Fine,' he said.

'Fine and dandy,' she replied.

Ray Deedes's computer was a state of the art box, which meant that it was immediately underpowered the moment he had bought it. It worried him. He felt cheated, even though the multifaceted software, computational speed and fine screen resolution impressed him and would impress anyone who knew about such things. His pride in the machine was short-lived because he had known it was out of date, seriously passé, before he had had a chance to get it out of its carton. He had almost refused to walk out of the store with it. The moment of pleasure had lasted as long as a card swipe. He had felt the tension building as he was signing the receipt.

He had gone to the store, happy, eager to buy the specification that he had carefully selected after hours of browsing innumerable computer magazines and Internet sites. But as he opened the boot of the car and watched the assistant set the huge cardboard box in the trunk, he fumed with inner rage. He wanted to yell at the ponytailed youth that he *knew*, that he, Ray Deedes, the sharpest investigator in Orange County, was being cheated. Not only did he know that the specification had already been superseded and that the manufacturers were working on something smaller, faster and better value for money, but he knew that when he got the thing home, the whole system would be crippled by an antiquated telecommunications structure he was forced to use. He had been sold the electronic equivalent of a three-year-old Mercedes, and if that was not bad enough, he was obliged to use it on the data communications equivalent of surface streets.

This aspect of the whole sorry purchasing affair infuriated him the most. He had all that power and speed, the best available for purchase at that time – he understood that, he could accept that, in spite of the enormous irritation that blighted his joy – but he had no *bandwidth*, he wanted to scream, and images took up bandwidth.

The images he was dealing with today were of the company that Dr Peyronie had kept on a happier day before his cruiser was blown to pieces by a careless cigarette end. There was no reason to let his database of human frailty deteriorate simply because he was on to the biggest deal of his life. Stella Gates was going to have to find that money, and he had no doubt that she had it: the place she had on the hill, the art gallery with its high price of entry, the rich lovers.

Deedes had always felt that he had missed something with Dr Peyronie. He felt sure that the man had got more than bronze and paint from her for his money. She'd put out for sure, for what he could offer her: another high-value sale and another high-value introduction. Deedes could vouch for the fact that she didn't need any help from him otherwise. She could wait another ten years before things started to drop, though he'd seen women a lot younger paying for premature alterations of their natural stock. She had confidence in her body, and that counted for a lot more than a scoop of silicone and a pinned-up jaw.

The plastic surgeon was connected with Newport property developers and their wives. That was her prize. The good doctor would have made the appropriate introductions, but why should he do that for nothing? She'd put out, Deedes was sure of it, and he'd missed it. What Peyronie would have paid to keep unconnected from her right now deepened Deedes's frustration. He had his file on the dark-haired woman, Elizabeth Wiener, which was some consolation, but not enough. She was the curvaceous wife of a small-time computer dealer, Alfred Wiener, and Deedes had snapped

her with her arms around a wise-ass realtor by the name of
Charlie Pappas, who thought sophistication was his middle
name because his sister was Eleni Pappas, a fashionable
installation artist hereabouts. Charlie brought that fact into
any conversation where his appreciation of culture was
called into question.

Deedes felt sure that Mr Wiener would not be too pleased
to see his wife with her hand tucked down the front of
Charlie's shorts. He assessed the situation correctly: that Mrs
Wiener wouldn't have the money, but that her friend Charlie
might want to pay for the negatives just to keep his accom-
modating little lady happy. Deedes had photographs of Mr
Wiener too, walking into a Best Western with a blonde sales
representative of a local computer consumables firm. Whatever it had been for Wiener, it was certainly a double
whammy for Deedes.

The gumshoe leaned back in his chair and sucked content-
edly at a pencil, while the hammer of a honky-tonk piano
played in his ears. It was all small change compared to what
he was going to get out of Stella. In a way, he felt almost
embarrassed taking it from her. They'd kind of worked
together. They were almost a team. She'd directed him and
she'd paid him well. Sometimes, he felt just like one of her
artists, only without their additional compensations. It
amused him to think that he was only just behind her
husband on the food chain. At the very minimum, they both
got to watch.

She wouldn't take any shit either. She inspected the photographs and she wouldn't let any pass unless they were just
right. There couldn't be a lot of her in the photo. She liked
the shots that he would have thrown away. The shots that
had the heads cut off. The ones which showed the back of
the man, her arms and legs wrapped around. The street shots
also had to have the man's back to the camera, if possible,

so that she was facing, but hidden, the man leaning across to caress or kiss her.

She knew what she was about. There were times when it had been pretty hard just watching her and shooting film, not ever getting to play. He could live with that as long as he could get the money, that quarter of a million. He laughed to himself. She was definitely a one-off. Most people would pay just to keep those photographs out of circulation, but she didn't care about that stuff. But she did care about the tape. She cared very much about the tape. She was begging that boyfriend of hers to off her husband. She didn't want anyone to hear that, not with all the accidents the poor guy was having. And now he had all the new stuff. Her face didn't change much when he had told her. There was no dramatic stuff, just a slight tensing, like someone had tweaked at her skin. It was almost as if she was expecting it, like she knew it was coming and it was just a matter of time.

'I sympathize,' he had said to her when she opened the envelope, 'I really do.'

'Save it,' she said.

'Like I said, I sympathize,' he said. 'It was real tough how you got caught.'

She shook out the old photographs of herself and the newspaper cuttings and placed them in sequence on the table. She touched each one carefully, almost reverently, and inspected every picture and read every line.

'The kid's in the river and who's to know?' Deedes said. 'Except it's got a handprint bigger than its own on its face. Then some neighbour puts two and two together and wonders about a funny noise one night, starts thinking what happened to the pregnant woman who had nothing to show for all that time spent in big dresses, you know, with those cute little flowers and white lacy collars.'

'It was something like that,' she said.

183

Deedes lit a cigarette. He offered her one but she refused. He had begun to circle her like a shark.

'A baby's greased up like a little pig when it's born. What they call that stuff?' he said.

'Vernix. Vernix caseosa.'

'Drown the kid in the basin and dump its little body in the river. I see how that could have worked. Missed the prints on its face. Pity. You couldn't have been thinking straight.'

'Motherhood affects some women that way.'

'Beats me how you didn't even do time. You'd have got a darn sight more than that in the US of A. But, here you are, Mrs Gates, with a fancy house and a fast car, a pool, a hot tub, a lover and snooty artsy-fartsy friends. Did he know about the kid? This Fiennes. *Fee-enns*. That how you pronounce it?'

'*Fines*,' she corrected him.

'Was it his kid?'

'It was mine. My baby.'

He was still checking up on her. He'd put in some calls to the Spanish authorities and he was sniffing around with his dog computer. He wanted to know all about her. He wanted to know who Gates, the man with no credit history, really was, though he suspected he already knew. A quarter of a million dollars was cheap, Deedes thought, unaware that his information was being devalued as it arrived, just like his computer. His brief golden moment of satisfaction and contentment was interrupted by a telephone call.

Deedes turned the music down and smiled as he listened.

'Sure,' he said. 'I'll be there in twenty minutes.'

Johnson's hangover had finally abated. It was five-thirty and the street lights were spreading enough artificial luminescence around to bleach the colours of the day and blank out the velvety evening sky. There were three cars in the lot, and Deedes's old Chrysler wasn't one of them. Johnson was about to get out when a blue Taurus swung in off the street and the driver had near enough jumped out. Johnson stayed where he was and watched the stocky, crop-haired individual in the grey pants and white shirt enter the building. He was on his own and in a big hurry. Johnson timed him. From the moment he lit his cigarette and walked in, to when he returned to his car, empty-handed, it was ten minutes at the most.

Johnson noted the number on the licence plate and waited for the man to drive away before he got out of his car, checked the number on the board with the one he had scrawled on a piece of paper and opened the door of the building that housed Ray Deedes's office. He walked down the dim corridor that smelled of dental mouthwash and musty carpeting and waited outside the door.

Once he could smell the smoke, it took him three minutes to locate the alarm and five to clear the building of one Asian dentist, his assistant and a bumbling patient, whose mouth was numb with Novocaine. Johnson checked that no one else could possibly be inside before walking over to his own vehicle and putting a trace on the Taurus. He waited a full five minutes before radioing the fire department. The nose-to-tail traffic on the distant freeway suggested that they would be some time.

Chapter Twenty-one

Ray Deedes's body was found in his car at seven-thirty a.m. the next day in a business district of Laguna Hills, one street away from Lake Forest Drive off the El Toro Y. His car was parked on an empty stretch of road that wound behind the low buildings and sparsely landscaped parking lots. He was slumped across the front seats with his precious raincoat all bloodied, and a .38 calibre bullet in his head. The path report put the actual time of death at around four-thirty p.m., an hour before his office had been burned out.

Alfred Wiener denied that he had done it, denied he even owned a gun. In fact, he denied everything except the fact that he had been at Ray Deedes's office at the time Detective Lieutenant Lee Johnson said he was. He said that he had supplied Ray Deedes with a computer system and had been called out, for the zillionth time, by the private detective, who had demanded that he come and fix some little glitch. He *sold* computers. It wasn't his job to *fix* computers. He had a service company that dealt with that, but Deedes had been such a pain since the day he bought the thing that Wiener told the police he drove right out there after the last call to pack the whole thing up, give the gumshoe his money and take the system back.

'He never freakin' stopped,' the man said. 'If it wasn't the modem, it was the screen, the drive, the ports, the cable, the software. I had enough, I tell ya. I went in. I banged on his freakin' door. He wasn't there. I left. I didn't see, hear, or smell no fire.'

The Orange County deputy looked at Johnson and raised an eyebrow, and Johnson returned the compliment.

'Was he expecting you?' Johnson enquired.

Alfred Wiener held his head in his hands and then said, 'He called around two. I told him I was coming over.'

'Did you give him a time?'

'Late afternoon, was the best I could do.'

'Been there before?'

'I just said. Weren't you listening? I went there all the time. The service company refused to go. It was like checking into the freakin' Hotel California. You can never freakin' leave.'

Wiener made a big show of being frustrated and nervous about the situation that he found himself in. He was, to some extent, but he was also as happy and relieved a man as Johnson was. Of course, he didn't realize that he and the black detective had more in common than he could ever imagine. In fact, Wiener, his wife and the detective, all three had more in common than he could ever imagine. Ray Deedes had, or might have had, something on them all. The only difference between them was that the detective had not had to pay out a single dime.

Wiener hadn't gone to Deedes's office for the computer. It *was* true that Deedes had been like a monkey on his back about it since he came into the store and bought the darned thing. Wiener had gone to meet with Deedes because Deedes was blackmailing him. He had gone there to try to make the private detective back off. He was going to tell him that he couldn't afford more than two instalments. The expense was killing him and would have been worse, but his wife had lately stopped asking him for money over and above her allowance.

Deedes had made his first attempt at blackmailing Wiener

about a couple of months ago, and the computer store owner hadn't had a good night's sleep since. He knew his wife would divorce him and, frankly, he couldn't afford that either. Paying Deedes was expensive, but it would be cheaper than paying her alimony, giving her half the business, which she would certainly go for though she'd never done a day's work in her life. He wanted Deedes to cut him some slack, but the detective wasn't at home to negotiate with. Wiener hadn't set the fire in Deedes's office, but he was glad it had happened.

The black detective had looked him right in the eye when he told him the place was a burned-out shell, made a point of it. Wiener thought then that he might be trying to trick him into saying something about the photographs and the tapes of him and the 1993 Comco Computer Consumables Salesperson of the Year. Deedes had caught them interfacing, in the old-fashioned way, in a Best Western before they rode the lift together. Somehow, he even had a shot of them in the hotel bedroom, but how would the cop know that?

Wiener decided he wasn't going to fall for the man's reassuring gaze. All he had to do was make sure he got rid of the sample copies Deedes had given him and he could breathe easy. There was nothing to connect him with Deedes, other than he'd sold the fat man a freakin' computer system.

For his part, Johnson had told the fire investigators that he had assumed the door was locked. He had felt the heat behind it and had decided not to bust it open, for obvious reasons. Any fire inside would come out looking for oxygen. He'd have got flames, hungrier than fleas in an empty house, shooting out and jumping all over him. They told him he had done the right thing. Flash-overs can hit a standing person at 3000 degrees C. If a door just *has* to be opened, the advice is to duck, real quick.

When Wiener had finished, Johnson nodded to the deputy

and the two police officers stepped outside the room together.

'The door had a busted lock, whaddya think?' the deputy said.

Johnson sucked at his teeth.

'It's possible he busted in, started the fire, for whatever reason, and closed the door best he could to make sure it got nice and hot in there.'

'Did you notice it was busted?'

Johnson shook his head.

'The door was shut, and *hot*.'

'You didn't check the door?'

'No. I could smell smoke, and see it. I sure as hell didn't want to open it.'

The deputy stuck his hands on his hips. He was a big man, white, Orange County born and bred, about the same height as Johnson and about the same age.

'He set the fire,' he said.

'Maybe, but why?'

'Concealment. A private detective has files on people. Maybe he was blackmailing Wiener with something.'

'You think Wiener would have broke open the door and left the freakin' computer in there?'

The deputy laughed.

'Yeah, the freakin' computer,' he said, shaking his enormous head.

'We should ask him straight out if Deedes had anything on him.'

'Your call, but it could have been an accident. Deedes could've left a cigarette burning in there. He have cigarettes in his car?' Johnson said.

'Yeah, he did, but you think that's what happened, with a busted lock?'

Johnson pursed his lips and looked doubtful.

'You think it's connected with your stalker?' the deputy asked, and Johnson shrugged.

'If it is, it sends us in a whole new direction,' he said.

'Time of death could put Wiener in the frame. Even with traffic, it shouldn't have taken an hour and a half from Anaheim. Anaheim, Lake Forest, and back, maybe.'

The deputy eyed the detective slyly. They both knew there was another possible suspect, for the fire at least, and if for the fire, then the homicide. The first rule of homicide investigation: *everybody*'s a suspect. Johnson knew that the deputy would think what he wanted and would do nothing about it. Johnson had been there in his capacity as a police officer in the conduct of his duty, and the deputy wasn't the kind of cop that was so desperate to alienate his cop buddies that he'd call Internal Affairs just so he could get a sneaking suspicion off his chest. Even though he was black, Johnson had a stand-up reputation and Deedes hadn't. He was a police officer and Deedes wasn't. In fact, the deputy'd have been less than honest if he'd admitted his conscience was in the slightest bit troubled by the chuckle of satisfaction he'd had when he'd heard that someone had finally iced that slimeball Ray Deedes.

For his part, Johnson said nothing about the tape he had demanded of Stella Gates, or that he was worried that Deedes might have had a copy of it. He said nothing about the snub-nosed Smith and Wesson .38 he'd seen in the drawer of the desk in Steven Gates's study, either.

'Let me have the ballistics report soon as you can,' Johnson said, and the deputy said he surely would.

Steven Gates sat by his swimming pool, and, as he watched the tiny brown leaves and twigs floating on its shimmering surface, he tried to understand the logic of what he had been through. He had come back to his home in the early hours of the previous morning and had searched for his gun and found that it was missing. Panic had jabbed at his heart. Anxiety surged through his veins and crackled in his nerve endings. He hadn't thought of the who or the what, just the appalling implications of the weapon's absence. It had gone and with it the immediate means with which he could protect Stella, and himself, from the man who had followed them all down the years to this place and time.

He had shut the drawer carefully, and, just as carefully, opened it again. The gun had most certainly disappeared. He shut the drawer and chewed at his lips. Fear began to cook inside him. What had happened to her? He ran out of the room and searched frantically about the house, but she was nowhere to be found. He had half expected to discover her corpse in the bedroom – shot to the head, shards of bone poking out through her hair like peaks of ice in a glass of Coke. He had almost *wanted* to find it. However monstrous, the sight would end the nightmare of panic and despair he was enduring. It would end the tension that gripped his mind and body and drove him to search the house over and over again to the point of exhaustion. It would have enabled him to collapse into grief and sink to rest in a slow, still ocean of mourning. But, dead or alive, she was not there. When he had finally convinced himself that he was alone, he had driven to Michael Revere's studio. Her car was parked close by. He had waited outside in his, watching the silent building with its sleepy windows and reshaping the blueprint of Michael's apartment in his mind. She would be in bed with him and he knew where that was. He knew the shade and texture of the sheets, and the smell of them. He had watched and entered. He had walked around. He had seen in the photographs. He knew what they looked like when they made love and when they slept. He built the pictures of their union in his mind, but could gain no satisfaction, and as the morning sun backlit the black hills with a sky of sapphire blue and a delicate crown of stars, he had driven back home again, far from the restless ocean, where he had collapsed into unconsciousness. He lay on his back, alone in his own bed, his wife present only in his dreams.

The following day had passed in watery visions of murder through which he floated like a drowned man, bloated and partially dismembered. He woke some time after six in the evening, his mouth dry and his body aching. He could not eat. He drank a beer instead, and had gone into his listening room where he noticed that there was no tape in the machine. He opened the drawer of the desk and saw the gun.

Steven still had doubts. He couldn't be sure about the tape. He couldn't remember if he had removed it. He hadn't checked if it was in the machine when he had returned the first time, but he felt sure about the gun. The gun had not been there and now it was. He felt as if he was standing on a dune of sand, the whole side of which had slipped away under his feet. He had moved with it. He was still upright, the view was the same but the perspective had changed.

He ran a fresh tape through the machine and set it up to record once again. The scanner was functioning. Everything was ready. He remembered the tape before had been a mess of colour, one conversation after another topped and tailed by red and yellow, words of love whispered and promises made. He had said he would kill him for her. He had told her that he would, and now he had a gun.

He opened the drawer and looked at it. It was still there. He had wanted that gun and there it was, just when he needed it. Why hadn't he seen it before? Was it the same phenomenon as had occurred with the keys? He had found the keys in his pocket, and yet he had searched everywhere for them.

Who am I? he asked himself, and before he could answer, the scanner clicked and the tape began to spin automatically. He listened to the conversation between familiar voices.

'*Can you talk?*' Johnson said.

'*One moment,*' she replied.

Stella was in the parking lot of the hospital. She was searching for a ticket machine.

'*Where are you?*' Johnson asked.

'*I'm visiting Steven.*'

'*You seen him?*'

'*Not yet. I'm about to.*'

'*Deedes is dead.*'

Stella put the quarters in the ticket machine, the phone tucked between her ear and her shoulder.

'*He is? The son of a bitch. How come?*'

'*Bullet in the head.*'

'*Nice.*'

'*.38.*'

'*Smith and Wesson?*'

'*Maybe.*'

'*I'd have used a knife.*'

'*Would you?*'

'*Yes – oh, maybe not. He was a big man.*'

'*I thought he worked for you.*'

'*He tried to blackmail me.*'

'*How?*'

'*He's not doing it now, is he?*' she said.

Johnson paused, he heard her mocking laugh and felt the tingling of adrenalin inside. He'd have to be very careful what he said.

'*I'm not concerned about him.*'

'*Oh. I understand.*'

'*There was a fire at Deedes's office.*'

'*Was he in it?*'

'*No, I told you.*'

'*He could have been shot and the place set alight. Paint me a picture.*'

'*He was shot and about an hour later there was a fire at his office. The whole place was completely destroyed.*'

'*Look, are you breaking the good news, or interrogating me? I'm out of the parking lot and walking towards the doors. I won't be able to talk very much longer. I'm going to say goodbye to my husband and then I'm going to Palm Springs with Michael, unless . . .*'

'*Palm Springs?*'

'*Yes.*'

'*Why?*'

'*It's getting cold here.*'

'*Tell me about Duran.*'

'*What?*'

'*Eduardo Duran, Spanish drugs wholesaler. Missing, presumed dead. You were on the boat.*'

'*I have to see Steven.*'

'*He's not there. He discharged himself the day before yesterday.*'

'*Where is he?*'

Stella spun around and began to hurry back to the car.

'*Tell me about the baby, Stella. The other one, the one that died.*'

'*I can't talk about that.*'

Steven sat by the pool. He had gone over everything, but his mind had still not cleared. He could remember only two things with certainty: the stranger at the gallery window and the nightmare of Stella's bloody corpse. A breeze ruffled the water and he felt a tingling in his stomach, followed by a burning ache that seemed to vibrate within him, radiating up towards his chest and clasping the muscles on either side of his spine in a hot, acidic grip. He felt as if he were being consumed. He clenched his fists together and closed his eyes, but the blazing sun illuminated the blood-red membranes and dark, snaking vessels of his eyelids, searing the tender corneas beneath with heat and light. He jumped out of the chair and hurried up the steps and into the house. He had to speak to her.

The tape had stopped, so he rewound it and listened. Johnson's voice was almost irrelevant. It was her voice he tuned in to. Her voice was the raw material of his dreams. He could hardly wait to get to work and mine the rich seam of sentences that were threading their way through the machine. He visualized her mouth close to the phone and the tiny movements of her tongue behind her teeth as her lips shaped her words. He listened to the undulations of her familiar accent and the inflections she now used that betrayed her assimilation into West Coast living. He heard her laugh. He was going to steal her laugh. He needed it. He took the microphone, and with a fresh tape mouthed his words for a hoped-for shot of intimacy. He took the razor and splicer and began to work quickly and expertly. This time it was not Michael Revere's voice that was sliced from her conversation but Detective Lieutenant Lee Johnson's.

'*Where are you?*'
'*I'm visiting Steven.*'
'*You seen him?*'
'*Not yet. I'm about to.*'
'*Deedes is dead.*'
'*He is? The son of a bitch. How come?*'
'*Bullet in the head.*'
'*Nice.*'
'*.38.*'
'*Smith and Wesson?*'
'*Maybe.*'
'*I'd have used a knife.*'
'*Would you?*'
'Yes. Something slow. Something I could repeat.'
'*I thought he worked for you.*'
'*He tried to blackmail me.*'
'*How?*'
'*He's not doing it now, is he?*' she said.

She laughed and so did he, for they shared a similar sense of humour, dry as bones.

'There was a fire at Deedes's office,' he said.

'Was he in it?'

'No, I told you.'

'He could have been shot and the place set alight. Paint me a picture.'

'He was shot and about an hour later there was a fire at his office. The whole place was completely destroyed.'

'Look, I won't be able to talk very much longer. I'm going to say goodbye to my husband and then I'm going to Palm Springs with Michael, unless . . .'

'Palm Springs?'

'Yes.'

'Why?'

'It's getting cold here.'

'Tell me about Duran.'

'What?'

'Eduardo Duran, Spanish drugs wholesaler. Missing, presumed dead. You were on the boat.'

'I have to see Steven.'

'He's not there. He discharged himself the day before yesterday.'

'Where is he?'

'Tell me about the baby, Stella. The other one, the one that died.'

'I can't talk about that.'

'Talk to me.'

'To ask. You know, so why ask?'

'Who was the father? Was Duran the father? What happened out on that boat? Did he rape you? Was Duran the father?'

'No. No one raped me. Steven was the father. It was Steven's baby.'

As he rewound the tape his own self seemed to press out

of his fantasy and into reality like a diver surfacing from the deep into the light and air.

'No. No one raped me. Steven was the father. It was Steven's baby.'

Steven wanted to be sure that he'd heard correctly.

'It was Steven's baby.'

'Steven's baby.'

'Steven's baby.'

'Steven's baby.'

Enraged, he opened the drawer and peered in. There was the gun, the Smith and Wesson. He was going to kill her; his beautiful, faithless, murdering wife.

Chapter Twenty-two

Johnson felt uneasy. He watched Stella Gates walk back to her car and pull out of the hospital parking lot. She wasn't in any hurry. She knew he was there, watching her. Her frankness had disarmed him. She told him she had killed her own child, Steven Gates's child, without a tremble in her voice. Honesty and directness were qualities most Americans valued, but in her, they acquired the lustre and danger of automatic weaponry. If she could tell him this, then what would she hide? Nothing. She wanted him to know everything.

A man had been murdered with a .38 calibre bullet. She was a suspect. Her husband was a suspect. Her lover was a suspect. The mysterious stalker was a suspect. Alfred Wiener was a suspect, and he would not have been surprised if Wiener's wife was also on the list. If the murky truth be known, so was he. Everyone, bar Wiener and his wife, had at one time in the past couple of days had access to that gun in the Gates's home. They all had a motive. Although, he figured, in Wiener's case it wouldn't have been Deedes's unreasonable demands for computer maintenance.

Everyone. Suspect everyone, the golden rule of homicide investigation. He watched her black hair flick about in the breeze as she followed the circular route of ramps through the lines of shining vehicles towards the exit. He had seen the Smith and Wesson. She had shown it to him along with

the tape, but he was in an awkward position now. He had
to protect himself. How could he accuse her? What could he
do except trust her? And want her. Want her, and hope she
would keep her mouth shut.

Stella knew exactly where Johnson was. She had seen him
while she had been walking towards the hospital and now
she saw him in the rear-view mirror, leaning against his car,
appearing closer than he was. She had known that Deedes
was dead. In fact, she had been waiting for Johnson's call. It
had been on the television news, and she had watched the
no-nonsense reporter in the Lake Forest parking lot telling
her audience just who had been found murdered there but
not suggesting why, arousing in them the deliciously fretful
anticipation of a whodunit. The reporter gave them the
additional information of a coincidental fire at the dead
man's place of work, and in doing so placed them in the role
of spectators, reassuring them that the crime was unique to
the victim. Only Deedes, the dead man, had served a purpose
for the murderer. They would not be chosen. The murder
virus would not be transmitted to them. This was not the
inclusive work of a strange and secretive Famalaro for whom
any woman, stranded off the freeway or waved down for
assistance late at night, might do.

She was much safer with Deedes out of the way, if the
policeman kept his nerve and understood the situation,
which she was sure he did. They were both more secure with
Deedes dead. Involving Johnson had been a gamble, but it
had paid off. He had to trust her, and the price of having to
had just risen. Her heart was beating a little faster than
when she had driven into the parking lot. She wasn't as
relaxed as she might have been. There were so many vari-
ables, but she had been right to assume that the police would
begin mining their past, looking for that defining event that
might explain the present. Johnson knew a lot about her. He
knew about Duran. She hadn't wanted to give away so much

information to Steven quite so soon, but he had discharged himself and she had had to think quickly. After all, he might have been at his listening post, and she had to take advantage of the opportunity. He now understood the precise payment she had exacted for his betrayal of her love that night under the stars. He knew how deep her hatred was rooted.

Sitting in the car, Dandy also watched her leave, and when Johnson finally opened the door to get in, she said, 'Nothing?'

'They're going to Palm Springs.'

'Let's haul 'em in, now.'

Dandy glanced in the rear-view mirror and pulled out of their space in the parking lot. Johnson wasn't saying much, and she kept silent as she turned the car on to the Pacific Coast highway. Johnson gazed out across the almost deserted road and tapped his fingers on his thigh. *It was Steven's baby*, he repeated to himself. It was not the face of a stranger, not the face of the man who raped her, if such a man did, or ever went with them on that boat and never returned.

'Stop by the gallery,' he said, as they drove through Laguna.

It was closed for business. They stood outside and stared at the silent space within. Johnson stood back and tried to master the scene as a whole before taking his time to study each piece in turn. Dandy was less interested in the art than what was on her colleague's mind. He was perplexed, and when he finally turned to her, his eyes were tired with looking at the stuff.

'I'm not sure. Look at that painting.'

Dandy peered through the window. 'I've looked and looked at the darned thing. What of it?'

'The kid look like anyone you know?'

Dandy studied the picture again.

'No. Maybe . . . no,' she said.

'Give me that strip.'

She handed him the black and white police photographs of Steven Fiennes. He looked from them to the painting of the child a couple of times before giving them back.

'See a resemblance?'

'No,' she said.

'No, neither do I.'

'If it looks like anyone, it looks like Michael Revere.'

'You think so?'

'Yeah. I think it looks like him.'

Dandy waited as Johnson contemplated the portrait through the heavy-duty glass of the gallery.

'What if it did look like Steven Gates?' she said.

'Then there would be an explanation for all of this,' he said.

'What do you mean?'

'All this stuff in here. She's telling him something.'

'You think she's rubbing his nose in it? A last look at something he's lost for ever? Does she have to? My God, what could be worse than having your wife leave you for another man whose child she's carrying?'

Johnson didn't reply, and Dandy, once again, felt uncomfortable in the vicinity of Johnson's own memories.

'It's Michael Revere's Installation of Memories,' she said. Johnson turned to her. He looked like a man who had been woken from a dream.

'What?'

'It's his show.'

'But it's *about* her,' Johnson replied.

'She posed for him, that's all.'

'Could it be his memories of her?'

'Maybe. That'd count.'

'It's not art if she just posed, but if it's *about* her, it is?'

'Or someone else. Or life. The model isn't important. The

201

model is like meat to a chef, just something for him to work with.'

'Is that right? So, if this is art, this exhibition has to be something more, it has to say something, about life. That it?'

'Yeah, because he's given the damned thing a title. It's supposed to say something about Michael Revere's Tits and Ass Memories, and maybe our own.'

Johnson scanned the pudenda and thighs, the breast and arms.

'I mean, it would still be art if he called it *Stella, a Study*, or whatever. Then you'd be looking at beauty and truth in the human form. But he didn't. It's about his memories and so to be art it must communicate that.'

'These are just pieces of her. I think she's trying to tell us something,' Johnson said.

Dandy stood away from the window, a little closer to the kerb.

'Sometimes if you stand back, you get the whole picture,' she said.

Johnson straightened up, unfolded his sunglasses and slid them on to his face.

'Let's go see,' he said.

Stella was lying down on the bed in Michael Revere's apartment, pillows plumped up around her. Her face was grey with exhaustion. The two detectives sensed the palpable aftershocks of a major domestic argument.

'Give me a cigarette, Michael,' she said.

'You think you should?' he replied.

Stella's vitriolic glance directed him almost immediately to where her handbag rested on the large and untidy table. He obeyed, took out a pack and threw them on to the bed beside her. Stella lit up and took a deep, grateful drag.

'Do you know where your husband is?' Dandy said.

'I don't know where my husband is. He's not at home,' she said.

'When did you last check?'

'When did *you* last check? I don't want her going up there again,' Michael insisted.

He was clearly more anxious than Stella was. Her attitude was weary and matter-of-fact. She had the composure of a woman who had been through a lifetime of emotional challenges and discovered that the worst aspect of these daily traumas was their predictability. A surprise, no matter how hideous, would almost be a relief.

Dandy pressed on.

'Deedes provided your husband with photographs, Mrs Gates.'

'You think my husband would kill Deedes for taking photographs that he wanted to see? I don't,' Stella said.

It was obviously the first time Michael had heard about the photographs. He ran a restless hand through his long dark hair. To Johnson, he looked like a bad B-movie actor.

'Photographs? What photographs?' he said.

'Photographs of you and Mrs Gates, together,' Johnson replied.

Michael grabbed at his hair again and the lieutenant had to look away. In a perverse kind of way, he considered Steven Gates a worthier rival than Michael Revere. He gazed across the large and spacious apartment to where the living quarters merged into the studio. Beyond a half-covered work in progress was a plain wooden chair and a red cape. All that was visible of the canvas and subject were the charcoal lines of a seated woman's single naked buttock and thigh.

'You ever use another model?' he enquired.

'What?' Michael replied.

'For your *Installation of Memories*.'

'No,' he said.

'What's the show supposed to be about?'

Michael wasn't in the mood to talk about his work. He was pumped up with anger and frustration. He almost shouted at Stella.

'He had photographs? Yeah, why not? He had everything else. Photographs? OK. Tell them about the tape. Tell them how crazy the son of a bitch really is. Tell them. Right now.'

Johnson felt his stomach turn.

'You tell them,' she said.

Johnson wiped his top lip with his finger. Through a break in the floor-to-ceiling drapes, the sun was lighting dust trails in the room. He could see a fire escape, and he wondered if it was there that Deedes had stood, or Steven Gates. He glanced over at the large wardrobe. Its door was ajar. It was big enough to hide a man inside. Johnson walked over to it, opened it wide and shut it again before turning to face the three people, who were now staring at him.

'Tell us about the tape, Michael,' Johnson suggested, walking across the artist's apartment towards the window and the fire escape, where he drew back the drapes and let the sun spill its heat into the room and illuminate the bed on which Stella lay.

'I'm sorry,' he said, as she shielded her eyes.

'God damn it,' Michael shouted. 'Steven tapes our conversations, that's all. He's been watching us, listening to us. He videoed us. I might have known he'd have photos.'

'You've been having an affair with his wife,' Dandy observed. 'What did you expect?'

'Goddammit. Tell them about the tape,' Michael yelled.

Johnson was standing close to the end of the bed. He was conscious of Stella's bare feet resting on the bedcovers. He could have reached out and enclosed her narrow ankle in his hand. She lay still and looked at her burning cigarette for a long minute before leaning over the side of the bed and stubbing it out on the wooden floor.

'I gave this up a long time ago, but as soon as I felt I was pregnant, I seemed to need it. It's unusual. Most pregnant women say that the taste of cigarettes, or coffee even, is quite unpleasant. It's the baby telling you what's bad for it. I don't know why I'm different. Maybe my baby is prepared to take a risk. You know, live fast, die young.'

She swung her feet away from him to sit up, cupping her hands around her belly as she did so. Michael Revere started towards her but she raised her hand to stop him. Dandy spoke up, almost sick with indignation.

'Where were you at four-thirty p.m. Monday, Mrs Gates?'

'I've already told your lieutenant that,' Stella lied. 'I was with Michael. We were making preparations to go to Palm Springs.'

'Why?'

'The cold. Look. I didn't kill Ray Deedes, obnoxious and incompetent as he was, but if I had wanted to I reckon I'd have had to join a long line.'

Michael interrupted her. He was afraid of Stella's flirtation with the facts.

'It was on the news. We watched it on the TV,' he said.

Johnson's memory lit up like three bars on a fruit machine. It replayed the bytes of faulty information. She had said, *He is? The son of a bitch. How come?*

Meanwhile, Dandy's freckled face had flushed red with embarrassment at her small betrayal of her boss. To have asked the obvious question meant she didn't trust him to do his job, at least as far as Stella Gates was concerned.

'Why would you have had to join a line, Mrs Gates?' she said.

'He tried to blackmail me. I'm sure I wasn't the only one.'

'What about the tape?' Johnson said, gently.

The square flat box was on the table. They watched her walk over, pick it up and open it. Johnson felt a flutter of false hope when he saw the pristine henna shine of the curled audiotape. There were no slivers of colour betraying the psychotic splicing of one voice for another. Of course, Johnson reminded himself, why would it: *he* had that. He felt like laughing out loud. It must be a different tape. The one Stella held and displayed to them, as if she were a Byzantine saint clasping a holy icon, was a *different* tape. He started thinking quickly. She'd given him the tape straight off the machine. It must have been the last tape Steven had been working on. He wouldn't have had time to make a back-up, or maybe he never made back-ups – why should he? Did she? Did she make a back-up? It was a different tape. He was hoping to hell that it was.

'Have you played it?' he asked.

'Yeah, up at the house,' Michael replied.

'And?'

Michael stared intently at the detective.

'There's stuff on there that needs a lot of explaining,' he said.

'Are we going to hear it?' Dandy asked.

'I don't have a machine,' Michael said.

'I'm sure the police do, Michael,' Stella said, shutting the box and handing the tape to Johnson.

Johnson cleared his desk to make some room. He gestured to a couple of chairs and Michael and Stella sat down.

'I haven't heard the whole thing. Get to the bit near the end,' Michael said.

Dandy hit the button and the numbers spun on the counter as the reels turned. It took a few stops and starts before they heard her voice.

'That's it. Start it right there,' Michael said.

They all listened to the desperate voices of Stella and Steven Gates.

'*He tried to kill me. He hurts me. He hurts me, all the time. I want him dead. I want to kill him. I want him dead.*'

'*Leave, Stella. Please leave him.*'

'*I can't.*'

'*Tell me.*'

'*I can't.*'

'*Why?*'

Pause.

'*You love me, don't you?*'

'*I love you, you know that. I love you.*'

'*Kill him for me.*'

'*I'll kill him for you. I'll kill him for you.*'

The conversation stopped and the tape hissed its way across the recording heads.

'That it?' Johnson enquired.

'Fast-forward,' Michael said, and listened as Johnson jabbed and released the stop button. 'There. No. There.'

'*What about me? Do I exist? Now. In you. Do I? Do you love me? Do I exist?*'

'*Yes,*' she said, '*you exist. Yes, you exist. You exist.*'

'*You sing the blues, ba . . . by?*'

'*I could murder you.*'

'*You sing the blues, baby?*'

'*I love you. I love you. I could murder you.*'

'*I'll do it. I'll do it. Say you love me.*'

'*I love you.*'

The voices stopped again.

'Anything more?' Johnson enquired, his finger hovering over the machine.

Michael shook his head.

'That's it.'

'Oooo . . . kay. What have we got here?' Johnson said, struggling to hide his relief as he rested his clammy hands on his hips.

'Pieces of *our* conversations,' Michael said, pointing a finger at Stella and then at himself. 'That son of a bitch taped our calls.'

'Are you saying that's you?' Dandy enquired.

Michael ran both hands through his hair this time.

'It's him. He cut what I said and copied it using his own voice. Now *he*'s having that conversation with Stella.'

'You had a conversation with Stella about murdering someone?'

Michael stopped like he had taken an electronic prod to the head. He looked at Stella, whose stone face gave him no comfort. She took a packet of cigarettes out of her bag and prepared to light up.

'This is a no-smoking office,' Dandy reminded her, pointing at a sign clearly displayed on the beige-coloured wall.

'May I?' Stella asked.

It took a moment or so for her to gauge the look in Dandy's eye and put the cigarettes away.

'As I recall,' she said, 'my husband and I had argued that day. He tried to drown me. I got away from him and drove to Michael's. I phoned him on the way. Steven must have scanned the phone call and recorded it,' she said.

'You asked Michael to kill your husband?'

'Of course not. Not literally. I was furious. I was just saying that I felt like killing him, you know how it is.'

Johnson allowed himself a small smile.

'No, you *asked* Michael to, you just said so. "Kill him for me". We all heard it,' Dandy persisted.

Michael didn't like the way the interview was going.

'I said "no",' he said.

'I said "Someone kill him for me",' Stella insisted. ' "*Someone kill him for me*". It was something like that. He must have cut it. Of course, I didn't mean it literally. I was mad. We'd had a fight.' She pointed at the machine. 'I certainly didn't have *that* conversation, detective.'

'He's been almost killed, twice.'

'He almost drowned me.'

'What did you fight about?'

'Michael.'

The colour had ebbed from Stella's face.

'Are you OK?' Johnson asked.

She nodded, but Michael leaned across to put a protective arm around her. She gently removed it and patted his hand reassuringly.

'This man recorded our conversations, cut out my voice and replaced it with his own. Get an expert in. They can tell,' Michael said.

'Do you have the original?' Dandy asked.

Johnson stared at the machine.

'What do you mean?' Michael said.

'The original would be a mess of splicing. Where your voice was cut out, then his voice would have to be spliced in. If you're saying you had this conversation, then this must be a back-up copy, a re-recording.'

'There are lots more like that in his room at home. One of them must be the original. Search the place. You might even find the bits he cut out,' Stella suggested.

'Why would he re-record it?'

'I have no idea.'

Just as Johnson felt as if the room had emptied of air, his telephone rang. It was the county deputy calling with the ballistics report.

'He got smoked with a Smith and Wesson .38,' he said.

'Great.'

'Yeah, I'm with you, pal. All we need is a description to go with it: medium height, average build, wearing jeans, sneakers and Nike T-shirt.'

Johnson put the phone down and rubbed his finger over his top lip. The seesaw of good fortune had just tipped his way. He walked around his desk and sat on the edge of it. He gazed at the couple, and Dandy took her cue from him and stared directly at them too. Only Michael was uncomfortable with the silence. Stella kept cool, despite the surge of excitement she was feeling. The tension had left

Johnson's face. He was relaxed and sure of himself. These were clues that she picked up on because only she knew the pressure he was under. With Deedes dead, she felt no pressure at all. She had cooperated with the police from the beginning. Her fate was tied to so many others, and she could rely on their self-interest, for, by protecting themselves, they would protect her. They were only human. For most people, the price exacted for self-sacrifice was always too high.

'Mrs Gates, does your husband have a gun?' Johnson enquired.

'Yes, lieutenant, a Smith and Wesson .38,' she replied.

Chapter Twenty-three

Steven's saliva had left a diaphanous line on the cigarette paper. Pieces of moist brown tobacco spilled out of the thin tube as he rolled it between his fingers and lit it. The taste on his tongue was sweet: he hummed lazily to himself. Nothing came as close as this to perfect pleasure. He couldn't remember much else that had, except for taking a piss. Not even murder, if the truth be known. He could sit by the pool in just his shorts, smoke and do nothing, maybe listen to the breeze, the cicadas, the damn hammering to rebuild million-dollar homes with ten-million-dollar ones, and watch the baby swimming in the pool.

It had his face. He could see himself swimming there. It wasn't impossible for a baby to swim. They could swim underwater. They had to come up for air like everyone else, but they could swim. He made a good baby. He had blue eyes and a fuzz of blond hair. His arms and legs floated upwards before the rest of his body which popped up, his head stretching for the sun, his eyes closed, his mouth smiling and water streaming over his perfectly smooth skin.

'Never mind,' he said and began to laugh until the tears flowed and the cocktail waiter asked him to leave.

'There's no smoking by the pool,' he said.

Steven pinched the end of his cigarette and slipped it into the pocket of his shorts. The waiter hovered. He was a lot younger than he was, white, with short, slicked-back brown hair.

'Are you staying at the hotel, sir?'

Steven looked around. The pool was shaped like an amoeba that was stretching out its transparent pseudopodia to ingest a scrap of something, a floating fragment, in this case a miniature island of white marble. Two blonde women wearing Jackie O. sunglasses and gold earrings were in the pool with their snorkelling children. A large white man in his late forties lay on his side on a substantial lounger, reading a thick paperback entitled *Men are from Mars, Women are from Venus*. Black hairs covered his back like matting.

'I'm waiting for someone,' Steven replied.

The waiter raised an eyebrow. Steven stood up.

'But it seems like they're not coming,' he said. He bent down, picked up his holdall and his folded short-sleeve Hawaiian shirt and limped away towards the exit. The waiter had thought about calling the police until he heard Steven's English accent and guessed that the man wasn't a vagrant after all.

'What happened to you, man?' he said.

Steven turned and smiled.

'Car accident.'

'Hire car?'

Steven smiled and said nothing as the waiter politely held open the wire-mesh security gate for him.

'You got to get used to driving on the right side of the road,' he said.

'You mean the wrong side,' Steven replied, and walked outside past the purple bougainvillea into the moist gardens that smelled of vanilla and were dense with banana plants and hibiscus. He had a Smith and Wesson in his bag and he was driving to Brentwood, to the corner of Rockingham and Ashford. He had no real idea why he should, except that he felt the need to see O. J. Simpson's house, now a tourist attraction in a resentful, well-maintained neighbourhood of countrified real estate that protected itself from the city of Los Angeles like a hydroponic ecosystem on a hostile planet. Unlike its wealthy suburb, Los Angeles was not ashamed to show its dynamic infrastructure of ferroconcrete freeways, signs and utility power lines. Along the discreet boulevards of Brentwood, however, the moneyed homeowners hid their spacious, high-security houses behind the shady trees and disguised their overused conduits for electricity, entertainment, communications, water and garbage behind voluptuous non-indigenous vegetation and green paintwork. Steven had been there before the murder. He had wanted to see the tomb of Marilyn Monroe in Westwood, and a premature off-ramp on the 405 had led him to Brentwood. The slumbering greenery had shocked him. It had reminded him of Surrey, and when he had told Stella that, she had said that every image has its history.

Steven stood by his hire car and looked back across the lines of other vehicles, whose bodies shone like the glass that sheathed the smooth form of the hotel and reflected the sky, the clouds and phalanxes of helicopters above. He wondered about the baby in the pool, and felt a rush of concern that grew into panic and sent him hurrying back through the miniature Eden of irrigated flora towards the wire-mesh fence and the security gate. The waiter was collecting up the thick white towels that had been used but once. The man with the hairy back was still reading and the women were reapplying high-factor sun lotion over their tanned leathery skin.

The blue water in the swimming pool was still, and there was no panic around the perimeter. He wanted to look into the water for the child. It was possible that no one else had seen it and that it had quietly sunk to the bottom, unheard and unnoticed. The waiter looked up and saw him and

Steven remembered that he had somewhere to go, someone to kill. He stopped for a moment. Or was it save? he wondered.

'I just don't believe it,' Dandy said.

'That she didn't lie about it?' Johnson said.

'How could immigration have let it pass? She knew *he* was lying. She must have done.'

'Let's focus on him. He's the one with the Smith and Wesson.'

Dandy stamped on the accelerator to haul the vehicle up the steep gradient to the Gateses' home.

'What do you think they're doing now?' she said.

'Meeting with their attorneys?' Johnson ventured.

The drive of the house was empty. Dandy pulled in and Johnson opened his door and stepped out on to the gravel. He could hear the drone of a pool filter and smell the slight taint of chlorine in the air. The gears of construction trucks engaged and disengaged in the distance. Dandy shut the driver's door and her feet crunched across the tiny brown and grey stones as she walked up beside him. She didn't speak. They both waited but there was no sound from inside the house and the blinds were drawn.

'Is the alarm disabled?' Dandy enquired as Johnson searched through the fob for the correct key.

'Yes,' he said, placing the key in the lock.

'Nice and slow,' Dandy advised. He turned to her.

'You want to do it?' he asked. She made a face.

The house was quiet, empty, but they checked all the rooms – he told Dandy to take the bedroom – but Steven Gates was not there. He wasn't home at all.

The two police officers stood in the lounge. Dandy had stopped in front of the marble torso. Johnson recalled the moment when Stella had run her fingers across it and he felt an ache of sexual desire. He remembered her perfect smile and her imperfect teeth. He wanted to obliterate those memories, obliterate them all, rip out all the little hooks she had pierced him with. If he could go back, he told himself, he'd have said no, no, no. Like hell, he would. Like hell.

'OK. You've been scanning the catalogue for clues of their damaged psyches. Tell me this. How come there's a man in here and not one single sketch of a woman, not one painting, not one sculpture, just this one of a man, the trunk of a man?'

Dandy was right. The gallery was full of depictions of the female form, never quite entire, but definitely female. Here in her home, in her and Steven's home, was one sexually complete male, with no head, no arms and no legs. It was a study in trapped masculinity. The milky whiteness of its breast and smooth contours of its loins were irresistible, even to Dandy. She pressed against the sternum and her fingers smoothed over its cool surface, stopping just above the navel.

'You think Chuck here came between them?' Johnson said, fighting to seem as disinterested as possible. She took her hand away and wiped it on her skirt.

'I don't know about that, but all *that* might have done,' she said, nodding at the television and the stacks of pornography beside it.

Johnson bent down and picked up a couple that were untitled.

'Home videos. What do you say?'

'Later,' she said without humour. 'I want to find the audiotapes.'

They went back to the study that contained Steven's home recording studio to search through the tapes. Johnson had to go through the motions with Dandy, knowing that there would be no original of the tape that Stella had given them. He had that, and with Deedes conveniently dead and his office, all his records and the computer destroyed, it was the *only* traceable copy of the original conversations apart from the discarded cuttings, wherever they were. Deedes had lived on the office premises, his bedroom with its single bed was through the shattered frosted-glass door, so there would be no secret stash of revelatory files on his clients past, present or future elsewhere. At least, Johnson hoped not.

The only problem was, he had to trust Stella and she had already lied to him. She had expressed surprise at Ray Deedes's death, though she had known the man was dead when Johnson mentioned it. Funny how one little lie could contaminate every statement someone had ever made.

There was a tape already in the machine. Dandy rewound it and they listened.

'*Tell me about the baby, Stella. The other one, the one that died.*'

'*I can't talk about that.*'

'*Talk to me.*'

'*To ask. You know, so why ask?*'

'*Who was the father? Was Duran the father? What happened out on that boat? Did he rape you? Was Duran the father?*'

'No. No one raped me. Steven was the father. It was Steven's baby.'

Johnson bent down and sifted through the pile of shaved tape. This time the chalk letter J was marked on several of them. Dandy was rewinding the tape and listening to the spliced conversation.

'That's definitely Steven Gates's voice,' she said. 'But who had the original conversation?'

'Me,' Johnson said, straightening up and showing her a length of audiotape with a yellow initial J marked on it. He opened the drawer of the desk. There was no Smith and Wesson.

'Did we mess up, lieutenant?' Dandy enquired, an unfamiliar tinge of self-doubt in her voice.

'No, not you. You didn't mess up, I did,' Johnson replied.

Dandy stood with her hands on her hips and took a deep breath.

'This was the call you made to her when we were in the parking lot of the hospital, right?' she said.

'Right.'

She stared at the machine, a slight frown of curiosity marking her face. She reached forward and replayed the tape.

'*Deedes is dead.*'

'*He is? The son of a bitch. How come?*'

'*Bullet in the head.*'

'*Nice.*'

Dandy pressed stop. The frown was still there.

'Didn't Michael Revere say that they had heard it on the news?' she said. 'That means she already knew Deedes was dead when she spoke to you.'

'She might have done, but let's assume she didn't do it.'

'Why?'

Johnson pulled at the boxes of audiotapes that lined the shelves, twenty per shelf. There had to be at least a hundred tapes that had been spliced with re-recorded fragments of Steven Gates's voice. He had removed other men from his wife's life, other men she had said he had welcomed. Maybe, Johnson thought, he wanted something he just couldn't have, a goddamned *conversation* with her. A conversation that included the words 'I love you'. He'd do anything for her. If she could just say something that might make him feel like he *existed*.

'Why, sir?' Dandy said.

'If she didn't do it,' he said, patiently, 'which Michael Revere will alibi, then there's the possibility that someone else told her. Steven Gates, for instance. He could've called to tell her that Deedes was dead, that he had killed him even.'

'With a Smith and Wesson.'

'Right.'

'Why'd *he* kill him?'

Johnson dragged his finger down along the filed boxes of tapes.

'Because he thought she asked him to?'

Dandy whirred her fingers around her temple. Johnson copied her.

'Aren't we all?' he said.

He pressed the rewind button once more. Dandy waited. He pressed play.

'*.38.*'

'*Smith and Wesson?*'

'*Maybe.*'

'*I'd have used a knife.*'

Dandy understood.

'She guessed?'

'She must have known her husband had a gun and what type it was.'

'We didn't have the ballistics then. I think she was trying to let me know, but she was nervous about saying too much in a phone call. I mean, look at all this.'

Johnson gestured to the boxes of tapes and the surveillance equipment.

'We better find Steven Gates,' she said.

'Yeah. Whoever *he* is.'

Johnson stepped outside into the garden to cool himself down. He looked at the pool and breathed deeply. Stella had seen through him in a moment, assessed his weakness and used him. He was working for her. She'd probably done the same with Michael Revere, used him. Johnson felt like laughing. He had to hand it to her. She'd seen the sham, seen right through it. The well-maintained black lieutenant tooling around Laguna like a Lexus driver in an Oldsmobile, going from A to B but not in any style he wanted or at any speed he could. Ella had seen that too, but it had taken years. She'd told him that he was as bored with their comfortable home in suburbia as she was, only he'd convinced himself that that was what they had to have. Hell, she had screamed at him, there weren't any *cops* living around there, never mind *people of colour* like themselves.

Dandy stepped out beside him.

'You think all this is the drug money?' she said.

A sudden breeze maddened the ripples on the blue water. No sooner did they hit the sides, but they rebounded back against each other. Their rapid ruffled shadows looped and entwined in the depths and shallows. Patterns emerged and fell back into chaos. Johnson was so mesmerized by them that he hardly noticed Dandy walk down the steps until she was suddenly there, crouched by the edge of the pool, sticking her hand in the water. Her rounded milky knees pressed against her chest as she leaned on one strong freckled arm for support. Wisps of ginger hair whipped across her face. She was smiling.

'I can never resist doing this,' she said. 'My dad had a little fishing boat and we'd go out in it. I just liked to sit there with my hand in the water as it splashed along. He said the big fish would think my fingers were something nice and tasty, but I was never afraid.'

Johnson ran his thumbs around his belt and looked around.

'I don't think they were that heavily into narcotics.'

Dandy stood up and followed Johnson's line of sight out across the garden to the canyons beyond.

'You think that's the only one they did? The one where they got caught?'

'You think she'd have been stuck on welfare in a cheap motel, what they call it – bed and breakfast – if she'd had any money?'

Dandy pushed the untidy strands of hair from her face and walked briskly towards the house.

'I still can't believe immigration let that go,' she said. 'She murdered her baby and she got a green card.'

'I'm not surprised. They let that Arab in, didn't they? The one that put *Terrorist bombing* as an occupation on his form?'

'Yeah, they must have thought that meant he bombed terrorists and that made him a goddamned hero.'

Johnson grinned, but he wasn't comfortable with the chit-chat. He was thinking about the kid too. Her husband was in jail. She had no means of support. It was possible that she'd been raped. If she had been raped by Eduardo Duran, and she didn't know who the father of her child might be, then she might have had a reason to kill her child, if it had turned out to be Duran's. But the child had turned out to be Steven's. She had said so. She had killed *their* child. The simplest and most comforting explanation was that she had lost her mind in post-natal depression, that it didn't matter whose eyes, ears, nose, feet and hands the child had, she just couldn't cope with it. Johnson took one more look at the Gateses' fireproof spread and left with his partner.

Chapter Twenty-four

Steven Gates called George Peyronie on his way back from Brentwood. It was late. George wasn't asleep, but he had taken a tranquillizer to help him on his way. The nightmare that his life had become since the boat had gone up, taking several others with it, had robbed him of his peace of mind.

'Listen, George,' Steven had said. 'It's all right if I call you George, isn't it?'

'For Chrissakes, Steve.'

'I need to talk to someone.'

'Talk. I'm listening.'

'It's not safe. We need to meet.'

'Look, Steve, whatever trouble you're in, I'm in enough of my own. I don't need this.'

'I'm not in any trouble, George. I've kept my nose clean. I've been a model alien, believe me. You've been a good friend. I have some information that might be of interest to you but I can't talk on the phone. Someone's been taping my calls.'

'You think they could be . . . Shit, give me ten minutes.'

The two men arranged to meet in a tourist bar in Balboa, a thin peninsula that helps form the natural bay of Newport. George Peyronie shouldn't have been driving anywhere at all with the sedative inside him, but he had no desire to invite Steven Gates to his home. The doctor figured the way their luck was running, there would be a flood or something, or

Steve would spontaneously combust and cause problems with his house insurance. He didn't want to meet him anywhere where he might be recognized either, and when he saw Steven limp towards him in a cheap, white suit, a Hawaiian shirt and the grubby bandage still on his hand, he praised himself for his good thinking. The two men ordered Cokes and sat in a booth together like reformed alcoholics.

'I've just been to Brentwood,' Steven said.

'Oh?'

'You think he did it?'

'Who?'

'O.J.'

George, who was already fighting to keep his eyelids from closing, and had watched at least an hour of O. J. Simpson-related news bulletins that evening, wondered if at some point along the way he had died and gone to hell. He felt like screaming but he had to humour the man.

'He did it,' he said.

'Funny that. How all the white folks think O.J. did it.'

'He's as guilty as hell. What's race got to do with it?'

'You'll find out when they show you what a black boy who can *pay* can do.'

George supped irritably at his drink.

'You have business up there, in Brentwood?'

'No, I just needed to find myself,' Steven said.

'Oh, Jesus. In Brentwood?'

'It's a little like Surrey, England, all rural charm and money.'

'That where you're from?'

Steven began to laugh. It gave George the creeps because he laughed like a dopehead, but his faded blue eyes were on him all the time. George was beginning to wonder if he had gotten himself into a Charles Manson situation.

'I had a sweet life,' Steven said.

'Well, if Surrey's like Brentwood, it couldn't have been at

all bad,' George replied, and moved swiftly to the point. 'What was it you needed to tell me?' he said.

'Can you understand anyone beating up his own wife, George?'

'Yeah, I can imagine O.J. doing it.'

'I mean, take someone like Famalaro.'

George acknowledged that the name sounded familiar but he had no idea who or what Steven Gates was talking about. He certainly didn't feel like he was having a conversation with anyone. It was like Steven was talking to himself. He just wished the man would tell him who he thought was taping their calls, so that he could call his attorney and get some sleep.

'Famalaro had no personal interest in his victims, so, in a way, he is more moral than a wife-beater like O. J. Simpson or Bill Clinton's dad.'

'Victims?'

'Famalaro, the painter and decorator, the guy who killed those women. He kept one dear lady frozen in a truck in his drive.'

'Oh, *that* Famalaro. Man, I don't even want to think about what sort of moral being *he* is.'

George was struggling to keep up. The tranquilliser was making him feel like he'd shared a bottle of wine with the man instead of half a glass of Diet Coke. Steven wouldn't let up.

'He had a basic need. Like hunger or thirst. You could no more condemn an animal than Famalaro,' he continued.

'I believe Famalaro is an animal.'

'A shark,' Steven said. 'A shark. I'd say a shark.'

'A shark wouldn't keep his prey deep-frozen in his drive.'

'You're right. Yeah, good point, George. Shark'll smell blood and eat whatever is leaking it then and there. A shark wouldn't bugger about with feeding its imagination. That's the real difference between humans and animals, isn't it?

We're serious about our pleasure, and you have to be able to imagine, to think and feel like a human being to get pleasure from cruelty.'

It began to dawn on George that what he had first thought were minor cultural differences between the English-speaking peoples were in fact part of an individual pathology in Steven Gates. He looked at him for the first time as a doctor might look at a patient who might be suffering some sort of pernicious malaise, as opposed to a personal representative of an alien upbringing, a childhood of different landscapes, language and values. Steven Gates, he decided, was a sicko.

'What did you bring me out here for, Steve?' he said.

'George, I think whoever killed that detective Ray Deedes . . .'

'Remind me, Steve.'

'The PI who was found dead in his car out at Lake Forest?'

George shook his head, so Steven explained who Ray Deedes was, the circumstances of his demise and the fact that it had been on the news.

'Stella hired this guy?'

'She hired him to trace the stalker. We had this *someone* hanging around. Stella's car keys disappeared. The brake cable of my car, remember? Your boat?'

'The PI was Deedes? What are you saying? That somehow this stalker got to him?'

Steven nodded.

'And Deedes might have had some sort of proof. How?'

'He took pictures.'

'Wow.'

George fell silent as he contemplated the repercussions Steven's story might have for him. He was still finding it difficult to concentrate, but at least the dumb blockhead sensation that he had compared to a bottle of wine now had some bubbles in it. A stalker would get everyone off his back. A stalker was a goddamned criminal. George could be a victim like everyone else, instead of liable because he had employed a flake with a criminal record as a favour to someone he had once fucked.

'I knew you'd come up with something, Stevie. I *knew* you wouldn't let me down. This has been a bad time for me, you understand?'

Steven's face grew serious. He saw the doctor's happiness and wondered why he hadn't understood.

'The stalker's not dead. Deedes is.'

'Yeah, but you're telling me that this Deedes had pictures of the stalker, the guy who blew up my boat. You are saying that, aren't you, Steve? This guy's been taping your calls. That's why you brought me here, isn't it?'

'There was a fire, in Deedes's office. There is no evidence left at all, George.'

George held his head in his hands. He felt as if he had been up all night at the Manic Depressives' Ball.

'Kill me. Someone kill me,' he said.

'I know how you feel,' Steven replied.

It was one in the morning and Johnson was alone at the station. Dandy had gone home to get some sleep, and he said he'd wait for news of Steven Gates. He said he'd wake her.

'I'll go through as many of the tapes as I can,' he had said.

With the headphones on, he listened to the tape that Stella had given him and watched its colours spin before his eyes. He'd heard it all before.

'*He tried to kill me. He hurts me. He hurts me, all the time. I want him dead. I want to kill him. I want him dead.*'

'*Leave, Stella. Please leave him.*'

'*I can't.*'

'*Tell me.*'

'*I can't.*'

'*Why?*'

225

Pause.

'You love me, don't you?'

'I love you, you know that. I love you.'

'Kill him for me.'

'I'll kill him for you. I'll kill him for you.'

'What about me? Do I exist? Now. In you. Do I? Do you love me? Do I exist?'

'Yes,' she said, *'you exist. Yes, you exist. You exist.'*

'You sing the blues, ba . . . by?'

'I could murder you.'

'You sing the blues, baby?'

'I love you. I love you. I could murder you.'

'I'll do it. I'll do it. Say you love me.'

'I love you.'

Stella had insisted: 'I said "*someone* kill him for me".' Michael Revere had tried to cover himself.

'I said "no",' he had said.

'No' was not the answer to *Someone kill him for me.*

It was the answer to *Kill him for me.* Stella's explanation had gnawed away at him the whole day. *Kill him for me* must have been exactly what Ray Deedes had heard, and had decided to blackmail her. He must have started doing his sums when Steven Gates was almost killed in a car crash and then blown up by an exploding boat. Johnson replayed the conversations and listened to the tone of her voice. It was hard to tell her intent because the anger was plain.

The tape spun around and Johnson listened to himself. The way he was taking her was raw and punishing. He couldn't let anyone hear that. He had built up an image for himself, a career. It was important to him. It was all he had. She'd trapped him because she had to. She'd made a mistake, for sure. She hadn't wanted anyone but one person to hear what was on that tape. She didn't want anyone to be able to analyse the tape that Steven had cut and rejoined, for each splice was original and only the original was evidence. Forensics would be able to tell if she had said *Kill him for me*, if any word, the word *someone*, for example, had been removed. The only person with a copy of the original uncut conversation, the one before Steven had remade it as their own, must have been Ray Deedes. He had heard exactly what she had said and had probably been blackmailing her. And now Deedes was dead and everything he owned, everything he may have had on her and anyone else, was burned to nothing. Johnson winced as if a thorn had snagged his insides. She had exploited his little weakness and recorded it. She hadn't offered it. She was too clever for that. He had free will. He could've turned her down, and if not, he could've taken the tape and played it for Dandy or whoever, just faced it out, told them all to go to hell and look at the evidence. He could have, but it was too hard. She had learned a few lessons about how a woman could be destroyed, and, over time, he had learned a few lessons about how a man could be.

'You think Deedes could have anything on us?' he had asked her that day.

'Why not? He has everything else. You can find out. Why don't you pay him a visit?' she had said.

So that's exactly what he did. Her suggestion was planted in his mind, waiting like a seed for the right conditions so it could burst from the brown, dry earth. He paid Deedes a visit but the PI wasn't there. He knew he wasn't because Wiener had left so quickly. He didn't know Deedes was dead, of course, so he'd worked fast, thinking the fat man might return any time. He'd set the fire and cleared the building. He had wondered how far he would have to go, how far she would need him to. He was hoping for a little luck and he'd got it. He set the fire, but someone else had iced Deedes. He didn't have to, but the question he kept asking himself was, would he have done? He'd never know.

And what about her? She'd trapped him to try to save herself, he understood that. She could unmake him. But would she? How far would he go then? Could he kill *her* if he had to? If he really had to?

Johnson was tired. His head ached and the back of his neck was knotted with tension. He was thirsty too, for whisky, not water. The flavour was coming back like a fond memory and he had to fight it. He'd come too far to turn back now. It was one thing to be a thirty-year-old drunk with a wife and family, and another to be a forty-two-year-old drunk, divorced and alone. If it hooked him again, who would he struggle for against it? Not himself. He couldn't go down that road again.

As the tape came to an end, he rewound it to the last splice and edged it along until his voice and hers began. He took a razor from his pocket and cut. The tape fell away on to the desk and he rolled the detached strand into a tight coil and placed it in the pocket of his jacket. He lifted the reel off the machine, tidied up the tape and tucked the loose end into the plastic holding. He placed it in a box and then on to the pile with the others that he and Dandy had collected from Steven Gates's room. The last thing he did was take the headphones off and sling them to one side.

He was sweating when the phone rang.

'Sir.'

It was Dandy telling him that she couldn't sleep either. Her voice was low and soft, quite unlike the brisk, matter-of-fact tone she used at work. He tried to imagine her in bed, but the pictures wouldn't come.

'Where are you?'

'At home in my kitchen with a cup of warm milk and a shot of brandy. It isn't working. Did you find the original?' she said.

'Yeah, it's here. Voices all cut about and spliced together just like the others.'

'Is there anything else on the tape that's not on the copy?'

'Like what?'

'Oh, I don't know, sir. I was just wondering why he'd make a copy.'

'I've thought about that too. There isn't anything else on this tape.'

'There had to be a reason for making one.'

'Who knows? We're hardly talking Mr Reasonable when we're discussing Steven Gates.'

'Are there any other copies of other conversations there?'

'I haven't found any.'

'See?'

'No, I don't see.'

'The only one re-recorded is the one *she* handed over. I just thought there might have been something else on the one he put together originally.'

'Like what? I told you, there's nothing here.'

'Maybe something he didn't want to listen to any more, or something *she* didn't want anyone else to know. Whatever or whoever, they made a copy and left it out.'

'I'll get forensics to check on it. Nice work, Ruth. I'll be sure and let you be the first to go through the out-takes of the thoughts of Michael Revere.'

There was silence on the other end of the line.

'You still there, Ruth?' Johnson said eventually.

'I was thinking, sir.'

There was another silence.

'Are you doing it now? How long do you need?' Johnson enquired.

'It's too crazy. You'll laugh at me.'

'Try me.'

'You think it's got something to do with Famalaro?'

Johnson reassured her that it was the most dumb-assed thing he'd ever heard, and told her to get some sleep.

*

Stella had returned to her home in the hills. She had no desire to stay with Michael. She thought he had behaved like a fool, and that they were fortunate that Johnson was not quite as big a fool as he. She had undressed, loosened her hair and wrapped herself in a long robe so that she could sit outside and smoke a joint.

A neighbour had told them that it wasn't a wise thing to sit out too far from the house, because there were coyotes and mountain lions in the hills. They hunted the domestic cats and dogs thereabouts.

'Something has survived!' Steven had said, excited at the prospect, but neither of them had ever seen anything wilder than themselves in their garden, so they ignored the warnings.

Stella liked to swim in the pool at night and Steven, of course, liked to watch her. He would drink, or smoke a joint, and she would swim up and down in the moonlight, or, if the night was black and filled with stars, the lights by the side of the pool. Now that she was pregnant, it was more comfortable to swim on her back. She stepped into the icy water and floated effortlessly away from the edge, her hair spread around her like a net thrown from a little white boat. She placed both hands on her swollen belly, squeezed and whispered.

'Baby grow. Baby grow. Grow. Grow. Grow, baby.'

An engine whined up through the hills and around the hairpins. She spat a spout of fresh water into the night and kicked her feet, her hands circling gently and propelling her body slowly round and round the pool. She lifted her head and looked down at the curve of her stomach, which swelled above the waterline and shone with moisture like the pearly lining of a shell. The sound of the car got louder and then stopped. Stella laid her head back in the water so that she could hear nothing but the underwater drone of the pool filter and the rhythm of her breathing. She imagined she could hear two hearts beating, and the vibration of another body turning in its own pool of liquid inside her. Up above, the light of a trillion dead stars and living suns shone coldly down on her as she spun slowly around like a wheel.

'You're hard to see in the dark,' she said as Johnson stood by the side of the pool with a gun in his hand.

The muzzle followed the arc of her body as she lifted her arms and swam back to the shallows. He watched the splashing of her feet and the slow dip of her hands. Her breasts were white and the hair between her legs was sparse and dark. When she stood up her hair dropped down, black as the road he had just travelled. Her waist was thicker, and her hand cupped the gentle mound of her belly automatically as she stepped out of the pool. She dragged the excess water from her hair and bent down to pick up a towel.

'You can trust me, you know,' she said.

'Can I? You tricked me.'

'I know. I had to. But I wanted you, too.'

Johnson's throat was dry.

'You asked Michael Revere to kill your husband and Deedes got it on tape. That's why you wanted me.'

His hand was shaking a little. He had never killed before. He had never fired his gun at a human being. He had swung his revolver against a few skulls and knocked a few run-of-the-mill boneheads out. He had stared down the muzzle of a gun himself more than once, been fired *at*, but, like most cops, he never killed anyone. The cops who had never wanted to talk about it, and, if they did ever talk about it, they said they never wanted to *think* about it. He had never met a cop who had killed a woman before.

'Have you come to kill me?' she said.

'No. No, I haven't come to kill you, Stella, I've come to protect you,' he replied.

She picked up the remains of the joint she had been smoking and lit it. She was shivering. Her eyes focused on the gun in his hand and then she looked at him, her eyes soft and vulnerable. She was drawing him to her. His mouth was drier than chalk. He tried to work up some saliva but it wouldn't come. He took a step towards her but she didn't move. She trembled and dripped cold drops on to the ground until an inky patch spread like a shadow around her pale feet.

He dropped the length of tape down like a satin ribbon, pinching one end between his thumb and forefinger. The night breeze tugged at the long, shining tail. She held up her lighter and stretched forward. The tape caught fire and they watched it burn like a fuse. This was the beginning and the end, the alpha and the omega. She was laughing, and the light of the flame was in her eyes.

'See, I've set you free,' she said.

In a moment, he was holding her and she had her arms about him, tugging at his clothes. Their lovemaking was too fast and frantic. He couldn't hold on, and, as the moment came, she sank her teeth into him to stifle the hot moan that escaped from her mouth like the growl of the last remaining wild thing in the hills.

'Do you know what's going to happen?' Johnson asked, buttoning his creased and damp shirt when it was over. Stella stretched over for her robe.

'My husband is coming to kill me,' she said.

'Did you think I was him?'

'I thought you might be.'

'Why didn't you try to get away?'

'I wanted to see if he could do it. I wanted to see if he could make the choice.'

Johnson sat down on a sunbed with his jacket in his hand as if he were sweltering under the midday sun instead of freezing in the Californian hills on a winter's night. Stella put on her thick towelling robe and wrapped her hair in the towel once more. She knelt in front of him and held his face in her hands.

'Lee, my husband is destroying himself,' she said.

'And you're helping him. That's right, isn't it?'

She kissed his mouth and he felt her tongue pressing in. It tasted of fresh water and he wanted to make love to her again. He couldn't let her die, but could he kill Steven Gates? Would he need to? Could he draw his gun and shoot for the first time in his career, in his life, at another human being? He'd pointed the gun at her. He could have killed her but she had known. She had known exactly how it was going to be. It was all planned.

'Why?' he said.

Stella took her hands from his face.

'I'm leaving him, that's why. I'm finally going. We had a strange arrangement.'

'I'd say.'

'No stranger than I had been used to, and with people more hateful. But we were equals. I wasn't a victim with him. I was free to do as I pleased, and I pleased him. That was what I wanted.'

'So what happened?'

'I thought there were rules. I thought I chose, that my happiness meant something to him, but I found out that I was nothing to him, nothing more than a collection of body parts. Like I'd been to everyone else. What I wanted didn't matter, not really. I killed his baby *because* it was his. You know that, don't you? I know you know.'

'Yes.'

'It was our baby, our sweet little life, and I couldn't look at it. I couldn't. But that wasn't the worst thing. What was worse, what was so much worse, was that I couldn't let it look at *me*.'

He knew she wouldn't cry. She had done that. She didn't look away from him either. She looked into his face with her clear eyes and told her story. She told him how much she had loved Steven Gates, and that everything she had ever done for him and with him, she had done willingly. She told him how he thought he was so smart, and how he really *was*. He had told her that if you use your brain, you can always be in control, however complex life is, however complicated it becomes. He was young then, she said. He had to learn that there are a few surprises in life, and he was going to find out that the biggest surprise of all was going to be himself.

He had told her once that she kept him on the edge, and made him believe that there was something beyond his own plan. Back then, the plan was making money, in the short term and the long term. It was the only plan. He made good money delivering the boats and he never had to cut any throats doing it. He took her with him most trips because he liked to have her around. He liked to listen to her sing and watch her move. He said he couldn't ever get enough of her, her body, her chit-chat, her funny little ways. They had made love all the time. He told her that sometimes he could almost see themselves making love, like it was an out-of-body experience. It was a fantasy, and he wanted it to become a reality, and it did. She made it happen for him. He said it released him. She released him by letting him have what he wanted. It began with that, those out-of-body experiences, like the ones you have when you are close to death.

'How did you feel about him?' Johnson asked.

The question seemed to baffle her, as if she had never really thought about it.

'I trusted him and he betrayed me,' she said.

Johnson knew Steven Gates hadn't betrayed her with any woman. He wanted her to tell him how. She spoke of pain, a pain so deep that her hands shook as they fluttered up to her lips. He watched her, and she may have believed that she was telling him, but all she was doing was reliving it in her head. When she finally spoke, she said that he'd let someone try to rape her, not actually rape her, but try to rape her. Steven had gone to jail. She'd given birth alone, in that dingy, single-bed room. She had nothing, no one, but she had wanted that baby. She saw its face with its faded blue eyes looking up at her and she couldn't feel love.

'I couldn't feed it,' she said. 'I cut the cord, I don't know how, but I couldn't let it near me. Its mouth was searching for my breast and it began to cry. I wanted a child so much, but not that one. It was a horror. I lost my mind,' she said. 'Can you understand how that feels, to lose your mind, to lose your self? He does. That's what he's doing now.'

'Why did you marry him again?'

'I had to. I wanted a new life. I had to.'

'Did he know the baby was his, Stella?'

She didn't answer. It was all he was going to get. It should have been enough, but he wanted more because he wanted to feel better about loving her. He had no doubt that she had powerful reasons for doing the things she had done, the things she was still doing, the things she had begun to do to him. He just wanted to hear them for himself, all of them. He reached over and brushed his fingers against her lips. She caught them and kissed them until he dropped his jacket and pressed his other hand between her legs.

'I won't let him kill you, honey,' he whispered. 'I can't let him do that, no way.'

Chapter Twenty-five

The bar closed and the two men stood out on the street. The occupants of the big houses across the bay were asleep in their beds. Their security lights blazed down on to the ocean, where their bright reflections shone back like the many moons of Jupiter. George had wanted to call the police and tell them, but Steven had said there wasn't any point. They hadn't protected him and they couldn't protect Stella. He knew who the stalker was and where he was. He was going after him himself. He had a Smith and Wesson .38, which he showed to the doctor.

'George, I killed a man.'

George's anal sphincter tightened a tad. He was cold and tired and he wished he was home in bed instead of out by the seashore at gone two in the morning, a stiff wind blowing in for Thanksgiving and an armed sociopath for company.

'You had your reasons, right?' he said.

Steven tucked the gun back in his jacket.

'I was a soldier.'

George was about to tell him that a soldier killing someone didn't count, that it was his job like his was tightening butts and breasts, but Steven wasn't listening.

'He wasn't the only one I killed.'

'No?'

'But he was the only one who deserved it. I'm sorry you

had to get involved in this, George, but it was me and not you he was after. He's trying to kill me.'

'But . . .'

George thought better of mentioning the word *killed*, but he had begun to wonder how a dead man could come back.

'Haven't you got any proof, anything that you could go to the cops with?' he said.

Steven suddenly grasped the doctor's pudgy shoulders and, sedated or no, the man's heart beat so fast he thought he was going to faint.

'I told you. I killed a man. I did it to protect my wife. My wife was raped. I cut him to pieces and dumped him in the sea. He was a face. A face. a big-time drug distributor. A face. In the end, he wasn't even that. Do you understand now?'

George understood.

'This guy's business associates have found you? Is that what you're trying to say? They blew up my boat because they were trying to kill you?'

Steven shook his head.

'It's *him*, George. I'd recognize him anywhere.'

'How can I help you, Steven? How can I help you, man?'

Steven looked intently at the doctor, who gazed back at him with the purest expression of sincerity that he could muster. Steven's hands dropped from George's shoulders and he shook his head.

'You can't, mate. I just wanted you to know. I wanted you to know that it wasn't my fault.'

'Why don't you leave this to the cops, Stevie? You could get yourself killed, man. Come on, you and me, let's call the cops, let *them* sort this out.'

Steven wasn't listening. He was already walking away into the night, his shoulders hunched against the wind. He'd gone about one hundred yards and was about to round a corner away towards the shore, when the doctor turned and ran as fast as his fat little legs would carry him in the opposite direction, back towards his BMW. Ten yards from the vehicle, he pointed the key fob desperately at the car. The warning lights flashed comfortingly as the automatic doors unlocked and the interior lights switched on. But, lit from within, the sleek, isolated car no longer looked like a place of safety. It looked like a steel trap, and George approached it filled with foreboding. He was close to crying as he peered through the glass into the back seats and checked around. When he was sure no one was in there, he yanked open the driver's door and sat inside before swiftly applying the central locking.

His hands trembled at the ignition and froze as he saw Steven's car coming down the empty street. Steven saw him, flashed his headlights and drove on past. He didn't appear to be in any hurry. The doctor watched the rear lights receding in his wing mirror, and when they had gone, he opened the car door once more and almost fell on to the sidewalk.

This time he peered underneath the car but the shadows there were blacker than tar. He couldn't see anything, and if he did, he wondered if he would recognize it. He had never looked underneath his car. He didn't know what was supposed to be there. He didn't want to touch anything inside, not the car phone, nothing. He looked around. The street was empty. He didn't want to walk anywhere. He couldn't remember if he'd seen a public phone. He thought that maybe he could just sit in the car and wait for a cop car to come by, or even wait till morning when the stores and coffee bars opened.

'Why *my* car?' he reasoned. 'Why not *his* car? Guy's after him, not me. Why not *his* car?'

The doctor got back in the car and placed his hands on the wheel.

'Come on, George. Come *on*, man,' he said, and though his confidence was shattered, he turned the key.

When the engine started and a saxophone blew loud from the radio, the perspiring doctor gingerly engaged an automatic gear and pressed the accelerator pedal. He drove straight home to Newport, poured himself a large one and called the police.

Steven had his radio tuned to a different station, one that operated out of Santa Monica. It was playing a song by an English guy who was singing about a time when he would call up his girl and put down the phone, but now he couldn't care less. He sang that he couldn't be him, if she wasn't her, and Steven sang along as he drove down the coast. His hands looked large and bony on the wheel, and he remembered the hands of the man he had shot in Northern Ireland, the man with 'love' on one hand and 'hate' on the other, and little smudged blue crucifixes on each thumb.

He'd thought it was corny at the time but he was thinking about it now, about the letters *love* on the left and *hate* on the right. He wondered if the man was right- or left-handed, and if he felt hate more strongly than love, or love more strongly than hate. He looked at his hands on the steering wheel and it was clear to him that he was using both, *love* and *hate*, and a little blessing on each thumb.

About an hour later, Johnson called Ruth Dandy and told her where he was.

'I've been trying to raise you for the past half-hour,' she said.

'We got him?'

'No.'

'So what's going on?'

'You tell me.'

'Don't like your tone, detective.'

239

The line went quiet. Johnson spoke first.

'Stella Gates rang to tell me that her husband was not home and she was afraid. She was afraid to go into any of the rooms or outside. She wanted someone to look around and then to sit with her,' he lied.

'What about Michael Revere?'

'They've had a fight.'

'What about me? I could have gone up there.'

'Lack of empathy, detective.'

Dandy took in the fact that she had overstepped the mark, and apologized before reporting that the station had had an early morning call from Dr George Peyronie's attorney. The doctor had met with Steven Gates. The attorney explained that Dr Peyronie had felt obligated to meet the man. Steven Gates was armed.

'He say what with?'

'A Smith and Wesson.'

'OK. What else he say?'

'Gates told him he was being stalked by someone. That this man had threatened his wife and he was going to do something about it. He said he'd killed someone already, but Dr Peyronie couldn't work out who.'

'Get Michael Revere some protection and get on up here yourself, Ruth, with some help.'

He put the phone down and turned to Stella. Her face was white and her eyes alert with fear.

'He's here,' she whispered.

Johnson stepped back into the darkness.

'I got you covered,' he said. 'Turn on the light in the lounge.'

Steven let himself in and saw her standing by the torso. He felt disorientated, as if he were looking down on her from above. His head ached and his hand throbbed. He scanned the sculpture and the stumps of its arms and legs. Stella said nothing. He walked into the room and sat down. He could barely handle the tobacco tin, but he managed to open it and roll a cigarette.

'Got a light?'

Stella lifted the table lighter, and as he took the flame he grasped her wrist.

'His eyes looked into yours. He looked right into them and he took what he wanted. He wanted it. He took it. From that moment on, he was a dead man and he never knew it. Christ, if he had known, he would have taken the bloody knife and used it on himself.'

Johnson strained to listen. He wanted Gates away from her. Her head was too close to his. He didn't want Ruth arriving with the cavalry, either. He saw Gates push her away and hold his head.

'I never saw it. My eyes were closed. I swear, Stella. I woke up and I did what I could. I thought it'd be OK, but it never was, ever. I did hard time. I did it all for you. You killed him, I know that. I saw it but I never told a soul, a single black soul, because I loved you and I knew you had to kill him. I saw it all.'

'I thought you said your eyes were closed.'

He hit her then, and, as he stood over her, he said, 'It blew up in his face, pieces and pieces of it falling down on his head and he didn't die. He lay on his back looking up at the gulls and he was still breathing. I did what you said. I tried. I fucking tried.'

Steven walked towards the French windows. He looked out at the pool and opened the doors. Stella got up off the floor and looked across to where Johnson was, but she couldn't see him. She felt a surge of anxiety. She didn't want the detective to make any mistakes, by reflex or will. It was the end of the game. She had played and she was about to win. She wanted to win.

Steven wandered out into the night towards the water. The

wind was strong and cold. He thought of home, of the cold and the rain and the patchwork green and yellow fields of England, its villages and towns with their gardens of roses and chrysanthemums and hanging baskets and two dustbins by a gate. Here, the brown, creosote-covered hills rolled on into clipped lawns and swimming pools. They were waiting for their time to come, when they would rise up and tear the land apart. He had nothing to live for. He belonged nowhere, with no one. He had given his life and she had drowned his child, drowned him. He'd thought it was Duran's. He never thought it was his. The messages she'd sewn together in her fucking exhibition, her fucking installation of memories that never let him forget. He was going to fucking kill her, and he'd have killed her a long time ago if he had known Duran hadn't quite made it, hadn't quite fucked her.

Stella stood in the doorway and Johnson began to panic. He had no line of sight. If he fired, he'd shoot her in the back. She had to move, she had to know that. If he called out, Steven Gates might jump the gun and kill her. He thought about all of this as if he had hours.

She knew. Steven was turning around. It didn't matter. He held the gun. The Smith and Wesson .38 that had killed Ray Deedes was pointing at her. It was all over. The past came hurtling to meet the present. *The mind*, she whispered, *has a thousand eyes, the heart but one, but the light of a whole life dies when love is done.*

Johnson screamed at her to hit the floor so he could take him, but the flash of gunfire had already lit her up.

Stella. Stella. Stella. Steven said her name in his head. A hiss and then a flick from the top to the bottom of his mouth with the tip of his tongue. Stella, la, la. Hair, skin, breast, belly and thigh, his sweet cat of a wife was all around.

I am not what I am, he thought as he put the gun to his head. I see myself outside myself, but whoever I am I see her.

Steven seemed to float above himself and watch the world below. The man in the white suit and the Hawaiian shirt was lying on his back in the pool. Johnson was holding Stella, holding her, and Steven knew it was all wrong. Why wasn't she in *his* arms? He had saved her from the man who came to kill her. He had watched over her. He had said he would. They'd talked about it. She had begged him to. '*Kill him for me*,' she had said, and he had done. He wondered why he had never seen them or heard them, and why it was so cold, so wet and cold. Police in uniform were looking at the man in the pool. They ran around the cool lozenge of water like shadows. Her arms were outstretched. She was screaming at the man who was floating and the black man was pulling at her, pulling her back. He was calling her name but she was calling her husband's name. She was calling his name and he wondered why.

'Steven, Steven, Steven, Steven,' she was screaming.

I exist, he thought, as he looked up at the twinkling stars in the black dome of the sky and saw them spiral into a small dot of light.

Chapter Twenty-six

Johnson and Dandy stood in the shade of the bank, drinking ice-cold Cokes, their sunglasses protecting their eyes from the spring sunshine. Johnson had worked out more than he had needed to that morning, and his shoulders ached a little.

In the pavement café opposite, Stella Gates leaned back in her cane chair and closed her eyes. She had taken off her broad-brimmed hat, and the warm sun lit up her face. The straps of her dress had slipped from her shoulders and Michael Revere drew his fingers across her bare skin. Her breasts and stomach were swollen and ripe. It was seven months since her husband had committed suicide.

'She could drop at any minute,' Dandy said.

'She's sure looking heavy,' Johnson replied.

'And she's carrying low.'

'High and round means a girl.'

'She'll have had tests.'

'Think she knows?'

'Might, might not. Some people like surprises.'

'Not Mrs Gates.'

Johnson and Dandy didn't talk so much about the case any more, but, for differing reasons, it never left their thoughts. For Ruth Dandy, it was that the events had apparently proved her wrong, but the explanation was too pat for her satisfaction. Steven Gates had been obsessed with his own wife, and when he finally understood that she was leaving him for another man, he had killed himself in a deranged effort to prevent himself from killing her. Johnson had reminded her that it fitted in nicely with her theories about victims serving a purpose for their killers.

Dandy believed Steven Gates had seen his wife raped and had murdered her attacker. She also believed that, quite possibly, both had murdered him, and Steven Gates had taken the rap because he loved his wife. His wife had been raped and he had failed to protect her. Stella Gates denied that she had ever been raped by any Eduardo Duran, or that she ever met him. Her child was her husband's, and she had killed the baby for no other reason than post-natal depression. She said her husband could not accept the fact that she was pregnant by another man and that she was leaving him. It would have meant the end of their arrangement, by which she allowed him to watch her having sexual intercourse with a string of lovers. She had not lied on her immigration papers but Steven had had to, because of his record. She had built up a successful business, supported her husband, and her powerful friends were helping her fight deportation.

For Johnson, the case had meant that he, like every other lover Stella Gates had ever had, shared a guilty secret with her. He had gone down a road from which he could never return. He had seen the gunfire and smelled it. She had had her back to him, and he could hear her screaming his name, as if the devil had left her and she wanted him back. Johnson had wanted to fire his gun. His fingers had twitched as the front door caved in under the weight of his fellow officers. He had run to her instead, and taken her in his arms. He could not escape the feeling he had that Stella had fired at her husband. In that moment, he thought only of himself, of how he would never be able to hide what she had done. A dead body floating in a pool was not a length of recording tape that he could roll up tight and unroll into a flame. He had looked for a weapon in her hands and found nothing. There was a Smith and Wesson at the bottom of the pool. It had dropped from Steven's dead fingers.

'*Kill him for me*,' was what Steven Gates had heard, and that's what he had done. He had killed himself. Johnson gazed at the pale body leaking blood as black as oil and realized that she had been killing him for years, paying him back every moment of every day. Steven Gates was a dead man the moment he had allowed Eduardo Duran to touch her.

'My wife's mother used to use a needle and cotton,' Johnson said to Dandy.

'Oh, that old wives' thing?'

'Yeah. She'd make Ella lie down and bare her big belly, and she'd stand over her and hang a long piece of cotton and a needle just above the navel. We had to be very quiet and wait. If the needle began to spin round and round, it was a girl. If it swung backward and forward in a straight line, it was a boy.'

'Was she right?' Dandy asked.

'Hundred per cent, three times in a row.'

'She had a fifty per cent chance of being right every time. Those are good odds.'

'She got all my wife's sister's kids right too.'

'You're divorced.'

'What of it?'

'I just wondered when a wife becomes an ex-wife.'

Johnson took a drink. The outside of the can was running with condensation and soaking his hands.

'You want a hot dog?' he said.

'Sure,' she said, and they walked twenty yards up the road to the stand.

'Two,' he said to the proprietor, and turning to Dandy he

246

said, 'You tell me how you eliminate someone from your life.'

Dandy glanced over to where Stella was sitting. She was partly obscured by the other lunchtime customers but she could see the back of her head. Her dark hair was held in a silver clasp that shone as if it was melting. There was someone who knew how to do it, she thought.

'I have memories. I have kids,' Johnson said.

'A mother-in-law with a needle,' Dandy replied.

'A mother-in-law with a needle. Right. Believe me, you have to have special skills to junk all that. You have to have special skills just to junk the junk.'

'Think they want a boy or a girl?' Dandy said, breaking finally.

Johnson chewed at his hot dog, which was burning the inside of his mouth. He didn't care if it was a boy or a girl. He knew it wouldn't be black. He still had a career and a pension to look forward to because there was never any proof of their relationship, nor would there ever be. He had to trust her and she had to trust him. The gun that Steven had used to kill himself was identified as the murder weapon in the Deedes killing, and though Steven Gates got the blame, Johnson knew different.

'I had to,' she had said. 'He knew about us.'

'What about us?' he had said.

'Exactly,' she had replied, and touched his hand lightly with her fingers. 'You remember that.'

Stella wondered if the baby was facing the sun. She imagined its face, Steven's face, pressing against her belly, its tiny hands open and its blue eyes shut. It was a nice thought, but not a pleasant position for her. It would be agonizing if the baby stayed that way. It would have to behave itself and turn its back to the light, turn into her. She remembered the first time, when there had been no sun. She had been full of hatred and pain. This time it was different. This time she had light and space and money. There was the relatively trivial irritation of whether or not she could remain in the country, but her attorney had assured her that she had a good case. If she had been a little pregnant Latina, she would have been packed off home in a pick-up, but she was rich and white, and connected. Her boyfriend was a friend to the stars.

Stella smiled to herself. Michael had been very attentive, but she knew he had another woman. He had not kept his nerve like Lee Johnson had. She hated cowards: weak men were everywhere, but not all were cowards. Michael was both. She was glad he wasn't the father, though it would never do to tell him. He was lucky that a slap in the face, though unforgivable, was forgettable. He was lucky that she had never loved him like she had loved Steven Gates.

'I'm hungry,' she said.

'You've just eaten, Stella,' Michael replied.

'Obviously not enough.'

'You want a pizza?'

'No. I want real food. Meat. Something bloody with fries.'

Michael studied the menu. It was a vegetarian restaurant.

'Oh, I'm tired of waiting,' she said.

'We haven't ordered yet. Fact is, there's nothing bloody here except Mary.'

Stella laughed. Her eyes were still closed. She would wait another minute, before hiding them behind her sunglasses and shading her face with her hat.

'For the baby, you fool. I'm tired of waiting for the baby.'

Michael closed the menu and took a sip of his O.J. He didn't know how he really felt about the baby. He just knew he had never reconnected with her. The show had ended and he had done nothing since. She had made no suggestions. She had spent more time up in the hills than down a the studio. He was going to have to come up with something, something different, but it was hard. He'd lost something, he knew that, but what he wasn't sure of was whether he had had it in the first place. She had had it, his love and the talent. She was better than him, and now that he needed her more than ever, she had withdrawn. That was it, withdrawn.

'What do you think it'll be?' Stella asked, putting on her hat and glasses.

'I don't know.'

'What do you want?'

'Don't keep asking me that.'

'What about names? You never mention names.'

'They don't have anything bloody.'

They both got up and walked to the car. He drove to a place close by where she could eat a quarter-pounder rare. The little restaurant overlooked the sea, and she told him a story about a long time ago when someone a lot older than her had sent her photographs of himself.